MW01146881

I BET YOU

ILSA MADDEN-MILLS

Copyright © 2018 by Ilsa Madden-Mills
Cover Design/Paperback Formatting: Shanoff Designs
Photography: Wander Aguiar
Editing: C Marie
Content Editing: Evident Ink
Formatting: Champagne Formats

Paperback:
ISBN-13: 978-1727893878
ISBN-10: 1727893875

All rights reserved. Without limiting the rights under copyright reserved above, no part of this publication may be reproduced, stored in or introduced into a retrieval system, or transmitted in any form, or by any means (electronic, mechanical, photocopying, recording, or otherwise) without the prior written permission of the above copyright owner of this book or publisher.

This is a work of fiction. Names, characters, places, brands, media, and incidents are either the product of the author's imagination or are used fictitiously. The author acknowledges the trademarked statue and trademark owners of various products referenced in this work of fiction, which have been used without permission. The publication/ use of these trademarks is not authorized, associated with, or sponsored by the trademark owners.

TABLE OF CONTENTS

DEDICATION

This book is for all the cool, smart girls in the world, especially dedicated to those who love hot football guys, bodice-ripping historical romances, men in sexy button-up shirts, *Twilight*, *True Blood*, *Buffy the Vampire Slayer*, and of course, it goes without saying, cherry red lipstick and lollipops.

Wall Street Journal **bestselling author Ilsa Madden-Mills returns with an all-new swoon-fest of a novel about what happens when you look beyond labels and take a chance on love.**

I BET YOU

Sexy Athlete: I bet you…

Penelope Graham: Burn in hell, quarterback.

The text is random but Penelope figures out exactly who "Sexy Athlete" is. And why she shouldn't take his wager.

Ryker Voss.
Football star.
Walks on water and God's gift to women.
Just ask him.

His bet? He promises Penelope he'll win her the heart of the guy she's been crushing on. His plan—good old-fashioned jealousy. Once her crush sees her kissing Ryker, he'll realize what he's missing. Sounds legit, right? The only question is…why is Ryker being so nice to her?

Penelope Graham.
Virgin.
Lover of sparkly vampires and calculus.
His mortal enemy.

Penelope knows she shouldn't trust a jock, but what's a girl to do when she needs a date to Homecoming? And Ryker's keeping a secret, another bet, one that could destroy Penelope's heart forever.

I BET
YOU

CHAPTER 1

PENELOPE

The door to my bedroom flies open and I grab my chest, my fingers clutching the bodice of my sapphire-blue dress. Standing in front of me with his cravat slightly askew is none other than the devil himself, Lord Ryker Voss, the Duke of Waylon. He thinks he's the best thing since crumpets and scones. Maybe he is. But I hate him.

"I'm here to ravish you, Lady Penelope."

"No," I gasp, but I suspect he knows I don't mean it.

"I know you don't mean it." He gives me a cocky smile, whips off his dark coat, and tosses it on the floor. His white linen shirt is next, the buttons flying around the room. My wide eyes linger on the rippling muscles of his abdomen, wandering to the deep V on his hips that leads to—

Dear me.

His male length juts out of his trousers, and it's hard and long…and magnificent.

Will it even fit?

"I'm a virgin," I say, darting around the canopied bed even as I imagine him spreading me out naked on those velvet covers, his tongue sucking my peaks one by one—

He captures my arm. "Are you imagining me fucking you, Lady Penelope?"

I tremble and melt into him. "Yes."

"Good." Caressing my bodice with his palm, he tugs on the fabric until it rips and my voluptuous breasts pop out. Desire glows in his aqua-colored eyes. He pushes me down on the bed and gathers my skirt up, his fingers finding the opening in my undergarments. His huge length teases my entrance, and I moan, my hands clutching his shoulders—

"Yo! *Garçon*, we need some help back here," comes a deep male voice from somewhere inside the restaurant. I jump at being pulled from my concentration and nearly fall off my stool before righting myself, my face a deep cardinal red. I slam my journal shut with an emphatic bang and tuck it under my laptop on the bar to make it less conspicuous.

I'm on my break, but I stand to see who needs help, groaning when I see the football table waving at me.

Of course it has to be *him*.

I exhale as my eyes drift over the players and jersey chasers before coming back and landing on Ryker freaking Voss himself, the center of attention and Mr. Golden Boy Quarterback of Waylon University.

I swear I can smell the testosterone from here.

And to think I imagined him ravishing me…

Please. I grimace. Ryker is such a douche. Everyone knows his bedroom is a revolving door, and he wouldn't know what a real woman was if she walked up and hit him on the head.

He cocks an infuriating eyebrow at me and calls out,

"Today would be nice."

Ass.

I glance at my journal. I probably inserted him in my bodice-ripping scenario because school is back in session—senior year, baby—and Ryker just happens to be here in Sugar's. I waited on his table earlier, and once I get going with an idea, it gets a life of its own and the words just flow across the page.

I make a mental note to go back and scratch his name out of my notebook.

Clearing my throat, I stick my hands in the pockets of the half apron tied around my waist and head to his table. Of course, I could get one of the other servers to wait on them, but most of them are dealing with their own customers or cleaning up in the back.

And his table *is* in my section.

I exhale. Since the moment he waltzed in with his buddies an hour ago and requested me as his waitress, I knew it was going to be a long night. School started two weeks ago, and he's been in a few times, always asking for me.

He enjoys me being at his beck and call.

His gaze is arrogant and riveted on me the entire forty feet or so it takes to get there. It's a little intimidating to be the focus of his scrutiny, as if I'm his serving girl and he's the lord of the manor, but I straighten my shoulders and give him my brightest, sweetest smile—the one I reserve for people I don't like.

Which I suspect he knows.

The truth is I wrote a scathing editorial about him a few

months ago in the *Wildcat Weekly*, an article that carefully detailed his part in a football fighting ring spring semester. Once the smoke cleared and the NCAA exonerated him, I did write a brief follow-up...but too little, too late, I suppose. I already painted him in an unethical light, and I'm guessing those words are probably hard to forget.

He hates me.

I come to a stop at their table, my hand going to my hip like it does whenever he's near.

Our eyes meet and I hold my ground, not breaking our stare. I'll admit he's a magnificent male, all six feet, four inches of him. With his tousled mix of brown and blond hair, ocean-colored eyes, and sensuous full lips, he's the kind of gorgeous that makes you stop and blink. You might even rub your eyes to make sure he isn't some sort of sexy devil/angel.

"Yes?" I break our gaze, and my eyes sweep the table. Everything looks fine. Burgers and fries are mostly gone. Soda glasses are full. "Was there a problem with your check?"

Ryker's lips curl up. "No. We have a proposition for you."

Proposition?

My eyes narrow, and I'd like to tell him to suck it, but I keep my voice polite and sweet. Every Southern girl knows how to do this because our mamas taught us. "If it doesn't have anything to do with your service here, I'm not interested. Thank you."

One of the jersey chasers giggles. A buxom brunette with a ton of smoky eyeshadow—his usual type—she's sitting next to him and has her hot pink manicured hand curled around his arm. "But it's Ryker," she says in a high-pitched voice. "Don't you want to know what he wants?"

He *wants* to annoy me. It's obvious. I straighten my black cat-eye glasses. "Nope."

"But why not?" Her face is perplexed.

Bless her heart.

I sigh and break it down for her. I've been nice long enough. "A guy who calls me over by yelling *garçon,* which means 'boy' by the way, and then has a proposition for me... yeah, no. I have better things to do. Now, if you'll excuse me —"

"Wait. Don't run off," Ryker says, leaning forward on the table and easing the girl away from him. She points a pout his way, but his eyes are on me. "It's just a bet."

"I see. How...quaint." The football team is notorious for their betting shenanigans leading up to homecoming.

"All in good fun," he says, spreading his hands. "It's a tradition among the players. We even have a trophy that's been passed down since Waylon first got a football team. It's mostly the offense against the defense, but sometimes we do individual bets just to mix it up—which is why I called you over."

I give him a short nod and a tight smile. "I get it, but I have actual work to do, you know."

His eyes flick to where I was sitting at the bar. "You didn't look busy to me."

"I didn't know you were keeping tabs on me," I say, stiffening.

"I wasn't."

"Then how do you know I'm not busy?"

"I assumed."

I smirk. "Well, we all know what assuming does."

"You were sitting at the bar writing in a notebook."

My eyes flare. *Sweet baby Jesus, if he only knew.* "You're very observant. Is there something about me that interests you?"

He shrugs those impossibly broad shoulders. "Maybe I need more soda."

I look at his glass. "You don't."

"Maybe I need—"

Blaze, one of the players who's been watching our back and forth with wide eyes, interrupts him. "Um, this is getting weird. Can we get back to the bet?"

Ryker clears his throat, his thick and surprisingly dark lashes closing for a second as if he's shielding his expression. "Of course. Back to the nitty-gritty. The guys and I have been talking and were wondering if you'd want to earn a quick forty bucks." That infuriating eyebrow arches up. "Easy money."

I pause. Money *does* come in handy, especially when you hold down two jobs and go to school fulltime. Easy bets are also hard to resist. My roomie, Charisma, and I do them all the time, mostly to spur each other on. Last week I bet her she couldn't get an A on her first astronomy quiz, and she managed to pull one out. Her prize from me was a homemade breakfast complete with buttermilk biscuits and sausage gravy.

I exhale and look around at the faces. Besides the jersey chasers in between each player, I take in Archer, Blaze, and Dillon, all of them seniors and star players. I know Blaze best of all, a rather rambunctious puppy dog type of guy I tutored last year in algebra.

As a whole, they seem harmless enough, and I relax a little, pulling a raspberry lollipop out of my apron, taking the wrapper off, and sticking it in my mouth. They help me think. It's also a nervous reflex.

Ryker's aquamarine blue eyes are riveted on me.

"What's the bet?" I say, popping the sucker out and considering him.

He tilts his head toward the center of the table where someone has placed a bottle of ketchup front and center. "We bet you can't open that. Ten bucks from each of the players if you can."

Ha. I maintain a poker face, fighting back my grin. I open stubborn ketchup bottles on the regular. An hour ago, I managed to get a pesky jar of pickles open for our manager— who's a man.

"And if I can't?" Our eyes meet across the table, and I get a zip of heat from the intensity of his gaze.

"Then dessert is on you." He smirks. "I'll put my order in now: key lime pie."

He. Is. So. Freaking. Cocky.

I exhale, my hands flexing from thinking about opening the bottle.

They're all looking at me with expectant faces, and dammit, I know there has to be a trick here. They've probably been sitting here tightening it up for the past half-hour like overgrown kids.

But I'm no weakling either. I work out. I do yoga. I run. Heck, I do all the things.

"Do it, do it," Blaze chants, and I tell him to zip it.

"I don't think you have the balls, *cher*." This comes from Archer, his lilting Cajun accent reminding me he's from Louisiana. I take in his Billy Idol vibe: bleached hair, diamond studs in his ears, and full-sleeve tattoos. He gives me the creeps, but it isn't because of his bad boy appearance. It's the sly, beady look in his eyes that bugs me.

I move past him and look at Ryker—who grins.

Gah.

I know I should just ignore them and keep working, but something about him gets the rebel in me riled up. I want to win and rub it in his handsome freaking face.

"Fine, give it to me."

The guys clap and fist-bump each other as I hold my hand out. Ryker swipes the bottle off the table and stands to walk over and offer it to me.

I'm five ten, yet he towers over me when I look up at him.

"Good luck," he says with a smirk as he passes it off. Our fingers brush—accidentally—and electric sparks detonate. I realize it's the first time we've ever touched skin to skin, and my mind goes back to the sexy snippet I wrote. My entire body flushes.

I wonder if he feels the same current because he gets this peculiar expression on his face and drops his hand quickly, a scowl on his face. He considers me carefully, as if I'm a puzzle he can't quite figure out.

Whatever. I don't have time to dissect his reaction.

I look down at the full bottle, and it appears to have never been opened. I give it a try, testing it out with a strong tug, but the white cap doesn't budge. This might be harder than I thought.

"Need some help?" Ryker says as he takes his seat.

"Not from you."

He just grins. *Again.* Unfazed by my rudeness.

And I'll be honest, there's a dimple on his right cheek that does squishy things to my insides when he smiles. It always has. But, like I've done in the past, when it comes to a womanizing football player, I squash that feeling down. Football players are not for me.

Time to get serious and get this mother off. I take a break from twisting, set my sucker on a napkin on the table, and then wipe the sweat off my hands on my apron. I go in again, bending over and holding the bottle with one hand while the other tugs at the stubborn cap.

Ryker watches me with avid, intense interest, and it makes me more determined.

There is no way in hell I'm serving him pie on my dime.

"Penelope! Penelope! Penelope!" Blaze chants, and I glare at him to be quiet.

A few more twists and *pop!* it's free.

I let out a triumphant cry, but because of the angle and the pressure inside the bottle, red liquid spurts out everywhere. I look down at my *I ♥ Vampires* shirt, which now sports a blob of dark crimson ketchup that starts at my right shoulder, crosses my A cups, and then trails down to the waist of my yellow skinny jeans.

Great. I'm covered in half the bottle.

And it's my favorite shirt.

Ugh.

Everyone at the table bursts out laughing, and my hands clench. My gaze darts around the group and when I meet Ryker's gaze, he stops smiling, sobering as he takes in my face. "That wasn't supposed to happen."

"But fuck if it isn't funny," says Archer the Asshole.

"Dude, you look like someone shot you," Blaze adds.

"Thanks," I snap.

The jersey chasers giggle again.

"Shut up," Ryker says quickly, and then he looks back at me. "You okay?" He stands back up and hands me a wad of napkins, but I push them away.

My lips tighten. "I'm fine. I'm going to go clean up, but when I come back, I want my money."

He nods and gives me a long, searching look…one I can't decipher. "Done."

CHAPTER 2

PENELOPE

I stand in front of the mirror in the restroom and gasp. Holy moly, I'm a total disaster. Red is on my shirt, my neck, my cheek, and there's even a dab in my hair. I let out a heavy sigh as I wipe at it with a wet paper towel. At least my hair is auburn and the red will just blend right in. I scrub at the stain on my shirt, but all I end up doing is making a giant wet spot.

"Forget it," I mutter to myself a few minutes later as I straighten my lopsided messy bun and adjust my glasses. My makeup is faded, and I reach into my apron for a tube of cherry red lipstick then quickly swipe it over my mouth. Like that's going to improve the situation. I need a makeover and new clothes stat.

I walk out of the restroom and take in Sugar's Bar and Grill, a restaurant in Magnolia, Mississippi. The dinner rush is over, but a few stragglers will come in, mostly college students. Only a block from campus, Sugar's has a modern farmhouse feel with galvanized steel light fixtures, pale pine floors, and straight-back metal chairs, but the food...well, that's what keeps the place hopping. It's the only restaurant near campus to get anything you want served up with a side of fresh fried green tomatoes. Their menu also features Southern classics, such as chicken and dumplings or macaroni and cheese with bacon sprinkled on top. Just thinking about it makes my stomach rumble. I was so wrapped up in writing during my break that I forgot to eat.

I sigh and head to the football table, where they promptly hand over the money. "Nice doing business with you, boys," I say before flouncing off, feeling Ryker's eyes on me the entire time.

What's his deal with me?

I mean, you'd think he'd want to avoid me because of the article, but it's as if his mission is to be around me as much as he can. In fact, I'm not even sure he knew *who* I was before I wrote it since we don't run in the same circles. I suspect he's torturing me.

I push him out of my head and walk over to a table that needs bussing, picking up half-empty soda glasses and putting them on my tray. The door chimes, signaling that someone has come in, and I raise my head to see—

Whoa.

I freeze.

Bring out the angels and cue the hallelujah chorus.

Now *that's* the kind of man I should be writing sexy scenes about.

Standing at the door is Connor Dimpleshitz—yes, his surname is unfortunate, but his IQ makes up for it. I've been crushing on him since our sociology class last semester.

Framed by a golden halo of sunlight as it glints through the windows, I decide he's what would happen if Albert Einstein and Henry Cavill had a baby. "A hot genius. The perfect unicorn," I murmur to myself.

I chew on my lip, debating on whether to mosey up to him and say hi or hide.

Hide wins. I know, I'm a little ridiculous, especially since we have calculus together this semester and he'll obviously see me at some point in class.

But then I'll have good hair and ketchup-free clothes.

I quickly survey the possibilities for my escape as the hostess seats him in another server's section. My eyes land on the right side of the restaurant, where I could make a mad dash for the kitchen, but he's bound to see me darting since I'd have to walk past him. Plus, I want to hang around and watch him without him knowing.

I come to a decision. Wrangling the tray of half-empty sodas I cleared, I quickstep it over to the back left corner, the farthest away from the double doors of the entrance. I maneuver my body into an awkward hunkering position behind a huge potted plant with wide fan-shaped leaves. At least five feet tall with a gnarly brown trunk, the green monster is perfect camouflage.

I peek around a big leaf that's in dire need of a good dusting, judging by the motes floating around. Feeling paranoid that someone is a witness to my absurdity, I throw a quick glance over my shoulder to make sure no one's around.

Ryker. Shit.

He's staring at me from the football table, and there's a glint in his gaze, as if he's wondering what I'm doing.

I scowl and stick my tongue out at him. He makes me feel so rebellious and flustered and...excited.

I can't even stop myself. *Ugh.*

His expression deepens in amusement, and I grimace, realizing my butt is sticking out. His annoying eyebrow jacks up and says, *What the hell are you doing?*

With eye telepathy I tell him to *mind his own freaking business.*

I pointedly turn my back on him and focus on The Unicorn.

A few seconds later, a familiar deep voice resonates from behind me, making me start. "You look a little flustered, Penelope. Spying on someone for your next story, perhaps?"

I freeze. Blink. His voice is husky and lower than before when he was calling me *garçon,* the tone reminding me of languid summer nights under a starry Southern sky while he gives me deep, passionate kisses—

Good Lord. Stop your daydreaming. Must. Stop. Reading. Romances.

I heave out a sigh and turn around to face Ryker.

What the hell does he want now?

• • •

"I don't submit to the *Wildcat Weekly* anymore," I say.

I worked for them most of last year, covering the home games and a few random articles. With a dad who was in the NFL, I know a lot about football, but when Sugar's offered me more hours, I took it.

"No more football stories, huh?"

I shrug, my gaze taking in his chiseled cheekbones, the

curve of his full lips, the hint of scruff on his jaw. *Dammit, why is he so gorgeous?* "What can I say? I covered the most fascinating story last semester—you. Guess I went out on a high note."

He nods, taking that dig. "I always noticed you at the games."

I scoff. "I didn't think girls like me were on your radar."

"You sat near the third row at the fifty-yard line taking notes at every home game." His eyes drift over me. "And I didn't say you were on my radar."

"Really? Sounds like you did."

"Trust me, I have more discriminating tastes." He shrugs.

"Why, how sweet of you." My Southern accent has thickened, the way it does when I'm sassy. It's one thing to know he doesn't like me, but for him to say I'm not up to his standards…well. "Did you pop over here just to be nice?"

He exhales and rakes a hand through his hair, calling attention to the lighter strands that have been bleached by the sun. "Honestly, I'm not sure why I came over here." A conflicted expression crosses his face as he tugs at his collar. My eyes stare at the myriad of curly blond chest hairs that are poking out from the V-neck of the light blue Oxford he's wearing with the sleeves rolled up to his elbows. "I just wanted to make sure you were okay from the ketchup getting all over you, but everything I'm saying is coming out wrong."

Oh. This is different. And not what I expected.

"I'm fine, Baby Llama. No need to worry. You can go. Your girlfriends are waiting for you." I tilt my head back toward the football table.

He doesn't budge. "Baby Llama?" An amused grin flashes over his face.

I shrug. It's been my private nickname for him since sophomore year when I stumbled upon him coming out of an upstairs bathroom at the Tau house after a shower with only a white towel wrapped around his trim waist. Some jersey chaser was with him. His hairy chest had both shocked my virgin sensibilities and excited me at the same time. The unruly curls just made him seem *more* naked, as if I'd seen his cock. Much to my dismay, I'd later dream about rolling around on that bed of golden curls. Seriously, who takes a shower with a chick in the middle of a kegger? Ryker Voss, that's who. Because he can. And girls do whatever he wants.

But not this one.

I respect the game—even love it—but I don't fall for football players, especially high and mighty quarterbacks who think they walk on water. My dad was the star player at Waylon twenty years ago, and trust me, I know how they operate. They get what they want and then they walk out, leaving broken hearts everywhere.

"Have you ever seen a real llama?" he asks, continuing our conversation. It's as if he's actually trying to be nice. "I saw one at a safari park once. Little bugger tried to eat my hand off when I fed him, but he was cute. Maybe you need a poster of one in your room so when you see it, you'll think about me. I'll even sign it for you."

And there's the cocky again.

"Buy me one. I'll throw darts at it."

"Damn, you never stop." He huffs out a laugh, his eyes

lingering on my neck. "Oh, there's a bit of ketchup here too," he says, reaching out to glide his finger across the top of my collar, his knuckles barely brushing against my neck.

The feather-light touch is brief and not sexual, yet my body hums, tendrils of sparks racing over my skin. I suck in a breath and catch his scent, warm and spicy with hints of leather and sandalwood.

He blinks and clears his throat. "Um, I actually have this cleaner stuff that I spray on my practice clothes. It's a miracle worker. You're welcome to borrow it. Of course, you'd have to come by the football dorm to pick it up. We could even do laundry together if you wanted?"

He says the words softly, as if they're *nothing*, and I'm staring at him full on.

Do our laundry together?

I suspect Ryker Voss is flirting with me, though not well. The pimply-faced checkout boy at Big Star has better lines than this.

Yet...

Something warm grows inside my stomach and then flutters around, the sputtering of newborn butterflies. He *is* the hottest guy on campus. Still, I remind myself he's a player, gather my resolve, and shoot those butterflies down.

"You're being weird, Ryker."

"Because I'm being nice? Yeah. New year, new start. I want to forget all the bad stuff from last semester." He pauses. "And the article you wrote."

"Is that right? Even the part where I said you dishonored the sport and were a disgrace to college players everywhere?"

He stares down at his hands. "I had my reasons for what happened."

So I heard. He got involved in the fighting to help his friend and fellow teammate Maverick save his disabled sister.

"Ah, well, I did write a follow-up article, but it wasn't nearly as popular as the first one."

He shrugs, and somehow, he's closer now. I stare into his thickly lashed cerulean eyes and blink at the force of them. His irises...*God*, someone should name a crayon after them.

"So...do you want to do laundry together sometime?"

This again? My mouth parts. "What? Like a date?"

"Yeah."

I blink rapidly, my brain trying to wrap about this new Ryker. "No. I'm sure you already have jersey chasers lined up outside your dorm vying to do your laundry. I've heard they actually beg to rub your shoulders and do your homework. I imagine they even fight to be the one to suck your sweet little toes." I come to an abrupt halt. Suck his toes? SUCK HIS TOES? OMG. Where did that random comment come from? I don't have a foot fetish. I blame it on his presence and carry on. "And don't worry about me—I don't need your laundry advice. A little ketchup never hurt anyone."

Determination crosses his face and with a flurry of movement, he drops a small piece of paper onto the tray I'm holding.

I stare down at it. *Sexy as Hell Athlete* is written in masculine handwriting with a phone number after it. I look back up at him, my eyes tracing the enigmatic half-smile on his face.

"I wrote it down for you earlier and wanted to give it to you after the ketchup thing, but I chickened out."

Several seconds go by.

"Will you give me yours?" he asks after a few moments of us just standing here.

"My what?"

"Number." He grins.

I indicate the tray and my obvious impediment. "I don't have any paper on me."

"Just tell me. I'll remember."

I'm flustered, and that's the only reason I rattle off my phone number. He grins and repeats it back to me.

He lowers his voice in a conspiratorial way. "So...you're watching someone, I take it. Anyone I know?"

Feeling bemused by his attention, I shake my head, quickly losing control of this situation.

"For a writer, you seem to be at a loss for words. Do I make you speechless, Penelope?"

I scoff. "No."

"I'm curious as to what has your attention back here." He slides in next to me behind the plant, his shoulder brushing against mine. He's a giant next to my slender frame, and all at once, I feel protected and safe, which is entirely *wrong*. It's probably his male pheromones, lulling me into softness before the kill—and damn if it isn't working. He murmurs something about us hiding together and spying on people, but I'm distracted because my face is up close and personal with the chest hair that pokes out of his shirt. I want to trail my fingers through it and see if it's as soft as it looks. He smells like alpha male and sex. Hard, passionate sex that makes you orgasm fast and furious.

Not that I have any firsthand knowledge of that, of course, but I have my fantasies.

Gird your loins, Penelope.

Resist the quarterback.

But I'm getting sucked in.

I blame it on the dimple that appears when he smiles. My stomach does that fluttering thing again, and this time, I can't shoo the butterflies away. I'm weak. I move my eyes up the strong column of his tanned throat to meet his gaze. At least ten seconds go by as we take each other in.

What. Is. Happening?

"You're pretty," he murmurs. "Have I ever told you that?"

"We don't usually talk except for when I take your order."

His hand reaches up and briefly touches a piece of my hair that's fallen out of my topknot. He rubs it between his fingers. "Your hair…it's—"

"Auburn," I manage, clearing my throat.

"It reminds me of a new penny, the way the amber color catches the light…" His voice trails off, and he bites his bottom lip. "God, that has to be the stupidest thing I've ever said."

"You have worse lines. Tell me, is *doing laundry* code for sex?" I say, staring up at him. I'm itching to straighten my glasses, a nervous reflex, but my hands are holding the tray.

"I only use lines on jersey chasers. You're the kind of girl I have to work for."

"What about your discriminating tastes?"

"Pure bluff. I think we have a real connection, Penelope."

His face is closer now, and I swallow, wondering how we must look to everyone else in the restaurant. I realize that in the process of talking, we've backed up to the wall behind the plant, and I figure the only table we're visible to is the football one, but I don't tear my eyes away from Ryker to check.

"You smell like rainbows," he says.

My chest rises. I'm enjoying his full-court press. It's… intoxicating. "What does a rainbow smell like?"

"Sweet and delicious."

"It's the suckers." His eyes land on my lips, and it almost feels as if he's touched them. Heat rushes over my skin. "The red ones are my favorite. I think they're cherry or strawberry or raspberry…definitely not cranberry…that's disgusting," I say, rambling, feeling disoriented.

"It's crazy, but I really want to kiss you right now," he murmurs.

My eyes drift over his shoulder to where Connor's table is. I can't see his face, but I know he's there, and even though I'm drugged by Ryker's proximity, I remind myself *he's* the one I should kiss.

Not Ryker.

Ryker is a player—just like my dad was.

He watches the direction of my gaze and follows it. "You've been watching Dimpleshitz, haven't you?" he says, a frown line appearing on his forehead. "Are you into him?"

My stomach dips. "Why would you say that?"

"Because you hightailed it over here when he walked in and you've been hiding ever since. So, I figure he either did you wrong or you're infatuated, and since I haven't heard any gossip about you and him, I'm guessing you must have a thing for him."

Abort! Abort! He knows too much!

Sanity slowly returns to my brain in small increments, and I take a deep breath, orienting myself as questions race through my head. What if he uses my crush against me? Maybe he wants revenge for the article. *I don't know!*

Flustered and unsure, my eyes dart around the restaurant, looking for an exit so I don't have to answer his question.

My gaze lands on the football table he came from, and I notice Archer watching us with focused interest, a calculating look on his face as he whips his eyes from me to Ryker. He leans over and whispers to Blaze, who turns to peer in our direction. I pause, my brain analyzing and decoding. Why is Archer suddenly interested in what Ryker is doing over here with me—especially when there's a pretty co-ed sitting right next to him, tracing little circles on his bicep?

Yet Archer's eagle eyes are on *us*. Watchful.

I notice all three players at the table have suddenly given us their attention, anticipation evident on their faces.

Alarms go off in my head and things start to click into place.

How nice he was to me. How we 'have a connection'. *Yeah, right.*

Mortification washes over me.

How could I not have seen it sooner?

God, I am an idiot. I was so distracted…

I'm a bet. A stupid freaking bet.

I feel like someone just punched me in the gut.

My survival instinct tells me to get away from Ryker, and obviously, I could just walk away and hold my head high, but I want to make a point and show those football players they can't toy with me. I release the tray I've been balancing for what seems like days in his direction. The contents of the glasses spill out and crash to the floor, watered-down soda and ice drenching us before dripping down to the floor. The plastic glasses make a horrible clattering noise on the wooden floors, and I imagine most everyone in the restaurant heard it. I don't look to see their faces. I only glare at Ryker.

He jumps back and stares down at the mess on his khaki pants then looks back at me. "Remind me to never bring up Dimpleshitz again."

"Stop your games, Ryker."

His face stills. "What games?"

My teeth snap together. *Enough.*

CHAPTER 3

PENELOPE

Tension is thick as we eye each other, both of us ignoring the mess to continue our stare-down. The apron around my waist took the brunt of the water that came in my direction, but Ryker's pants are soaked—only he barely seems to notice now that we're facing off.

"It was nice chatting, Ryker. Oh, and by the way, it looks like you peed yourself." I move to walk past him to grab some towels from the back, but he takes a small step, blocking me.

"Wait, what's wrong?" Frustration flashes over his features. "Look, I never know how to ask a real girl out. Can we start over? Without all this water everywhere?"

Look at him. Still trying to win me over. He's persistent, I'll give him that.

I tilt my chin up and glare at him. "Why do you even care?"

He sighs heavily, and he seems to gather himself as he searches for the right words. "I don't know...maybe it's because you take great pains to walk around me on campus. You sit on the opposite side of me in class, and that was *before* you wrote that stupid article about me last year. It's like there's something about me that repels you."

"You repel me because you're a douchebag." Not waiting to see his reaction to that, I forget about getting the towels and bend down to pick up the glasses, setting them back on the tray. My hands are shaking as I whip off my apron and use the dry parts to dab at the floor.

"Here, let me help." He squats down next to me, raking the ice up into a pile and then scooping it onto the tray.

"Stop."

"No, let me help."

I pause what I'm doing and glare at him. "Just quit the acting, okay? Whatever bet you and the team have going about me, forget it. It won't work."

He stops and pales, and that's all the confirmation I need.

I was *right*.

Part of me, the silly girl inside who would be flattered to have the honest attention of the most popular guy on campus—even if he is a football player—wants to cry. I stuff her down in a box and throw away the key.

For half a second, I honestly thought the article I wrote didn't matter and he was being sincere. I thought he liked *me*. My hands clench. I let down my guard for half a second, and this is what happens.

I stand up. "You only came over here to talk to me for a bet." My lips flatten. "Just leave me alone. Please."

He's picked up the tray and is standing now, a look of unease on his face. "Wait, that's not the whole story—"

"And the next time you attempt to win a bet like this, consider the feelings of the person you mess with."

He swallows. "Penelope, it wasn't—"

I hold my hand up for him to shut up, and he does, his teeth tugging at his lower lip, a torn expression on his face. I flick my eyes back to Archer and company. Some of them are guffawing and chortling as they watch us, and anger tightens in my gut.

"Ignore them," he says. "They're just laughing at my pants. They knew I didn't have a chance with you, and now you've proved it."

I shake my head. "I guess the bet was if you could get me to kiss you? Go out with you?"

He rakes a hand through his hair and stares at me. "Look, I didn't mean for it—"

"*What* was the bet?"

His shoulders dip. "They bet me I couldn't get you to go out with me."

"A date."

He gives me a terse nod.

"Huh. So, you actually thought you and I would go out? Even though we don't like each other?"

"I never said I didn't like you."

"But you don't," I insist.

He hesitates, the words leaving his mouth reluctantly. "It was assumed I'd stand you up, but—"

My hands tighten. "So, your plan was for me to come over to do laundry and then you wouldn't be there?" My face scrunches as I try to picture the scenario. Hurt slices through me. "I have my own washer anyway, jerk."

He shakes his head. "I didn't have a real plan. I was just

winging it—"

"You knew exactly what you were doing and you lost, Baby Llama. *You lost.* I hope it was worth the laugh."

"I'm not laughing, Penelope." He frowns. "I didn't mean to hurt you."

"Only because you lost." Mustering up as much gumption as I have left, I turn my back to him and march over to the football table. I put my hands on my hips and make eye contact with each player. They don't faze me. Blaze reads my face and mouths *I'm sorry*, but I brush my eyes right over him. We may know each other, but right now, he's an asshole just like the rest of them.

"He lost, boys. Ryker Voss asked me out and crashed and burned. If there was money involved, I expect my cut of whatever the amount was. Understood?"

They all gape at me except for Archer. With a stare that seems to see right through my bravado, he grins. There's a carefree nonchalance to his stance as he shakes off the jersey chaser and stands to shake my hand. "Yes, *cher*. Absolutely," he murmurs. "You can have it all as far as I'm concerned." He pops the table with his hand and addresses the players. "Let's go ahead and give the lady our winnings. Ryker can even it up with us later."

Each player forks over a ten, and then Archer gathers up the cash and puts it in my hand. "I've never enjoyed anything as much as seeing Ryker get water dumped on him today. Thank you for that, and I hope you won't hold this little bet against me." His gaze is a bit too lingering, and I want to wipe my hand off when he releases it.

"You can all go fuck yourselves," I say.

Archer throws back his head and laughs. "You've got some spark to you all right."

"Whatever," I mutter, stuffing the money in my apron.

I give them one final hard look and then dash to the back of the restaurant, barely hanging on to my composure. My gaze darts to Ryker, standing in the corner with the tray in his hands. The glasses and ice are piled on top, and his face is expressionless, nearly granite as he watches me, and I resist the urge to flip him off. The only thing holding me back is that if my boss saw it, he'd rake me over the coals. Everyone loves the football players.

So, I fly right past him and blow through the double doors of the kitchen. Without a glance at anyone, I run all the way to the pantry, where I slam the door. I fight it with everything I have, but I can't stop the hot tears that spill down my cheeks.

The infuriating thing is I don't even know why I'm so let down and disappointed by a guy I knew was a dick to begin with.

CHAPTER 4

RYKER

My eyes follow Penelope as she storms across the floor to the bar and disappears into the back of the restaurant. *Fuck.*

Guilt washes over me. I have to fix this. I'm not a horrible human being, and I never meant to upset her; in fact, I never thought I'd get as far with her as she let me. I only meant to go over and make a half-assed attempt at asking her out, but once I got close to her and started talking...things just happened. True, the ketchup bet was my idea, mostly to annoy her, but this new one was orchestrated entirely by Archer.

I bet you can't get her to go out with you, he said earlier when she was cleaning up in the restroom. I resisted, mostly thinking there wasn't a chance in hell she'd agree, but he egged me on until I accepted.

Squaring my shoulders, I stride toward the bar at the front of Sugar's, but before I get there, a female form bounces in front of me. With her pink and black hair and petite frame, she's instantly recognizable as Penelope's friend Charisma. I've seen them on campus and at parties. I hadn't noticed her before, so she must have come in while I was talking to

Penelope.

"Charisma. If you don't mind, you're in my way." I give her the standard Ryker glare, which is pretty much guaranteed to make the guys on the team move their ass if I point it in their direction.

"WTF did you do to my BFF?" she asks.

I exhale. Charisma talks in acronyms, and sometimes it's like decoding another language. "None of your business. Please move."

I make a move to walk around her, but she steps in front of me.

"Hold on, QB1. I don't think you want to follow her right now." She gives me a hard once-over. "Out of all the girls at this school you could have messed with, you chose the nicest one." She crosses her arms. "Now, do you want to tell me what's going on?"

I widen my stance. I'm not telling her anything. Penelope is the one I want to see. "I want to talk to her."

She sends me a death glare. "No."

I rake a hand through my hair. *Dammit.*

Blaze jogs across the restaurant—because he never does anything slowly—waving at me. Tall and muscular with a carefully gelled brown faux mohawk, he skids to a stop and talks with his hands. "Dude!" He laughs, tries to stop, then gives up and lets out a hoot. "You screwed that up so awesomely bad. Dillon got it on video, and I've watched it twice already. Shit, that part where she dumps the water on you —your face is priceless!"

My teeth clench. "I know. I was there. Thanks for

reminding me."

"But you never saw it coming! You thought she was yours, man." He lets out a satisfied sigh.

I never thought she was mine. Penelope Graham is the kind of girl who would never give me a shot. I read her article—she thinks I'm a loser for letting Maverick participate in those fights last year. But the thing is, he's my best friend and he did it for money to help save his sister. Of course I supported him —even when it meant putting our team at risk. When he was caught, the entire scandal played out on national television for everyone to see—including my part in knowing about it. In all fairness, her article was a drop in the bucket of the bad press we received. Did it piss me off that a Waylon writer wrote shit about me? Hell yes. Do I hate her because of it? Let's just say it got my attention.

Blaze gets distracted by Charisma and gives her his famous head nod. "What's your name?"

Charisma rolls her eyes. "*My name?* As if. The question is: *Who are you?* A toddler on steroids. What did you do to hurt my friend?" Her head does the wagging thing.

Blaze backpedals. "Nah, nah, it wasn't meant to hurt anybody. I dig Penelope. She's wicked smart. She tutors me in math."

"Not anymore," she snaps.

Blaze looks concerned and eases in closer to Charisma, his hilarity forgotten. "I'm a good guy. So is Ryker here. True story. Now why don't you tell me your name?"

They're talking, and I figure Blaze is working his mojo on Charisma—which is the perfect distraction. I look past them, wondering if I can get to the back of the restaurant and find Penelope without Charisma tackling me. With a quick glance at her, I see she's up in Blaze's face, asking him about the details, and he's telling her about the bets in little spurts. Her eyes flash over to me, and I see the warning there: *Don't even try to follow Penelope.*

My lips tighten. I guess I could just sit here for a while and wait to see if she comes out. I take a stool at the bar, the same one where Penelope was sitting earlier. I recall watching her write in her notebook.

Yeah, I was checking her out.

Taking her in.

With her pouty red lips, nerd glasses, and mane of thick auburn hair, she's pretty in an understated way, nothing like the jersey chasers who hang all over us. She's not my type, to be honest.

Yet...

There's something about her.

She's... I can't find the words.

Sexy as fuck, a voice says.

Pfft. I push that thought away. Never going to happen.

I don't do quirky.

Or girls who can't stand me.

Besides, I'm focusing on football, not girls. I have a reputation to rebuild after last year.

My eyes land on her laptop and I frown. Granted, the bar area is a bit deserted, but there isn't a bartender in sight, and college students can get desperate for money sometimes. Computers aren't cheap. I gather up her laptop and notebook then take them to a cleared space behind the bar near a shelf of glasses. I'm sure she'll find it. I'm turning to go when my shirt catches on the notebook, tugging it out from under the computer, and I see what's written on the top. Surrounded by kitten and heart stickers are the words: *THIS JOURNAL IS PRIVATE. IF YOU OPEN IT, I WILL RIP YOUR NIPPLES OFF.*

Oh, babe. You can't throw down a gauntlet like that and expect me to not peek…

With a glance to make sure Charisma is still talking to Blaze, I flip open the first page, skim a few lines, and when I see my name, I start reading.

What the hell?

The words are enough to make me sweat.

I slam the journal shut, shoving it back under her laptop. Penelope has a crush on Connor, but her imagination goes all over place—*even to me?*

I push down the hard-on in my pants and go back to the stool at the bar. I thought she hated me…right?

She does for sure now—look what you did to her.

Hell, she's probably back there crying.

I swallow. *Shit*…that bugs me.

Feeling my neck prickle with awareness, I glance over at the table and see Archer staring at me, an amused sneer on his face. He raises an empty glass and mimics pouring it out on the table, obviously making a point about the tray Penelope dumped.

My jaw tenses and my hands clench. *Ignore him.* He's just trying to piss you off and get a reaction. It's no secret we butt heads, which can be expected when I'm offense and he's defense, but our personalities just...clash. He doesn't like that I'm the captain of the team and goes out of his way to nitpick at anything I do, whether on the field or off. In fact, he wasn't even supposed to eat with us tonight but somehow managed to wrangle an invitation out of Blaze.

Charisma has shooed Blaze off, and his shoulders slump as he goes back to the table. She focuses back on me, and if looks were bullets, I'd be dead. "As for you, I suggest you get out of Sugar's and don't come back. Penelope doesn't deserve what you did."

I heave out an exhale. "It's the best restaurant in Magnolia. I eat here all the time."

She purses her lips. "She might poison your food."

I shake my head. "Can you just tell her I'm sorry?"

She arches an eyebrow at me. "Go to hell, QB1. She doesn't like you anyway."

"Why is that?" I'm baffled by her bitter attitude toward me, and it must get across to Charisma because she gets this funny look on her face. She opens her mouth to respond but then shuts it.

"What?" I ask. "It's more than just the article she wrote, right?"

She shrugs. "She doesn't have the highest opinion of quarterbacks. Her dad was one and was a real jerk." She pauses as if she's said too much. "If you really want to make it up to her, how about doing something nice for her."

"Like what? Flowers?"

"I'm not telling you how to apologize, QB1. You're a smart

guy. You figure it out." She rakes her gaze over me. "BTW, wet khakis aren't a good look for you." With a hair flip, she's off to the back where Penelope went earlier.

After Penelope brought up the bet and I saw how upset she was, I mostly forgot about my pants. I look down at them now and grab a few napkins from the bar to dab up the water. It doesn't do much good. *Fuck.* It does look like I peed myself. With an annoyed exhale, I pivot around and head for the door to go back to campus, not interested in returning to the football table and dealing with Archer and his gloating.

Plus, a part of me is miffed that Penelope turned me down cold.

For some reason, my gaze lands on Connor.

I study him, taking in the dark hair and square glasses as he sits at a table near the window. He even has a calculator in his hand. What on earth does she see in this pasty dude? I guess he's handsome? Hell if I know.

Then I narrow my gaze, realizing all at once that he's pretty much the complete opposite of me—thin, dark hair, unathletic.

Observing Connor gives me an idea…and I think I have the perfect way to prove I'm not the asshole Penelope thinks I am.

CHAPTER 5

RYKER

Inside the locker room, Blaze's naked ass does the Whip and Nae Nae as several hoots and cackles come from the team.

"Get in gear," I call out as I saunter by out of the shower and slap him on the butt with my towel. "We have to be in class in thirty."

He keeps on dancing, hyper as hell, and I grin, glad he makes that energy work for him on the field as our star wide receiver.

Making my way to the lockers, my gaze lands on the golden wildcat statue that serves as the bet award and sits inside the glass trophy case on the far wall. My mood plummets. I take in the white board on the wall where the bets are listed. The one with Penelope is now there: *Ask Penelope Graham out and get a YES: Completed.* Points were given to Archer, Blaze, and Dillon, who bet that I couldn't. I have a giant goose egg.

The ketchup bet isn't listed since it wasn't players against players.

Coach Alvarez stomps into the locker room wearing a *don't*

tell me you're screwing off expression on his square face. Slashing bushy eyebrows accentuate his brown eyes as they spear every player in sight. His voice careens around the room. "Turn that fucking music off!" A mouthy man with a barrel chest and dark skin, Coach loves football—and cursing. "And why are y'all still in this goddamn locker room? Get the hell out of here and get to class."

My teammates pick up the pace, rummaging around in their lockers.

"You know the drill. I expect you back at three for practice with your heads on straighter than they were this morning. I need to see some fucking teamwork. You looked terrible out there. Get your shit together and stop acting like girls in a hair-pulling hissy fit. Our first game is this fucking Friday."

A few players hang their head. Yeah, we had a few scuffles on the field, a late hit and some shoving on the defense. Things aren't right with our team, and it's because our star defensive player, Maverick, is gone. Regret tugs at me, and I wonder if there was anything else I could have done to stop him from fighting last year.

Coach's militant gaze pins me. "Remember, Ryker's your captain. Listen to him and don't bring your shit onto the field. Got it?"

I nod. Coach and I get each other. We both want a championship this year, especially after the fiasco last spring.

"What about the defense, Coach?" It's Archer's voice, and I swivel my head toward him. "Don't we get a captain?"

Coach crosses his arms. "Maverick's your captain."

Archer shrugs and lifts his hands. "Yeah, but he's gone for

three games because of the NCAA ruling. Can't even practice with us." He pauses for dramatic effect. "With all due respect, sir, Ryker doesn't cut it for us. He knew what Maverick was doing and didn't tell anyone." His eyes are on me. "He was there at every fight Maverick participated in and should have stopped him."

My blood pressure spikes and my fists clench. I take a step toward Archer, but Coach holds his hand up at me, warning me to chill out. He looks back at Archer. "That was last year and this is a new season. We're moving on. What's your point, son?"

Archer straightens his shoulders. "Moving on is exactly right, sir. We'd like to elect our own captain—for the defense. It might be good for morale."

That sonofabitch. He thinks he can just slide in and take Maverick's place? I want to spit nails. No one can replace Maverick. Archer is just manipulating Coach to get what he wants.

"I've been talking to the defense, and they want me in charge." Archer takes another step until he's standing at the front of the team.

Coach looks around, his gaze taking in faces, trying to read us. "Is that so?"

Some of the defensive guys nod.

Coach thinks for a moment. "If the defense wants it, that's good enough for me, but when Maverick comes back, you'll need to work it out amongst yourselves. This isn't a competition, boys. It's a *team.* Got it?" Coach looks at me. "You good with this, Ryker?"

Fuck no. I think Archer is a piece of shit, but what can I say that doesn't sound like I don't have the best interests of the team in mind? My jaw pops. "I'm with you, sir."

He nods. "All right. Let's do it and move on. Got it?"

"Yes sir!" I say with several others.

He puffs up his chest. "Now get the fuck out of here and get to class."

I nod in agreement and do my best to shake off the practice. I need time to process the new Archer situation.

His face appears behind me as I style my hair in the mirror. My lips thin. "What do you want?" I say.

"Now, now, take it easy, number one," he says in his lilting accent. "I'm not trying to ruffle your feathers, just dropping by to say your arm looked real good out there today." He grins. "We're captains now. We need to pep each other up, keep our teams running smooth." He holds up his hands at my glare. "Just sayin'. I'm impressed, especially considering how *spectacularly* you got shot down yesterday. I figured your confidence would be in shambles today." He makes an exploding sound and moves his hands, mimicking a blast. A grin flashes on his face. "She. Nailed. Your. Ass."

A muscle twitches in my jaw. Archer has a knack of knowing what to say to piss me off.

"Goddamn, but she's a hot one," he says. "I wouldn't mind taking that out for a ride." He grinds his hips as if he's screwing. "Oh yeah, baby."

I flip around to face him, my face hard as stone. "You wanna try *me*, asshole?"

He reads me loud and clear and stops his grinding.

Yeah, that's right, my eyes say. *Pussy.* He might be our fastest cornerback, a big and capable player, but I'm taller and meaner and I fucking want it more, whatever *it* may be. I always have. Since the moment I walked out on the field for my first high school game as a freshman and smelled the grass, felt the bright lights of the stadium, I knew football was my dream.

I snatch my Wildcats shirt out of my gym bag and slip it over my head. I shove on my khaki joggers and forgo my sneakers for a pair of leather flip-flops.

"Losing that bet still bothers you," he murmurs, hovering around me. "I don't blame you, because honestly, who turns down Ryker Voss? And this girl, I mean—she hates you." A gruff laugh comes out of him. "I've been replaying that restaurant scene all damn day. It's like a movie in my head that I can't turn off."

I ignore him and throw my towel in the bin then bend over to pick up my dirty practice clothes and put them in my bag.

He holds a finger up. "I've been thinking…a girl like that, with all that fire…I really wanna go for it. Know what I mean? Tame her. Maybe wine and dine her then fuck her so good she begs me to never leave." He chuckles, his eyes sharpening. "That is, if you're okay with me moving in on her?"

A switch is thrown inside me, and it isn't so much about Penelope as it is about everything that's happened over the past few months. The thing is, I've been at a tipping point since the scandal. I wasn't docked games like Maverick, but I was investigated and lost any chance at the Heisman Award. You have to have a spotless rep to be named the best player in college football and, well, let's be honest...my name is pure shit in the media right now. That ship has sailed, and my anger and disappointment have been simmering for months, only heightening now that school is back in session, and I have to face everything and deal with it.

I'm not the golden boy everyone likes to describe me as.

And all I want to do right now is take it out on Archer's face.

My chest rises rapidly as I throw a quick look around the room, checking for any coaches, and when I don't see one, I move fast, getting up in his space and pushing my hand into his chest until he's pinned against the concrete wall.

He briefly squirms to try to get away from me, but it isn't going to work. When he sees that he can't get loose, he settles for puffing out his chest. "I didn't know you cared so much about her."

My open palm slaps against the concrete behind him. "This isn't about *her*. This is about you maneuvering to be captain. *Please*. You'll never take Maverick's place. Just stay out of my way. Got it?"

Blaze appears at my right, a hand on my bicep as he tugs on me, but I'm immovable. This little fight has been building for months. "Dude, let him go."

"Get out of my face, Blaze," I say, my eyes not wavering from Archer's.

"You're a leader, man. You can't be pushing people around," he says, bouncing around us.

I grit my teeth. "We're playing like shit. No one cares. Why should I?"

"I care, man." Blaze looks around for help, but the rest of the team is silent, waiting. I feel their eyes on me. Hell, everyone is watching me. All the damn time. I'm sick of it.

"This is exactly what Coach was talking about." He gives Archer a glare. "Plus, Archer was just kidding, right?"

He nods and attempts to raise his hands in mock surrender. "All I'm saying is it looked like you have a thing for her."

"I don't." I move in closer and put my nose to his. "And if I really wanted her, I could have her." The words feel wrong, but I can't pull them back. The truth is, part of me was wired up and excited during the bet—excited to see if she'd say yes. *What if she had?*

Would I have stood her up? Maybe. I don't know.

A sly expression grows in Archer's eyes. "Prove it."

I frown. *What the hell is he talking about?*

"Prove it," he repeats, louder and with a bit of shrill in his tone. He looks around at the players. "Everyone listen up. We're going to have us a doozy of a bet—one we don't put on the board."

My jaw twitches again. "I'm not playing your games."

"The bets are good for the team. We've been doing it for years," someone says, and I see most of the players nodding. A few rumble amongst themselves.

"…yeah, Ryker…"

Archer smirks and gives me a victorious look. "I bet you can't tap that, number one. I bet you can't score that girl before homecoming. Defense against offense for the whole shebang. If *you* lose, the whole offense loses. Got it?"

Some of the offensive players agree and clap me on the

back, offering words of encouragement.

"You got this, dude."

"Easy peasy."

"Don't you want that trophy?"

I eye the guys surrounding me, reading their excitement, and tension wraps around me. My teeth grind together. A bet to fuck a girl is not in my wheelhouse.

I release Archer with a push.

He gives me a hard look, one that tells me he isn't going to let this bet go. "It's all up to you, number one. If you want to win that trophy, you've got to bang Penelope." He curls his lip. "I don't think you can do it."

Bang Penelope.

My gut tightens and my fists curl at his crude words. Penelope and I may not like each other, but I do respect her, and I don't like him talking about her like she's a piece of meat.

"Fuck off, Archer." I give him and everyone a final glare then stalk out of the locker room with Blaze on my heels.

"Come on, man," he says as we walk out of the field house. "What's so bad about the bet? I don't think she hates you. There's something between you and her already."

I frown. "No, there isn't."

"I disagree."

I give him side-eye and he shrugs. "What? Everybody thinks I don't notice shit because I'm spastic, but it looked pretty steamy behind that plant before she dumped the water on you. She was *into* you." He sighs as we walk to the parking lot to get in our cars. "Besides, wouldn't it be awesome to get one over on Archer? It would bug the shit out of him."

I get to my black Chevy truck and unlock it with the clicker.

He watches me. "Dude, take one for the team. Ask her out again. Hell, you never know, you might really like her."

"Nope. Not interested." I motion to the passenger side. "Now, do you need a ride to class or what? You don't need to miss that upper level psych class. I saw the F you got on your paper. Focus, man—we need to keep those grades up. What if the NFL doesn't work out?"

"Yes, Mom, I'm going to class." He exhales and gets in the truck. "I just don't see why you won't at least play along."

"Football isn't fun and games," I tell him as I crank the vehicle. "It's serious shit and we can't screw it up. The draft is coming, and everyone's watching us."

"You thought the ketchup was fun."

I sigh.

"You like annoying her," he adds in a singsong voice.

"Maybe."

He exhales.

We pull out of the parking lot, and I should be thinking about my next class, but in the back of my mind I'm still replaying Archer's wager in my head.

I bet you can't score that girl before homecoming.

CHAPTER 6

PENELOPE

I'm standing in my kitchen, about to feed my bird when my phone pings with a text from an unknown number. I set the food down and study the message.

Hey, you there? I want to talk.

Hmmm. I study the text. *Talk?* Well, that sounds serious and it's obviously from someone who gets straight to the point. No bullshit—I like it. Studying the number, it seems vaguely familiar, but I can't put my finger on it. My brow wrinkles. It's the prefix for this area, so it could be anyone around Magnolia.

I shrug. Unknown texts *can* be intriguing. Once I got a series of messages about the best toga party on campus, and Charisma and I ended up asking for the address and crashing. It was out on a farm in the middle of a field, and there was free chardonnay—albeit, not the best, but I'll drink any kind of white wine. To this day, Charisma claims to have hooked up with some guy in the barn who blew her mind. Too bad she was too drunk to recall his name…

Anyway. Fun things can happen when you eavesdrop on someone's texts.

Talk about what? I reply.

It's better if we do this face to face. I got your address from someone in class. Would you mind if I dropped by? I need to see you.

I need to see you. I make a whistling noise under my breath. Oh, that's a tantalizing phrase, and it makes my romantic heart jump. It's so...emotional. Is this a guy or a girl texting? With the brevity of words and straight-to-the-point way of speaking, I'm guessing male. It's likely a college guy since he mentioned class, and obviously they don't know each other well since he had to ask where she lives...hmmm... My head pictures a lonely guy who's just trying to make things right with a girl.

But what if it's the mob and this is a lure so a hitman can kill the snitch who's squealed to the police? Maybe "face to face" really means *I'm going to whack you.*

Too much *Dateline*, Penelope.

Yet...

I'm fascinated as I pace around the kitchen. I decide to indulge my curiosity and text him back.

What do you want to talk about? Just text it. *I want to know all the things!*

There's a pause, and I wonder what he's thinking. What if this issue is a big deal to him? Worry pricks at me, and I feel guilty for being nosy.

Are you okay? I send.

His reply arrives fast. **Just a shitty day, but this isn't about me. Look, I'm sorry for what happened between us. I want to make it up to you.**

How will you make it up to me? I ask, excitement curling. **Type it here.** *Because this girl is dying to know.*

My mom always said I was too curious for my own good and it's landed me in trouble plenty of times, but I can't resist prying away layers to get to the heart of the matter. It's part of who I am. Maybe it's what pushes me to be a writer, to get all those emotions out and bounce them around to see what they can do.

He hasn't replied after several beats, and my conscience tugs at me again. I waffle about coming clean just as another text comes in.

What do you want? he says.

You, I send, biting my lip. What if I read this scenario completely wrong? Have I screwed everything up and given myself away?

Me? Are you sure?

Yes, I reply.

I mean, I could be wrong and this isn't a boy/girl love thing, but what if I'm not? I'm committed to seeing how this plays out now. *Romance must always win!* is my motto.

There are three dots on my screen for several moments, as if the person on the other end is typing and deleting his response over and over.

Come on, I think, clutching the phone in anticipation.

You can't handle me, babe, is his reply.

Babe? My eyes widen. Oh. This is a bad, bad boy. And his words send a buzz right through me.

He sends another. **Let's talk about this in person. Do you mind if I come by your house tonight? 8:00 PM?**

I study the words. Well, technically, I'll be at my sorority meeting and then off to dinner with some pledges, so…what's the harm? Maybe I'll reunite two people who obviously need to talk.

Before I can reply, another message appears.

You see right through me and don't take my shit, he replies. **I dig that.**

Oh, wow, he's getting sweet? I grab a raspberry sucker from the drawer next to the fridge and pop it in my mouth.

I believe you. We can work this out, I send happily and then announce aloud, "Call me Dr. Phil, people. I'm saving a relationship somewhere."

Can't wait to see you, I send. Wait…was that too much? *Nah.* **See you at 8.**

Got it, is his reply.

I set my phone down and focus on my bird, a pretty African Grey parrot who's been watching me the entire time, his small pale yellow eyes going from me to the box of Ritz crackers on the counter.

"*Jock* is today's word, Vampire Bill," I tell him as I approach his cage by the bay window. "I know, normally I have harder words of the day, but a certain person named Ryker has been on my mind and he's a real asshole."

I recall the episode at Sugar's and my chest hurts. Not to mention I saw him today in my upper level calculus class, one we unfortunately share. He attempted to speak to me in the hall before class started, but I sidestepped him, dashed into the room, and plopped myself between two people so he couldn't sit near me. As soon as the bell rang at the end of class, I was up and darting out of my seat.

Whatever. I don't care what he wants to say. He's already done and said enough.

I push my fingers into the cage and give Vampire Bill an encouraging scratch on his head. He's a small fellow by parrot standards, a runt really, only weighing about half a pound. One of his wings is also slightly smaller than the other. His beak is black and surprisingly delicate considering what a little pig he is when he eats.

"I know it's hard to say, but you can do it, buddy. *Jock.*"

"Shit!" he squawks in his high-pitched mimicry.

I roll my eyes. "That's not what I said, but I like where you're going."

"I want a cigarette!" he says, and I shake my head regretfully.

"No, and I apologize again for your previous owners who taught you those words. I just hope they never actually gave you a cigarette. Say, *Ryker is a jock.*"

He rolls his eyes at me and pecks at his soft gray feathers.

I sigh and we have a stare-off. He wins.

"Fine," I say, reaching for the box of Ritz crackers. He positively bristles in excitement, bouncing his feet on his perch.

"Oh? You asked for the meaning? Of course, let me get to it." I clear my throat. "A jock is a guy who thinks he's the best athlete in the world, but in reality he's going to end up selling used cars or pumping gas. Go on, say it: *jock.*"

He moves his head around, studying me as if I'm the crazy one here.

I pull out a golden cracker and wave it at him. "Say it. Go on."

"Jock! Ryker! Shit!" he squawks, and I hand over the Ritz.

"I'm glad you came along when you did, Vampire Bill. You make my days happy—even if you don't like me." I grin at him, and he uses a claw to grab some food pellets out of his bowl and fling them at me. Psycho bird.

My phone pings with a text, and I glance down at it.

Please come to dinner this weekend? You can see Cyan.

My fingers tighten around the cell. I definitely know who *this* sender is. The message is from my dad, and Cyan is his new baby. I stare at the words, imagining my father typing them out, sitting at his desk in his office at Waylon, dressed in his nice suit. My teeth grind together until I make myself stop.

After Mom passed away three years ago, he retired from the NFL and moved back to Magnolia. He said it was for many reasons: to get back to his roots, to teach at Waylon, but mostly for me. So I wouldn't be alone. So I'd have family around.

Liar. I don't believe him.

He came back because his knee was blown out, and he had contacts here to get a teaching job. Something hard twists inside me, and I suck in a sharp breath. I can't forgive him for not having a life with Mom while she was alive. They were college sweethearts—the cheerleader and the quarterback—but after she got pregnant their senior year, he left her to play for the Seattle Seahawks.

Magnolia is *my* town, the place *I* grew up.

Why did he have to come and mess it all up?

"OMG, are you still trying to teach that dumb bird the word

of the day?" Charisma says in her drawn-out New York accent as she bounces into the room. Petite, curvy, and sassy, she's the product of an Italian family from the Bronx. She was my first friend in college, and we've been inseparable ever since.

"Crazy is here! Crazy is here! Shit! Give me a cigarette!" Vampire Bill belts out along with a screech that's halfway between a wolf howling and a cat being murdered.

She flips him off. "I am *not* crazy. You are, bird."

"Be nice to him. His species is the most intelligent in the parrot family."

"I am nice to him. I gave him the pineapple off my pizza last night and still, this is how he treats me." She throws her hands up in exasperation.

I laugh.

"You ready to go to the meeting?" she asks a few beats later as she grabs her purse. "I don't want to be late for the first one of the year," she adds, and my eyes flare as I realize she's wearing slacks and a cute pink sweater. I check my watch and see we have five minutes to get there—ten if they start late. *Crap.* I haven't even changed clothes.

"Dammit!" I call out as I fly past her and run to my bedroom to grab my pink jersey that bears our Greek letters, pairing it with my red skinny jeans. I slap on some lipstick and throw two-inch suede booties on my feet to dress it up. I check my hair in the mirror, and it's a riotous mess. Oh well. It'll have to do.

Better to be on time than to look good.

CHAPTER 7

PENELOPE

Two minutes later, we're crawling into my car, an older model Toyota Camry I inherited from my mom. Also parked in the driveway is a brand new, white-silver metallic convertible Volkswagen Beetle—a gift from my dad a few months ago on my birthday. Boy, talk about an uncomfortable moment when he took me outside and presented my gift in his driveway, dressed up with a big red bow on top just like in the commercials. Confused, I looked from him to the car, trying to figure him out. Did he think a car would fix the fact that he abandoned me when I was a baby and now has a whole new family? Never going to happen. My pride refuses to enjoy it.

I pop in some Eminem and we peel out.

I break the speed limit driving the few blocks over to where sorority houses dot the street, all in a line. Pulling up to the curb, I manage to find a small parking spot and squeeze in after a bit of maneuvering.

"I'm glad you know how to parallel park," Charisma says quickly as we get out and dash for the Chi Omega house, a two-story mansion constructed of red brick with four Doric columns on the front. Built in the late 80s, it's got everything you could ever want in a grand house in the South: big front porch—all the better to dance on—and huge trees in the front yard with moss hanging from the limbs.

We rush inside to the large den and have barely taken our seats on one of the long benches in the back when the side door opens and our president waltzes in.

Made it! We fist-bump each other.

My gaze goes to the front. Everyone please welcome Margo Whitley, the Barbie at the top of the heap. From the top of her shiny, shoulder-length blonde hair to the little pink cardigan she wears around her shapely shoulders, she's the epitome of the perfect Chi Omega girl. She points her button nose toward the ceiling as she walks toward the podium at the front of the room. Definitely a snooty patootie.

She's also my new-ish stepsister.

My dad met her mom in a whirlwind romance and married her a year ago. Baby Cyan arrived six months later. Yeah, you do the math. The only thing that reverberates through my head is that Margo's mom was good enough to marry but mine wasn't.

She passes me as she walks down the aisle, but then backs up, her gaze critical, taking in my jeans.

Feeling defiant, I glare back at her. At one point during our freshman year when we were pledges together, we were friendly, even though we're obviously complete opposites: I'm fun and colorful; she's an uptight know-it-all.

She tilts her head toward me. "No casual attire." She looks pointedly around the room at the other girls in sundresses, skirts, and dress pants.

I send her a tight-lipped smile. "You're right, and I apologize. I was running late because I worked today. It won't happen again." My eyes dare her to say anything else. Sure, she has the rule on her side, and she could ask me to leave, but it wouldn't look good to start off the first meeting by kicking out a sister. Plus, I did say I was sorry—and I truly am.

I make a note to set an alarm on my phone for meetings. I'm a bit of a daydreamer, and deadlines do get away from me. I blame the mystery man who texted me.

She narrows her eyes. "Fine. Consider this a warning."

"Power-tripping," Charisma mutters as Margo continues down the aisle.

I nod my agreement and watch her as she maneuvers behind the podium, taking in the hair that's pulled back with a simple black headband. She looks perfect.

Yet...

She isn't happy—it's plain as day in the tight lines on her forehead and the dark shadows under her eyes.

"Hello, everyone." Her smile is brief. "Before we begin, I'd like to remind everyone to please dress appropriately when you attend our meetings."

"Oooo, she's talking about you," Charisma says while wiggling her eyebrows at me.

I laugh and Margo swivels her head in my direction, her eyes like lasers as they find mine. Great.

Charisma mouths, *Sorry.*

Margo inhales a deep breath. "Penelope, is there something you'd like to share with the group?"

I clear my throat. "No. I'm sorry for the disturbance."

"Good." She continues and levels her eyes at each fresh new face. "Let's discuss the first matter of business. It's recently come to my attention that one of our sisters has gotten caught up in the football betting hoopla. While we love the football players and want them at our parties, it only demoralizes a Chi Omega girl if we're the brunt of the joke. Please be aware of this danger."

My heart drops.

She's talking about *me*.

Charisma, who's been scrolling on her phone, puts it down and looks at me, her face flattening.

Some of the girls are whispering and looking around the room.

"…who was it…"

"…how awful…"

I inhale a sharp breath, embarrassed all over again that he almost had me convinced he really liked me. Just thinking about that stupid bet makes my face redden. Plus, I've been on pins and needles for the past few days wondering if the video Charisma said one of the players took would materialize and go all over campus, but it never did. Blaze swore to her he would make sure it was deleted, and I was just beginning to think the incident hadn't gone any further—but now…ugh.

Margo exhales. "Since there are no secrets in Chi Omega, I feel compelled to tell you it was Penelope Graham." Her gaze is flinty as she focuses on me.

Compelled my ass. She couldn't wait to tell them.

My teeth grit as I hear more whispering from the girls

around me.

I glare at Margo.

"Would you like to share the story with us and be our cautionary tale?" she asks, her lashes fluttering.

I push my legs to standing and scan the room. "Everything Margo says is true, but I beat him at his own game. My name won't be on their tally board again." I give them a smile. "Be vigilant this fall. Go Chi O."

Margo studies me for a moment. "Indeed. Let's move on."

I want to shove her *indeed* up her ass.

"The next matter of business is the homecoming party. The Thetas will be hosting their own party, and as Chi Omegas, we must *own* Sorority Row and beat them. I want to make their party seem like a preschool outing."

Several agreeing murmurs come from our sisters. There's no love lost between us and the other sorority, and I imagine it pricks at Margo the most—since she lost her long-term boyfriend to a Theta last semester. Gossip runs rampant at our university, and it's no secret she walked in on him screwing their president, a jersey chaser named Sasha.

Margo continues. "Our party will be the hottest ticket, and that means, first of all, invite the most popular guys." She's leaning over the podium and whips out a legal pad. "Personally, I've made a list of suggestions of people to invite, and I want us to ask as many as possible." She gazes around the room. "If you're willing, I'd love to have you pledge tonight to invite at least one A-list student from Waylon."

I frown, annoyed about the A-list student comment. Connor probably isn't on that list, but he's a nice guy, and I want to ask him.

First, I'd have to talk to him, of course.

I raise my hand.

"Yes?" Margo grudgingly nods.

I stand again. "Who are *you* asking?" We all know it won't be Kyle, her ex.

Margo's lips compress and her hands tense as she folds them into a steeple. "Why, the most important person on campus when it comes to homecoming—the quarterback."

Ryker? The jerk who made me the brunt of the joke?

Anger flies over me. "Football players go to the Tau house for homecoming. Everyone knows that."

Margo, who usually sports infallible confidence, seems to falter as her hands flutter around her notes. She clears her throat. "Which is why it will be a great coup for us to get him." She pauses. "I can convince him to come."

I scowl. "We should invite people we want to spend time with, not ones we don't know."

She stiffens. "Maybe I'll get to know him."

Oh. Well.

That shut me up. I didn't think he was her type.

She calls on one of the other girls who has her hand raised, and I plop back down in my seat.

Charisma levels me with a serious look. "If you don't want him here, I can take care of that real quick. I have connections."

I arch a brow and can't help the grin. "Mobsters?"

She rolls her eyes. "Just because I'm Italian and from New York doesn't mean I'm John Gotti, but one well-placed word in Blaze's ear and Ryker will never grace our party with his presence."

"Blaze?"

She shrugs, playing it off. "He likes me. I'm sure I can get him to encourage Ryker to stay at the Tau house."

Hmmm.

I whip out my red lipstick and reapply, my mind churning. "Hold off on that. I'll get back to you."

CHAPTER 8

PENELOPE

After dinner out at the local pizza place with some pledges, we pull up at our house, the one I grew up in, a rambling cottage-style bungalow built in the 50s. In the light of the streetlamp, I eye the late summer azaleas in the flowerbed, the ones Mom and I planted before she passed away.

A heavy feeling settles on my chest. *God, I miss her.* Sometimes I forget she's gone and half expect her to be inside, waiting on me so we can have one of our long chats. She'd know exactly what to do about Dad and Margo and Ryker.

"What's that next to the door?" Charisma asks me as we step onto the stone porch. She's ahead of me and bends down to pick it up. Turning to face me, she holds up a bag of suckers with a note stuck to it. "Oooo, it has your name on it," she says, waving it at me.

I take the note from her and read the sloping masculine scrawl.

I came by at 8:00. I guess you stood me up. Makes sense. I hope we're even now. Anyway, I thought of you when I saw these.

Later, Ryker.

The R is prominent and dominates his signature, big and cocky just like he is.

"Why is he leaving you your favorite candy?" Charisma ponders, an inquisitive look on her face. "Have y'all talked and you didn't tell me?"

"No." My brow wrinkles, a memory tugging at me, and then it dawns on me and I groan. "Oh my God, he texted me earlier, but I didn't know who it was…" I whip out my phone and reread the messages while she takes them in from beside my shoulder. I recall the phone number he tossed down on my serving tray at Sugar's, but it got dumped out along with everything else. Then I remember giving him my number. "These must be from him." I rub my forehead.

She chuckles. "WTF? You told him you wanted *him*."

Mortification flies over me. "Shit, shit, shit. I didn't know it was him. I thought he was some lonely guy pining after some girl." My face reddens. "I thought I was helping someone out with his relationship woes."

"That would be a BFN—big fat no." She holds the bag of suckers up to the porch light. "Look, he drew something on the side of the bag."

I take the candy from her and study the sketch. It's a creature with a long neck, small ears, and an oblong body with fuzzy stick legs drawn in black marker.

"I can't figure out what that is supposed to be." She looks at me. "Is he deranged? Should we call the cops?"

"No." A small laugh comes from me. "It's a llama."

"Oh?"

I shrug. "Inside joke."

• • •

Lying in bed later, I'm reading a romance book about a pirate, but my gaze keeps going to the note and the bag of candy on my nightstand. With a sigh, I put down the book and pick up the note—for the third time—tracing my finger over the confident strokes of his penmanship. The candy was a nice touch, but it hardly excuses what he did.

I nibble on my lip, thinking back to the sorority meeting and how Margo vowed she'd get Ryker to attend. He did say he wanted to make up for what happened, so what if *I* invited Ryker to the party? I mean, I can also ask Connor, but if I wrangled Ryker then everyone would know the bet fiasco is over and didn't bother me at all. I wouldn't have to be embarrassed, and everyone would think we're…friends.

But that's just silly, my inner voice says. *You hate him.*

Do I?

YES, YOU DO.

But my fingers aren't listening as I grab my phone and type out a message to him.

Got your note. We're not even close to being even, Baby Llama. And before when I was texting you, I didn't know who you were. I was just messing around.

I don't get a response for several minutes and am about to put my phone back down when I see the three little dots that tell me he's responding.

I still want to make it up to you.

Visions of him ravishing me on my bed come to mind. I

squash those thoughts down.

How? I ask.

I'll explain tomorrow. It's midnight and I need to be at practice by six. That means breakfast is at five fifteen.

Oh! I didn't realize he was so…conscientious. I guess I pictured him with two girls on either side, being rubbed down with oil as he drifts off to sleep.

Sorry I woke you, I text.

You didn't. I was lying here thinking about you.

A sizzle of heat ripples through me. Damn that sizzle.

Oh, so you're alone?

Uh-huh. You? Or is Connor there?

My teeth grit. I hate that he knows I have a crush on him.

Just me. I throw a glance over at Vampire Bill. At night, I put his cage in here. He doesn't like to sleep alone. Neither do I. **And you need to forget about Connor**, I add.

Don't worry, your secret is safe with me. Good night, Penelope. I'll find you tomorrow.

Find me tomorrow…?

I stare at my name typed by his fingers…and it feels surreal that I've just had a decent conversation with him.

Still, I'm not sure I'll talk to him when I see him.

With a sigh, I pick back up my pirate romance, and before long I'm asleep, dreaming of my own blond, curly-hair-chested pirate.

CHAPTER 9

PENELOPE

Someone clears their throat. A male. "Hey…you down there. Do you have any clue how hard you are to find?"

I stiffen at the husky words, embarrassed that Ryker has, once again, caught me with my butt straight up in the air. This time I'm scrounging around on the bookstore floor, looking on every shelf for the right workbook for my next class.

"What do you want?" I say without looking at him, tautness in my tone, although it's a bit muffled from speaking while bent over.

"You. I told you last night we'd talk, and here I am."

Ignoring him, I move another collection of books aside on the shelf, but my search is fruitless. A long frustrated groan comes from me.

"We do have a class to get to, so today would be nice," he says from above me, "although the view from here is *stellar*. Your curves are…lush."

He's staring at my ass.

"Keep your eyeballs in your head, quarterback."

"Hard to do when you're bent over."

"Try harder," I snap.

I huff out a breath and put my hand on the shelf above me to help me stand up. Ryker immediately extends a hand, his fingers clasping mine as he heaves me up. It's the third time we've touched skin to skin—yes, I'm counting—and I inhale sharply as the sensation ripples up my arm and out like waves from a skipped rock on the water. Breathlessly, I stare down at the place where our hands are joined, and he's looking as well, a look of speculation on his face. He swallows and drops my hand swiftly. His face changes, closing in and shuttering like a window, becoming contained.

No one really knows him, I think, except Maverick.

What I do know is he's a god on the football field, an authoritative kickass quarterback that has kept Waylon in the top ten of the SEC for the past three years. Back last year, there was even talk of Ryker being a Heisman candidate, but that day is long gone…

I glance down at my hand, my skin burning where we touched, as if an electric current has had its way with me. I press my palm against my leggings.

I blame my reaction on the early morning, my lack of breakfast, and the search for the missing workbook.

"What do you want anyway? I'm busy."

Amusement gleams in his eyes. "Damn. No one talks to me the way you do."

I shrug. "I see you for what you are."

A quick smirk. "A hot quarterback?"

"An asshole," I correct him.

"Some girls love assholes."

"I don't." My arms cross.

"I think you do. I've seen the romance books you bring to class, the ones with bare-chested men on the covers."

"Those are called alpha-holes."

"I see. This romance novel thing has its own lingo, then?"

"Doesn't everything?"

He grins. "What kind of football lingo do you know?"

"That you're a gunslinger."

He straightens, interest lighting his gaze.

I shake my head. "You really think I wrote that article about you and didn't research the hell out of it? And for your information, a gunslinger is a quarterback whose arm is good for long, deep passes."

He rubs his jaw. "Are you saying you're a secret Ryker Voss stalker?"

I stiffen. "The interest was strictly professional."

"So you've never checked out my Instagram or Twitter?"

"Never." Okay, I have. In fact, I did last night after texting with him. All I found were a few pics of him hanging out with Blaze and Maverick, some of his workout routine—damn, his body is tight—and a few random shots of a tiny white kitten.

But...

I won't let the fact that he likes small animals soften me.

He grins. "You blush when you lie, Penelope."

"I'm not blushing." My face is hot as hell.

He considers me. "You find what you were looking for down there?"

I huff out a breath and put my hand on my hip. "No. It's the stupid workbook for class. We're supposed to have it by today and here I am…scrambling." I run a hand through my hair.

"You're stressed out." It's a statement, not a question.

"Yes."

He fishes around in his black backpack and pulls out a paperback book, flashing the red and black cover at me, a small grin on his face. "This the one?"

"Don't tell me you got the last one."

He shrugs. "Someone delivered it to my dorm before classes started."

"Jersey chaser?" I smirk.

"No, just a service the administration provides for athletes." He pauses. "You seem to think I don't do anything for myself. I assure you; I'm a grown man."

Indeed, he is.

His broad shoulders shift, calling attention to his untucked, blue pinstriped button-up shirt that's rolled up, displaying his muscled, tanned arms. My eyes get hung up on his golden arm hair. It's nothing too crazy, mind you, but something about it on him is so fucking hot that my brain hurts.

I silently curse myself. This predilection for hair has never happened to me before. It's just…*him*.

His shirt hugs his chest, shaping and contouring to his muscles. My eyes drift down, taking in the khaki pants that are tight against his crotch.

How big is his cock? Is it in proportion to the rest of his body? Because *damn*—

"Penelope."

I blink. "Yeah?" My gaze finds his and is captured by his piercing blue-green eyes. They gleam as he studies me intently as if trying to suss out something important about me.

It's like we're both perplexed when we're around each other.

Again, I blame my lack of sustenance.

I don't know what his excuse is.

He continues. "I want to help you with something."

"How magnanimous of you," I say tartly. "But go on."

"Will you just listen?" He rakes a hand through his long hair and tugs on the ends.

My equilibrium is thrown by the earnestness in his voice, and I chew on my lip. "Fine. Talk." I lean against the shelf.

He nods. "First of all, the date bet at Sugar's was not my idea, and I know that's not an excuse and it's on me for taking Archer's bait…" His voice drifts off. "I wanted to apologize right away, but you ran off to the back, and Charisma refused to let me see you. Plus, I did have to get home and change my pants."

"So I heard." I cock my hip.

His eyes capture mine. "I'm really sorry I hurt you. It was shitty."

"It was."

He clears his throat. "I want to do you a solid and make up for the bet."

"Like what?" I could bring up the homecoming party, but I waffle. In the wee hours of last night, it seemed like a good idea, but I'm not sure being around Ryker is a good idea. He makes me feel weird things.

A slow smile builds on his face as he takes me in, sweeping over my red pointy-toed flats, gray leggings, and roomy black sweatshirt that reads *Forks, Seattle*. He looks around the bookstore with a bit of bemusement on his face as if he can't believe what he's about to say.

"What?" I ask, feeling cross at him because he's relaxed, and I'm still pissy because I don't have my workbook.

His eyes come back to me. "Who is it that you want? Answer me that and you'll know what I'm here to help you with."

My eyes flare. "You don't mean Connor, do you?"

He nods.

I pause. "You're going to get Connor Dimpleshitz as my— I'm just throwing out a guess here—*boyfriend*?"

A shrug. "Let's just say '*get you a date*' for now. It's up to you to make the boyfriend thing happen, although I don't doubt you can manage it. You're a pretty girl, and surely, you have game." His voice is doubtful as he stares at my sweatshirt.

"I have game!"

"Uh-huh." His tone is dry.

I shake my head. "But...why?"

"Because you like him, and I want to do something nice. In fact...I bet you I can get him to ask *you* on a date."

"Really?" I say skeptically. "Another bet? That's your answer?"

He inclines his head. "You know you can't resist a bet from me."

My eyes narrow. "Who told you that?"

His lips curl up in a grin. "You love to prove me wrong. It's obvious every time you see me."

"God, I do love knocking you down a peg."

He laughs, and I suck in a quick breath at the way it lights up his face. Some of the earlier tension related to the bet fiasco eases, but not all of it. He has apologized—very well, I might add—but I'm still wary. On the other hand, I remind myself I still need a date to homecoming in four weeks, and if he can get me Connor…

"And if you win and he does ask me out, what are the stakes?"

"No stakes. Just your forgiveness. I'm doing this for you."

Oh. That's unexpected. "You really are sorry aren't you?"

He gives me a small nod. "Yes."

With a wave of my hands, I indicate my body. "Basically, you're saying I'm so awful I need help getting male attention?"

"Awful? You're hot as hell, but I'm going to show you exactly how to have him eating out of your hands."

A full body flush washes over me. *Hot as hell?* I mean, sure my hair is long and wavy and my eyes are okay when I'm not hiding them with my glasses…

But I need clarification.

I push up today's eyeglasses, jade green with little jewels in the corners, and study him. "And just out of curiosity, how would you describe me to a friend, Ryker? Be honest. Am I the girl with the nice personality? What do I have that's working for me?"

Am I fishing for compliments from him? AM I? *Shit. I am.*

He rakes his gaze over me and strokes his chin, studying me. Then he maneuvers to walk around me in a circle.

"What am I? A horse?"

He makes some *hmmm* noises, the kind I make when I'm

working on a serious math problem.

I roll my eyes. "Well, do I pass inspection?"

He's back in front of me and gives me a nod.

"Verdict?" I ask, exasperated.

"How tall are you?"

I stand straighter. "Five ten."

"I dig tall chicks," he says and then clears his throat. "Tall works well with Connor, too."

"Mmmm."

His gaze lingers...everywhere. "Your ass is spectacular, but I can't see it for your sweatshirt—except when you bend over," he adds with a grin. "Personally, I like a girl who doesn't flaunt everything, but Connor...you might need to get his attention. He seems a little unaware of his surroundings."

He really is! I recall how I would attempt to talk to him last year, and he never noticed.

"So you're saying my ass is my best *asset*?"

"No." He meets my gaze. "Your gray eyes are pretty. I like the little flecks of white and gold around your pupils. They're nice."

Nice. I grimace. "Why, Ryker, you're a poet."

He shrugs. "Your best asset is your hair. You should wear it down more..." He pauses, his eyes roving over the wavy curls that drape over my shoulder. "Every man who sees it down imagines his hands wrapped around those strands as he's taking you from behind."

I can't breathe. What started out as a fun exchange is now layered with tension and heat. The air grows warm inside the bookstore, even though I'm clearly standing near one of the air conditioning vents.

A long silence follows as we both stare at each other.

I'm ticked that he's described a submissive scenario, but the hot-blooded woman in me only hears his sex-on-a-stick, husky voice, the one that makes my body vibrate and chime. My head goes to the book I'm reading. I picture us on a ship with billowing masts. He's wearing a white linen shirt—wet, of course, although I don't know why, perhaps from sea spray— and his golden hair is mussed. He's caught me and has me bent over the captain's wheel, my emerald green silk dress bunched up in the back and held secure with his fists as he slides his thick cock inside me, his breath ragged, his hands tangled in my hair…

Damn him.

I suck in a deep breath. *Forget the pirate! It's never going to happen!*

"I'm always saying crazy shit when I'm around you." His face is pink as he scrubs at the scruff on his cheeks. "I apologize for being so—"

He freezes, pausing mid-sentence, his eyes over my shoulder.

"For being so what?"

But his attention is diverted, and he grabs my shoulders to turn me so I see what he does. "Forget that. Look."

"What are you doing? Look at what?" His touch is fire, and it makes me nervous and excited at the same time. I wonder what it would feel like to have those big football hands slide down my arms and—

Focus, Penelope. I take a gander around the store, my eyes roving. "I don't see anything."

"Look to the left."

I scan the place. "New nose plugs for the diving team? A new rack of lipstick, which I should probably check out—" I stop on one person, and a small excited squeal of surprise pops out. "Oh my God, The Unicorn is here." Wearing his signature ball cap and a Wildcats shirt with his glasses tucked into the neckline is Connor, looking so studious and intelligent as he takes in the new line of mechanical pencils, probably to do his math problems with. I look back at Ryker, who's dropped his hands from my shoulders and is watching my face as I take in my crush. "So, what do I do? How are you going to help me?"

There's a quizzical look on his face. "Why do you like him anyway?"

"He's smart and nice."

An eyebrow arches. "That's all you require? Don't you think you deserve more?"

I squint up at him. "Like you?"

He shrugs. "Your words, not mine."

"Stuff it, quarterback."

"But you like him? He's *the one* for you?" He narrows his eyes at me. "Why can't you just talk to him? You talk to me."

See, that's the question...

"You're not shy," Ryker says.

I shake my head. "I'm a bookworm but not shy."

"So?"

I stare at my shoes. It's easier to be honest when I'm not looking at his chiseled face. "I know you and I will never be a thing, I guess, so it's easy to talk to you."

"Ah."

I nod, feeling the need to clarify. "I don't date football players." I play with the gold locket necklace around my neck, the one my mom gave me on my tenth birthday. There's a picture of her holding me on the day I was born. Just her. Not my dad. "I avoid guys who aren't likely to stick around. Connor is solid."

Ryker eyes the necklace then looks back into my eyes. "You could have a hundred Connors if you wanted."

Damn. That's sweet.

A small sigh escapes me. "I'm not like the girls you know, Ryker. I'm not a hook-up. I'm a vir—" I stop.

"What?"

I shake my head. "Nothing."

Several moments pass as we stand there. He's studying me and then Connor.

I can't take the silence anymore. "What on earth are you thinking about?"

"About how far you're willing to go to get the guy you want." He chews on his bottom lip, a focused look on his face as if he's contemplating robbing the place.

"You're scaring me," I say on a laugh.

A resolute expression flits across his features, like he's come to a decision. He hands me the coveted workbook. His hand doesn't touch mine this time, and I think it's on purpose, but I'm glad. I don't want to have those kinds of feelings about Ryker, and I guess the desire is mutual.

"First, take this. It's yours. I don't want you stressing out today in class."

I blink down at the workbook. "But then you won't have one, and Professor White is a hardass—he'll call you out."

"Don't you worry about me, Red. I'll get one." His eyes are focused over my shoulder, and I know he's watching Connor.

I straighten. "No one—and I mean *no one*—calls me that. Don't even try." I frown down at the workbook. "But let's focus on this. Why are you giving your prize to me?"

"So you won't be mad when I do this. Just slap me when it's over."

Slap him? *What?*

With a flourish, he drops his backpack, sweeps me into his arms, and kisses me in the middle of the bookstore.

CHAPTER 10

PENELOPE

What is happening?

His mouth takes mine, almost tentatively, his hands cupping my cheeks ever so lightly. Sensuous and soft, his lips sear me as his tongue touches mine, begging for entry. With a sharp inhale, I let him, and the kiss deepens, his lips insistent. He makes a sound —I can't describe it—and a spark is born, a fire that builds and burns until my toes curl.

My first instinct was to shove him away, but that hope is dashed. I'm lost in the spicy male scent of him, the sound of his shirt rubbing against my chest, the way his scruff teases my face. I'm not sure where to put my hands, and they falter, finally settling on the sides of his chest. His body is hard and tense, as if he's holding himself back…

I sigh into his mouth and he murmurs my name. Electricity dances over my skin where his hands touch. My face, the curve of my neck, my shoulders. His lips glide over mine as his palms press into my hips, guiding me against him. His cock is hard, and my chest heaves at the ache in my body. My inner self—the one who knows what a player he is—yells for me to stop, but I want this kiss to last forever.

Suddenly he's wrenched from me with force as if someone yanked him off of me, but when I open my eyes, he's only pulled himself back.

He's panting and his lips are lusciously pink and swollen. His hair is mussed—did I run my hands through those strands?

He says something, but I'm not paying attention.

He towers over me, his gaze deep like the ocean as he takes me in, lingering on my lips. We're still so close. I could kiss him again.

My lips are tender as I touch them. Ryker Voss kisses like he's gearing up for a season on *The Bachelor*. I picture us naked, on that pirate ship from earlier, only this time we're in the captain's quarters rolling around on the bed. He wraps my hair around his hand and pulls me to him for a deep kiss, our tongues tangling. I beg him to do it again—

He whispers, bringing me back. "Slap me!"

Why does he want me to hit him?

Somehow my foggy brain remembers the whole point of the kiss is to get Connor's attention.

Ryker's eyes widen as they look over my shoulder and then back at me. "Snap out of it. He's looking now."

Well, he *is* asking for it.

I slap him, mostly a nervous reflex.

"Goddamn, Red. You've got a mean right hook," he whispers in my ear before he takes a full step back and speaks loudly. "I'm so sorry, Penelope. I just couldn't resist kissing you…" He lifts his hand and rakes it through his hair, appearing to fidget as he moves from one foot to the other.

His voice carries the few aisles over to where Connor is, and I feel the gazes of several patrons move to us.

I'm impressed.

Has Ryker taken a drama class?

"Just keep looking at me like you're angry," he says in a lowered voice. "He's trying to get up the nerve to come over here."

"How do you know?" I hiss.

"Because I know dudes. He can't resist being a knight in shining armor."

I nod, his eyes steady on mine as we stare at each other, and I'm acutely aware that I *like* him saying those pretend words to me.

I just couldn't resist kissing you.

"Er, is everything okay over here?" comes a low masculine voice. It's Connor and he's moved to stand next to me, looking earnest and concerned as he takes us in. A tingle of excitement shoots through me. *Oh, wow...* This close up I see the luminous gold color of his eyes and the cleft in his strong chin. He really is handsome in a boy next door kind of way.

"It's none of your business, Dimpleshitz," Ryker says tightly, but his tone lacks heat.

Connor ignores him—*good for him*—and moves his attention to me. "Are you okay? Should I alert the security guard?"

I shake my head rapidly and clear my throat. "No, but thank you for checking on me. Everything is fine. Ryker and I just..." My words trail off. Shit, we don't have a backstory except for the article, and that doesn't fit here. "He's sorry. Right?" I look over at the first-rate kisser, and my eyes implore him. *Is this what I'm supposed to do—be the helpless female he rescues?*

Ryker gives me a little nod. *It's about time you figured out the plan*, his eyes say. Then a smirk dances across his face and I read it well: *My kiss really knocked you out.*

"In your dreams," I mutter.

"What was that?" Connor asks me, and I dart my eyes from Ryker to him.

"Nothing," I say, shaking myself. "Ryker was just…uh—"

He interrupts me. "I asked her out, and she turned me down. I thought kissing her might change her mind. Guess you can't win them all."

"Well, just don't do it again," I say as I cross my arms, playing my part.

"If that's what you want," Ryker says sardonically.

"I do."

"If you say so."

"I just did," I snap.

"Sometimes your body says more than your words," he retorts, arching one eyebrow.

How does he do that? It's virtually impossible for me to only lift one eyebrow.

"Sometimes you need to just move on," I quip back.

He smirks. "If you really mean that, why do you think about me all the time?"

How does he know I think about him?

I frown. "I don't."

"Uh-huh." He gives me a look like he knows something I don't.

I glare at him, widening my eyes. *What's his game?* He's

gotten Connor over here—shouldn't he be moving on now?

"Uh, did you guys used to date?" It's Connor speaking as he moves in closer, and he's definitely wearing Polo cologne. My nose flares at the familiar high school scent, and my first reaction is to recoil, but it's not the worst scent in the world, I suppose. It's not Old Spice.

"No," we both say.

"Ah, well, you heard her then," Connor says. "Maybe you need to give her some space."

A long exhale comes from Ryker. "I think you're right, Dimpleshitz." With that, he grabs his backpack, gives us one more look, and takes off down the aisle.

I shake my head, watching his broad shoulders as he walks away. "He might be a genius," I say, mostly to myself. Even though Connor does hear it, he doesn't appear to understand my meaning.

He watches him, a small scowl buried in his forehead. "He's an enigma for sure. Too bad about his involvement in the gambling thing."

I turn toward him, wearing a frown. "It wasn't gambling, and he was cleared by the NCAA."

He gives me a careful glance. "I see...but didn't you write an article about him?"

I nod. "I wrote a follow-up one as well."

"Ah, you're defending him."

My lips flatten. "No."

Connor's face is thoughtful. "But you're into him?"

I shake my head. "Absolutely not." *Work with this, Penelope.* Ryker has given me an opportunity, and I'm not going to screw it up. *Make conversation.* I touch his arm and smile brightly. "Trust me, we're just friends."

He smiles boyishly, one corner of his lips turning up in a crooked grin. "I thought you two didn't like each other, but then I can be a little oblivious."

I nod. "Same here. I barely notice anything. Look at us, two peas in a pod." I laugh. "So, how are you? How's calculus?" I'm rambling and gazing up at him with doe eyes, and the attention seems to be working.

He blushes and dips his head. "Great. I saw that you were in there. Are you on your way to class?"

I nod, and when he helps me pick up some of the books I scattered on the floor in my earlier haste, it's the closest we've ever been. I take in a small pimple near his chin and the tiny piece of pepper he has stuck in one of his teeth, probably from breakfast—I hope—and it's a decidedly unromantic thought, but I figure he's human like the rest of us. We make small talk, and I nod right along as he goes into a rather long and detailed discussion about Professor White and how much he enjoys his teaching style.

I try to pay attention—I really do—but before long I feel a pricking, as if someone is watching me, and I glance around the bookstore.

My perusal around the establishment lands one aisle over where I see a sliver of khaki pants behind a tall display of atlases. Craning my neck, I see his mass of wild hair.

I stuff down my grin. Ryker.

He's listening to us.

Maybe it's part of his…tutelage?

Admittedly, it does encourage me to try harder.

My phone vibrates with a text, and while Connor is checking out the mechanical pencils and going into detail about which one is best for each class, I pull it out stealthily and read.

Good job with the talking, Red. Keep it up and he's all yours.

"Hmmm," I say to Connor's question about paper choices as he bends down to look for a five-subject notebook.

What do I talk about? I text.

Find things you both like. Books? Chess? Dungeons and Dragons? Hell, I don't know. Nerd stuff.

I've seen you reading in the library before. Does that make you a nerd, Baby Llama?

I get no reply and focus on Connor, who's still talking as he stares at the notebook selection. I feel my phone buzz and arrange it on top of the workbook so I'm not actually holding it but I can still read it. Being stealthy, I peek at Ryker's response.

I'm guessing you call me Baby Llama because of my hairy chest, is his reply. **I see you looking at it. It hypnotizes you. I actually wore my button-down today so you'd get a good view.**

Oh, he is such a scoundrel!

I'M NOT FASCINATED BY YOUR HAIR, I reply. **Maybe I call you that because your face is rather long.**

I think you want to touch my chest, he replies. **Maybe later after Connor is gone I'll take my shirt off for you. I bet you won't touch my chest.**

Go to hell, quarterback, I text.

I remember that time you saw me coming out of the

shower at the Tau house with only a towel on. I saw your open mouth. You were…IMPRESSED. Do you have fantasies about my naked chest?

I'm going to slap you again next time I see you. Or pull out one of those hairs.

As long as I get to kiss you first, he says.

My breath sucks in. *Oh, he's just teasing me.* Then he sends me a string of laughing crying emojis with a string of llamas. *See.* A joke.

What a player, I think with a small smile.

It was a great kiss, I tell him.

I know.

I roll my eyes. Thank you for getting him over here.

Another text comes in a few minutes later. By the way, where is Forks, Seattle?

It's where the Cullens live. Hello, Twilight?

You're really into bloodsuckers.

If he only knew. I have most of the books and movies memorized.

Edward's face is on my pillow.

LOL, he replies. Maybe it's time you gave up your book crushes and focused on real life more.

And I assume Sexy as Hell Athlete is the one to help me with that?

Did I not just get you Connor? Now stop texting me and talk to him.

I'm chuckling when I hear my name and look up at Connor. His face is inquisitive.

"I'm sorry." I gesture to my phone. "Important message. Did

you say something?"

"I asked if you liked to play pool."

I squint. How did we get from school supplies to pool? I flounder, my eyes running around the store, trying to recall details of a game I played once or twice in my aunt's basement when I was a kid. I reach into my purse for my lipstick, a sure sign I'm nervous. I know there's an eight ball...

He gives me a slightly perplexed look. "You know the game with the balls and sticks? Billiards, if you're fancy."

"Oh, pool. I thought you said *tool*." I laugh. "I played in high school actually, was even in a league with...teams and such." God. *Do they have those?*

"I didn't know schools had those."

I nod. "They do! I went to a private school here in Magnolia, and it was all the rage."

His face lights up. "That's awesome. It's one of my favorite pastimes since my dad owns a pool hall back in my hometown."

I've read that widening your eyes when you talk to the opposite sex shows interest, so I flare mine open. "Where's that?"

"Memphis." He gives me an odd look. "You okay?"

I nod emphatically. "Yeah, why?"

"Your eyes got big."

"Oh, just a speck of dust. It's fine." I wave dismissively. "I love Memphis! Graceland's there, home of Elvis, right? It's the best. Lots of dancing and music...stuff."

He brightens. "You like Elvis?"

"Achy Breaky Heart guy with the great hair and shiny outfits? Totally."

He frowns. "No, that was Billy Ray Cyrus, and I'm not sure

where he's from. Elvis sang in the 60s and 70s—and he's dead. You know that, right?"

Oh God. I'm losing my mind. Of course, I know who the heck Elvis is! This is Ryker's fault...somehow. My eyes shift over to the map display where I swear I can hear stifled laughing. I clear my throat. "Duh. My brain is mush today. First couple weeks of classes and all." I pause and smile. "My favorite Elvis song is 'Love Me Tender'. It's very romantic." I briefly shut my eyes in mortification.

What is this nonsense coming out of my mouth?

I need a reboot. Stat.

"Yeah." He stares down at his hands for a moment before looking back up at me. "You know, I've wanted to talk to you several times, but I never seem to find the right time. I'm glad I ran into you today. Do you play chess?"

I blink at the non sequitur but smile at him, and he blinks a little, his eyes lingering on my lips. *Thank you, cherry red lipstick.* "Yes, I love it so, so much." At least that much is true.

He grins. "I didn't realize we had so much in common."

"I know. Amazing."

"I'm headed to a chess tournament this weekend, but maybe you'd like to get together soon—if you're not seeing anyone?" He blushes.

This is so easy. All I have to do is agree with everything.

"That sounds great. I work a few nights at Sugar's and at the library, but if I know in advance, I can ask for it off."

He nods. "Cool. I'd love for you to come to Cadillac's with me. Maybe show me some of your moves from high school?"

Cadillac's is a local bar where students from Waylon hang

out. There's a collection of pool tables there. Dammit.

It's like a soap bubble has burst.

"Uh…" I freak out internally as I emit a nervous laugh. "I may have to study…you just never know. I'll check my schedule."

He takes his glasses from his shirt and slips them on. He really is adorable. "Nah, just bring your books with you. We can go over whatever you need to do after we play."

But…

How in the hell am I going to fake play pool when I don't even know what end of the stick to hold?

"So, it's a date then? Maybe next week sometime?" God. He actually said the words…

Damn. Ryker did it. Connor actually said *date*.

I exhale. "Uh, yeah."

He asks for my number, and I give it to him, my gaze flicking to the area where I know Ryker is lurking.

Connor offers to walk me to class, and I give him a nod then tag along.

We walk out of the student center and head to the science building for our class. We're halfway there when I get another text.

You might need to brush up on your Elvis. And pool.

I smile to myself.

"Who's that?" Connor asks.

I sigh. "No one."

CHAPTER 11

RYKER

Penelope Graham. *Damn.*

Somewhere between hiding with her behind the plant and kissing her in the bookstore, something changed between us. I can't put my finger on exactly what, but I do know I'm fucking jealous as hell of a nerd who loves to talk about mechanical pencils and pool.

You have no right to your jealousy, I tell myself while I follow behind them as they walk through the quad.

Much to my surprise, I also notice that, at some point, she pulled up her sweatshirt and did some kind of tie thing on the side, so it shows off her heart-shaped ass. She must have done it while they were walking out of the bookstore, and I was lingering behind the display.

I take in several pairs of male eyes roving over her as she sashays past them and it annoys me.

But…

I shouldn't be surprised they're staring.

There's something mesmerizing about her that calls to the caveman in me and brings all my alpha instincts to the surface.

She's part goofy but clever. Hot but innocent. Her lips are a perfect Cupid's bow, full and red, and I admit to staring at them a little too long in the bookstore before we kissed. And her coppery hair that falls around her oval face? That's the stuff of wet dreams.

I half-smile. She isn't impressed with who I am, and that... that I fucking dig.

I walk briskly, my stride extended as I try to catch up to them without getting close enough to be noticed. Hell, I just want to be a fly on the wall for their conversation. Most of their exchange in the bookstore was about school supplies.

What I'm definitely not thinking about is the elephant in my head: *that kiss.*

Yeah, it was spur of the moment, but part of me wants to repeat it as soon as I can.

But...

That won't happen.

I'm getting Connor for her—not me.

I enter the science building, still following the...lovebirds? I watch their heads bend close to each other as they have a conversation that seems intense. What are they talking about?

Pool?

I was on a team in high school. Please. And just like that, I grin at nothing in particular. Penelope is...funny.

As I head down the hallway to class, I see Archer coming around the corner, his arm around Sasha, one of the jersey chasers.

Anger curls around me. These past couple of days at practice have been tense, but I'm hanging in there, as long as he can keep his trap shut.

I head for the entrance to the auditorium just as Archer ditches Sasha and hightails it over to me. His gaze sees the pair up ahead—Connor and Penelope—and a wide grin splits his face. A low whistle comes from him as he checks her out before she disappears through the door.

I hate that he's staring at her.

"What do you want?" I say.

He smirks. "Ah, poor Ryker, she's with a guy. That certainly makes things interesting, but I'm sure a handsome fellow like you can figure it out." He tosses his head back and laughs but then sobers, his eyes narrowing on my face. "Unless I'm wrong and you've tapped that already?"

I stare down at him, my fists tightening. "None of your goddamn business."

"Now that's a *no* if I ever heard one," he says in his slow drawl before giving me a slap on the back. "Don't worry, sport, maybe you can talk her into it. I mean, I know you've lost some of your game with the ladies this year, but surely you can get *this* girl." He considers me. "But then, maybe you're not feeling masculine enough? I mean, you've had some bad press lately. They say it affects the libido."

I exhale. "Don't you have better things to do with your time than worry about who *I'm* screwing? People who talk about sex are the ones who aren't getting it, bro."

He waves me off. "Actually, this is the highlight of my week. I'm going to win that trophy this year because you're too much of a pussy to get a piece of ass that should be so easy for someone like you—seeing as you're the big man on campus and all."

I smirk. "Sounds like jealousy to me, Archer. I'm not taking your bet. And as soon as Maverick comes back to the team, your ass is no longer captain."

His face reddens, and I'm glad I finally hit a nerve. He's a hard nut to crack under all that fake bravado. "You think you're so good, don't you? You think just because you're Ryker Voss everyone's just going to give you a pass."

I tower over him, inching into his space until I hope he smells my toothpaste. "Keep all this talk up and you're going to get hurt."

He laughs, a bit shrilly, and bounces away from me on the balls of his feet. "Whatever. It's all in good fun. Now, get back out there and try again, buddy. You're letting her get away with some guy who can't hold a candle to you—supposedly."

Then he's gone, vanishing down the hallway with Sasha by his side, leaving me fuming and ready to punch a hole in the wall. I settle for raking a hand through my hair.

Why do I let him get to me?

Because *everything* is getting to you now.

And something is going to crack.

It's going to crumble around me, and there won't be anything I can do about it.

I close my eyes briefly until a very Southern female voice interrupts me.

"Ryker? Oh, goodness. How are you? I haven't seen you in forever."

I whip around, and it's Margo...something. Maybe she's been lurking here for a while—I can't tell. I can't think of her last name, but I recall what I know about her: last year she dated some rich dude who screwed her over for a Theta. Apparently, she caught him red-handed at a party. I can't recall all the details, but the rumor mill ran rampant.

"You're just the person I wanted to see," she adds. A slow smile breaks over her face as she eats me up with her eyes.

Okay.

I know a come-on when I see it.

We don't usually chat, but I'll bite.

"What's up?" I ask, looking down in bemusement as she crooks her hand into the bend of my elbow and leads me over to the side next to the wall where we're out of the way of foot traffic. I've never taken her for the flirtatious type, or as one to dress skimpily—she's more of a CEO type—but today she's showing off, wearing three-inch heels and a short white sundress.

My ego is still a bit bruised from being brushed off for Connor, and that's what makes me malleable as she delicately and briefly fingers one of the buttons on my shirt. "You know, I've always loved how you dress. Even though you're this big strong football player, you certainly have style. Where do you shop?"

"Anywhere that has big and tall," I say dryly. "Is there something you wanted to talk about?" *That isn't about fashion?* "I have a class to get to."

She smiles again and leans in closer until I smell her perfume, something flowery and sweet. It's nothing like Penelope's candy scent—*dammit,* why am I even thinking about her right now?

Rein it in, Ryker. Rein it in.

She laughs up at me, big eyes wide. "I just wanted to say hi. We had a class together last semester, but you were always so covered up in girls I never really got to talk to you."

Uh-huh. Margo's the kind who gets what she wants if she wants it bad enough, and she's never made an attempt to talk to me.

"Well, here I am, ready and waiting. Let's talk." I give her a cocky grin. I can flirt with the best of them, and if it helps me forget that this year is sucking so far, so be it.

She preens. "I think you're an excellent football player. The way you throw the ball...and stuff."

Stuff? I scratch my forehead. *Is she serious?*

From behind me, I hear the sarcastic tones of Penelope's voice. I turn around and sure enough, she's standing there, minus Connor.

Her hand goes to her hip. "Well, don't you guys make the perfect Ken and Barbie." She says it completely without malice, but there's a glint in her smoky gray eyes as she measures the distance between Margo and me.

Margo takes her in, her lips pressing together tightly. "Hello, Penelope."

I sense tension and straighten. "You two know each other?" They eyeball each other like two dogs after the same bone. "Aren't you both Chi Os?"

"And stepsisters—since last year," Penelope says tightly.

Margo nods. "My mom married her dad, Professor Wainwright."

Professor Wainwright? My eyes flare. But he and Penelope

don't have the same last name...

"The psychology teacher?" He's also the chair of the department and my guidance counselor. I have a meeting with him soon to make sure I've got my credits together for graduation. A graduate of Waylon back in the day, he was a quarterback in the NFL for a few years.

Penelope gives me a short nod. "It's not something I go around telling people." She shrugs, a hard set to her face. "I barely know my dad. I happen to know a lot about football because I like the sport."

Ah. I know what it's like to barely know a parent. My mom left my dad when I was three and has been floating in and out of my life ever since. She only comes around when she's in between boyfriends and has nothing better to do. The last time I saw her was over two years ago at a football game in Austin, where I'm from. Despite the fact that I'm the quarterback, she's never been to a game here at Waylon. From watching the myriad of emotions flitting across Penelope's face, it seems we have that dynamic in common.

"Don't you have a class to get to?" Margo says to Penelope.

"It can wait."

Margo narrows her eyes. "I wanted to speak with Ryker alone."

Penelope stiffens and looks back at me, her eyes gazing at me accusingly.

The arch in my eyebrow says, *Are you jealous?*

Never in a million years, her smirk replies.

Then why the dirty looks?

She grits her teeth.

"I thought you'd already gone inside to sit with Dimpleshitz," I say pointedly.

"I did. I came out to find you."

Oh.

"Why?"

She eyes Margo and chews on her lip, obviously contemplating.

Did things go south with Dimpleshitz?

I'm about to ask her when Margo stumbles in her heels—how do you do that standing still?—and I reach out and grab her. She melts in my arms. "Thank you, Ryker. You're so strong." She bites her lower lip and pushes out her tits. My eyes, of course, go straight down to her cleavage. I'm human, after all.

I glance over at Penelope, who's glaring at me.

What?

"No worries," I say to Margo, setting her right. "Is there something else you wanted?"

She clears her throat, her hands fluttering. "Yes, as I was saying earlier...I think you're the best player in the country, and no one is more disappointed than me that you aren't being considered for the Heisman this year."

She definitely has my attention now. I frown. "The award isn't everything," I say, even if it so is.

"Good Lord, he could still win. He was cleared by the NCAA. How many times do I have to tell people?" Penelope says rather loudly.

"Are you...defending *him*?" Margo asks, an incredulous

look on her face.

Penelope shrugs. "Even if he doesn't get the Heisman, he's going to be a top pick in the draft. That's nothing to sneer at."

"But he did the betting thing to you."

"I'm right here," I add dryly.

Penelope looks at Margo. "And he apologized and has made up for it. Once I forgive someone, it's over and done. We're moving on. Isn't that right?" Her smoky eyes meet mine, and *fuck*, my heart kicks up a notch. My gaze drifts over her porcelain complexion, taking in the curls that fall around her shoulders. I stare at her lips, remembering that kiss.

She's not for you.

I swallow. "Yeah."

Margo lets out a heavy sigh, and this time her hand on my arm is insistent as she tugs. "Whatever." She focuses back on me. "Anyway, as I was saying, the Chi Omegas are having a huge—"

"*Willyoucometothehomecomingpartywithme?*" Penelope asks rapidly, running the words together as she stands with her hands clenched.

I whip my gaze back to her. "What?"

Did she just ask me to go to a party with *her*?

She nods. "It's a homecoming party at the Chi O house after the game. I know you usually go to the Tau house…" Her voice drifts off and she fidgets.

I grin at her, giving her the full golden boy charm. "I'd love to, babe."

She grimaces at the endearment. "And *I* invited you," she adds, a scowl on her face as she sends a triumphant look at

Margo.

"Whatever floats your boat." I turn more fully toward her, hoping Margo will take the hint and move away, but she doesn't. "What about Dimpleshitz?" I ask. "Is he going to be okay with that?"

She looks confused and waves me off. "I invited him too… just now. I was coming out to tell you. Aren't you proud of me? I mean, I was nervous, but he asked me out, so I think he's really into me. It gave me the confidence I needed." She smiles.

A frown scrunches my forehead. "I see. So I'm not *your* date?"

Penelope gives me an unsure look. "No. We can invite as many people as we want. We want to have a better party than the Thetas, and Margo insists we ask the most popular A-list students to come to the party. You're my pick."

A muscle ticks in my jaw. I get it now. I'm just a commodity. A means to an end. Get the popular jock there and everyone else will follow.

"Dudes! What's going on?" Blaze calls out as he waves. Dillon is next to him, the backup quarterback from Alabama with dreadlocks and a killer smile. They jog over to us, faces expectant. Carefree. Maybe that was me at some point but not anymore.

Blaze sidles up to Penelope, his gaze darting from her to me, a questioning look in his eyes. "So you guys are cool now?"

I just got her a date with her #1 crush—so yeah.

Margo is still attached to my arm, and part of me, the part

that's smarting after not being the only person Penelope invited to the Chi Omega party, decides to let her keep hanging on, especially since Penelope can't stop looking at me and Margo.

Charisma appears in our circle and throws an arm around Penelope then gives me a narrowed look. "What's up?"

Penelope says brightly, "I asked Ryker to the Chi Omega after party for homecoming, and he said yes."

An expression of surprise then understanding flits across Charisma's face as she looks at Penelope and then Margo.

Blaze's ears perk up, and he turns to Charisma, his eyebrows waggling. "I haven't gotten my invitation yet. How's about it, babe—wanna ask me?"

"Don't call me babe and *no*."

"I'm inviting you," Penelope announces.

He lets out a whoop and high-fives Dillon.

"Well, if it's going to be a big hoedown, I gotta be there too," Dillon mutters.

Charisma rolls her eyes. "Great. It's going to be one big football sausage fest."

Penelope gives Margo a smile. "Aren't you glad Charisma and I managed to invite all these great guys?"

Margo grits her teeth and pushes out a smile. "Of course. Our party's going to be the best."

Blaze gives me a long look. "Homecoming isn't that far away. Maybe we all need to hang out some before it gets here."

My lips tighten. I know what he's insinuating. He wants me to *bang Penelope*.

Penelope shrugs. "Sure."

CHAPTER 12

PENELOPE

Class is weird.

Ryker and I enter at the same time, and because we're a few minutes late, the only seats left are in the very back. Connor is sitting up front, where it's packed, and someone took my seat. Professor White is known to be a quiet talker, so if you want to keep up, it's best to sit close.

I'm glad I still have my backpack and workbook on me.

We head to the back, and Ryker's face is a mask as he settles in next to me.

While Professor White gives us a few moments to look over some notes before a quiz, I lean over to Ryker, keeping my voice low. "Aren't you proud of me?"

I expect him to flash that smile at me and be cocky.

But his expression is flat. Inscrutable. "You managed to get a date with Connor and invite me to a party and get a yes. Kudos. You've got some mojo. Everyone will be impressed."

I frown, searching his face. "Are you mad?"

He shakes his head and focuses on the board, where the professor is writing notes.

I replay the conversation, my conscience tugging at me. I can't come up with a viable reason for his surliness. Unless...

"Did you think I was asking you out?" I whisper.

Tension crackles in the air, and he inhales a deep breath then stares at me hard before looking back at the board.

"Ryker?"

A muscle pops in his jaw, but he doesn't respond for at least twenty seconds, his eyes holding mine, the color deep and mesmerizing, an iridescent sea-green color.

He opens his mouth to say something but then closes it.

"What?"

His gaze searches my face, as if looking for something, and I draw up, my body leaning toward his. God, how does he manage to create this tension inside me with just one look?

He exhales and breaks our stare. "Of course not."

He scribbles on his paper next to his laptop.

"There's something you're not saying," I murmur.

"I don't like being used to make your party cool." His voice is low. "I thought you were above all the labels at Waylon."

Labels? He's at the top of the food chain here. "Easy to say when you're the one looking down on everyone else."

"You don't know me. You don't know the pressure I feel to be the best."

"You're kidding, right? You have this entire school eating out of the palm of your hand. Everyone loves you."

"You're wrong." He shrugs, broad shoulders shifting. The movement causes his arm to touch mine, and I get sparks all over my body.

He gives me more room until we aren't touching.

"There's a shit ton of pressure on me," he continues. "My team wants me to bring them together. Coach wants a championship. NFL scouts are constantly watching and critiquing me. And, if I get hurt this year, everything's over. All that hard work...down the drain." He rakes a hand through his hair. "When it comes down to it, I'm just a twenty-one-year-old kid who's making some pretty big decisions."

I study his face, taking in the hard jut of his jaw and the shadows I think I see in his eyes. I've been imagining him as a carefree asshole, putting labels on him in my own way. Sure, he's not the golden boy I once thought he was, but black sheep looks good on him, too. Maybe I did get way too wrapped up in beating Margo at her own game. Sometimes we think everything is about *us*, but it isn't. And sometimes, we do and say not so great things to get the thing we really want, even at the expense of others. I think back to seeing Margo standing next to him in the hall and how angry it made me. Part of it was because I'm starting to think of Ryker as my friend, but I also didn't want her to get the upper hand. "You're right. I manipulated you." I look down at my hands. "I'm sorry."

A few ticks of silence go by as he taps his pen on the desk. My chest feels tight as I bring my gaze back up to study him. His stony expression softens. "Ah, Red. I'm not angry with you. It's just everything else really." He sighs. "I know you're not like other people. You don't even care who I am; in fact, I should still be begging for your forgiveness for that bet."

I shake my head. "No, we're past that. I meant what I said." I pause. "I don't hold grudges, Ryker. Starting right now, you and I have a clean slate. Friends."

"Friends, huh?"

I smirk. "It's better than enemies."

"You do have my workbook." He eyes the item in question as it sits on my desk.

"And thank you again. I owe you." I smile, and his dimple flashes at me. I get a high, like a rush of coke, straight to my head—not that I've ever done drugs, mind you, it's just...he brings out uncharted emotions in me, little by little.

He nods his head toward Connor, who's glancing over his shoulder at us. "He's looking lonely over there, and maybe a little jealous that we're talking. You best remedy that after class."

But...

I nod, and we turn back to Professor White.

Later, when class is dismissed, Connor walks over and offers to escort me to my creative writing class. I falter, part of me having hoped Ryker and I could talk more, but he doesn't wait around for me to decide; instead he runs his gaze between Connor and me, gives me a short nod and heads out the door.

CHAPTER 13

PENELOPE

Charisma and I sit inside a booth at Sugar's. It's my dinner break, and she popped in to keep me company. We eat burgers and fries as we strategize on how I'm going to figure out how to play pool.

I take a long drag from my soda and rub my forehead. "Why did I lie to him?"

She shrugs. "I assume because you like him and wanted to impress him?"

I nod, but there's a niggling in my head, a small voice that's beginning to grow stronger. Is Connor what I want? I'm not an advocate of lying, ever, and yet I started us off that way. It doesn't feel right.

She narrows her eyes at me as she stuffs a fry in her mouth. "What about Ryker? He's hot."

"There is no me and Ryker."

She looks at me.

"What?" I say. "I don't do football players."

She thinks on this, her finger tapping her chin. "What I find interesting is that Ryker chose to kiss you to make Connor jealous. There are a dozen other things he could have done, like told Connor how nice and sweet you are."

I shrug. "He had a gut feeling and just went with it, I guess."

She dabs at her mouth with a napkin. "Listen, I have gut feelings too, and mine is telling me Ryker has his eye on you. He watches you." Her gaze darts over to the football table in the back. "In fact, don't turn your head, but he's looking right now. And his face is so dang serious."

I stiffen, and it's everything I can do to not turn my head. It's been a couple of days since we had our talk in calculus, and it feels as if he's giving me space.

I lean in over the table. "What's he doing?"

Charisma's gaze brushes across the restaurant, lingers in their direction, and then comes back to me.

"Well?" I ask

She shrugs. "Looking hot and cocky as usual. Definitely a PILF." Player I'd Like to Fuck. "Not me," she adds, "but you know…the rest of the world."

"Who's next to him? Jersey chaser?"

She grimaces. "There is a jersey chaser there, but he's not into her. I've been scoping him out periodically and he's barely looked at her. Blaze is on the other side talking his ear off."

"He didn't ask for me to be his waitress tonight," I say, almost to myself.

"Interesting. No more *garçon*?"

I shrug. Honestly, I was a little disappointed.

She looks at me. "By the way, remember the guy I hooked up with at the toga party last year?"

"Yeah."

"Pretty sure it was Blaze."

I snort and nearly choke on a fry. After taking a long drink from my soda, I say, "How do you know?"

A sheepish grin crosses her face. "Just something he said. Apparently, he was also at that party and can't remember much of it." She gets a faraway look on her face. "All I can recall about him is this thing he did with his tongue—"

I hold my hand up. "Just stop right there. I want to be able to talk to him in the future without picturing what you're about to describe."

She giggles.

"And back to Ryker...I'm not his type, so nope. You're wrong."

Charisma thinks. "Hmmm, if you say so. But you did just bring him up again."

I tuck more fries in my mouth.

She sighs and smirks down at her curves. "I wish I could eat like you do."

"At least you have boobs." I wave at my chest area. "Underneath this vintage *Buffy the Vampire Slayer* shirt is a sixty dollar push-up bra. Thank you, magic brassiere." I look around the room and lean in. "With the cutlets stuffed in this contraption, everyone thinks I'm at least a solid B cup."

"Stop it. You have tits," she says.

"Correction. I have titlets."

She giggles. "That's not even a word! How do you come up with this stuff?"

I tap my head. "But in my stories, the heroine always has

big boobs." I twist my lips. "Maybe I should get a boob job."

She shakes her head at me. "Do it for you, but no one else."

I nod. "Of course. The man who falls for me will love my titlets."

"Please stop saying titlets."

We both laugh.

I shrug and check my phone for the time—my break is almost over—and eat a few more bites of my burger. "Will you feed Vampire Bill for me when you get home?"

"No. He hates me."

I wave her off. "The pellets are in the pantry, and if you can chop up some kale, maybe some banana, he'll be all set." I give her a grin. "Also, if you can tell him the word of the day again. We've been working on *llama*. Tell him I love him, too."

She glares at me. "Seriously. Anything else? He'll try to peck me. And *llama*? Ryker inspired?"

I shrug.

"It was!" A gleam grows in her hazel eyes. "I'm going to teach him something good, something that will definitely make him a cool bird."

I give her a look. "He already has enough dirty words. I know he learned 'shit' from you."

"I know nothing."

I sigh. "Just give him a little head scratch before you put him in my room, okay? Maybe turn on some music so he doesn't get lonely. Backstreet Boys is his favorite."

She takes a sip of her soda. "I don't mind. I just hate that you work so much. You know your dad would pay your bills, right? All you'd have to do is ask."

I exhale. He has offered to pay what my academic scholarship doesn't cover, but I refuse. Mom left me the house and some insurance money when she passed. I'm not destitute.

"I don't mind working. It keeps me busy." It keeps my mind occupied, too, and I've always been one who needs that.

The door chimes as customers enter. I glance up at the door and stop, eyes widening.

It's as if I conjured them.

I exhale. My dad, Carson, and his wife, Cora, waltz in with their new baby, Cyan. Yes, all their names begin with C.

"Ah, the new family," Charisma murmurs as we watch them talk to the hostess for a few minutes. They're probably up there requesting my section. I'm glad I still have a few minutes on my break.

"Looks like your dad is hunting you down," Charisma says, arching her eyebrow at me. "You probably should have said yes to dinner."

I sigh.

We watch as the hostess talks to them, and I study Cora. She's pretty in a girl-next-door kind of way with straight blonde hair and an oval face with high cheekbones. Her frame is small with a soft middle from being pregnant. She hides it with flowy tunic-style shirts, wearing them with style and confidence.

The hostess points over at me, and my dad tosses a hand up then Cora does the same. She's holding Cyan on her hip, and my gaze lingers there.

Perhaps he sees the trepidation on my face because he says something to the hostess and she leads them over to someone else's section.

Charisma's voice brings me back. "I'm heading home and crashing. You good?"

I give her a nod, and she takes off after leaving me cash for her check. I linger around the booth, taking my time, but eventually the laws of Southern etiquette demand I face them.

With a sigh, I clock back in and make my way to their table. It's on the far right side in an alcove that's rather secluded.

My dad is feeding Cyan orange baby food as I approach—something he never did for me. He looks up, sees me, and gets to his feet. "Hey, you," he says, brushing his hands with a napkin.

"Hey."

He towers over me, about six three, a handsome guy with auburn hair and gray eyes. He takes the few steps over and attempts to hug me, and I let him. It's this dance we do. He wants to make everything right between us; I'm not sure it ever will be.

I play with the gold chain around my neck, fingering the locket.

"I took that picture at the hospital the day after you were born," he says, indicating the necklace.

What? I blink up at him, my equilibrium thrown. I think about the faded picture inside the pendant. Mom is smiling down at me, wearing a white nightgown with tiny rosebuds on it. I'm mostly a blob, just a baby in a pink dress. My eyes are open and they gaze right up at her. It was always us, since the beginning.

I shrug. "I assumed you ran out of town before the big day. Was it the offseason?"

His face doesn't change, taking my shit well.

With a deep breath, he continues. "You were a C-section, and I was terrified when they wheeled your mom into surgery. The blood, the smell of the hospital, the scrubs we put on—but once they pulled you out and put you in my arms…" He stops and studies his hands for a moment then looks back at me. "It *was* the offseason, but that wouldn't have mattered. I wouldn't have missed seeing you born."

I frown at the emotion his words carry, my face tight. I don't want to feel soft toward him. "And then I didn't see you for ten years. Nice."

He pauses. "I took care of you."

"Child support."

His lips flatten—because he knows I'm right. "It's been three years since your mom passed. Maybe we should try to talk—"

"Her name is Vivien."

He nods his head in accord. "I cared for her too, you know."

"She never told me you were at the hospital when I was born."

He nods and looks away. "We didn't leave on the best of terms. I had a team to get back to, and she had her doctorate degree to work on here."

My jaw tenses, and I flick my gaze over to Cora, who I know can probably hear us but is pretending not to. I sigh.

"Some people just aren't meant to be together," he tells me.

"Your mom...she knew we were too young, and she only wanted the best for you. That was her."

Because he was busy living the baller lifestyle. Women. Parties.

"I made mistakes, Penelope. Having Cyan has made me see that."

"Now you see. How fortunate."

He watches me. "Just because there's a new baby doesn't mean we don't want to see you."

I frown. I don't know what to say.

"How are you doing?" Cora says brightly after that, standing to join him. She picks up Cyan from her high chair and places her on her hip. This close up I can see Cora's peach lipstick when Mom wore pink...how short she is when Mom was tall.

"Fine," I murmur. Cora *is* nice.

"You should come to dinner soon," she adds softly. "I've been itching to make a lasagna. I heard it's your favorite."

Cora doesn't wait for an answer, just holds Cyan out to me, and I take her and settle her on my side. I'm not sure how to hold her, but I loop my arm around her waist and her legs seem to just know what to do as they straddle me. Red hair sprouts and swirls from odd places, mostly in the front and back of her head. And her eyes—they're just like mine, the color of fog in the morning.

I can't help it. I smile down at her.

"She's six months today. We're celebrating," Dad says, watching me with Cyan. "We were hoping you were working, and here you are. Want to join us for a few minutes?"

I raise my head and meet his gaze. "I have to work, but thank you."

He gives me a short nod. "Of course. I admire your work ethic. Vivien was the same when it came to teaching." A brief smile crosses his face. "Everyone at Waylon adored her."

"She is—*was*—the best art professor here," I say, reminding him that she was part of Waylon before he came back.

Cyan blows a bubble with her spit, and I laugh just as the bell over the door jingles and Margo enters. She's wearing yoga clothes, and I figure she's popping in for one of our smoothies at the bar like she does sometimes. Our eyes meet over Cyan's head, and she frowns, her eyes flashing around our group. I don't think Cora and Dad see her and I'm about to wave—I'm not sure why, maybe because Cora *is* her mom and she's nice. Is it possible Margo has it in her to be a human being?

But before I can say anything, Margo's lips tighten as she hitches her bag up on her shoulder and marches back out the door.

I exhale. I don't get her.

But I don't understand life or people much since Mom passed away.

"Here ya go," I say, handing my half-sister back to her mom. "I need to get back to work. Glad you guys could make it out to eat."

Resignation sits on my dad's face. "I take it that's a no on dinner next week?"

"I'll have to check my schedule."

Cora puts her hand on his arm. "It's okay. School's just started, and she's busy. We'll have her over another time. Margo too."

I tell them goodbye and head in the other direction, my hand dipping into my apron as I grab a sucker.

• • •

A few minutes later, I look over my shoulder to the football table.

Ryker's watching me. He's got this quizzical look on his face, and before I know it, he's up and out of his seat and walking over to me. Blaze, who's sitting next to him, watches with a sardonic expression on his face, as if he's trying to figure him out. I also see the jersey chaser who was sitting next to Ryker—I don't know her name, but it's a different one than the last time he was here—watching him as well, a pout on her pink lips.

"Hey," he says when he stops in front of me, taking me in. He's wearing another button-up shirt, and part of me toys with the idea that he wore it for me. My eyes drift over his chest and move up to his face. He's as gorgeous as ever, hair a tousled mess, eyes intense and searching.

I must look frazzled. My wavy hair is in low pigtails and drapes over my shoulders. It did look cute this morning when I fixed it, but it's late and stray hairs are starting to poke out around my face. At least I'm wearing cute skinny jeans, a royal blue velvet designer pair I bought at a consignment store downtown. Soft and silky, they cling to my muscles and accentuate my long legs.

And points for not having any ketchup on my shirt.

"You okay?" His voice is gruff as he watches me.

"Yeah. Why do you ask?" I pat my head. "Is my hair crazy?"

He flashes a smile. "No, it's fine." He looks past my shoulder to where my dad and Cora are. "I saw your dad talking to you and things looked tense. Just making sure you're all right."

"I'm good," I say. "Thank you."

We stand and...well, just stare at each other. It's how we are, I think. We've done this in class a few times this week, neither of us quite knowing what to say to the other. There's a tension between us, a tugging of sorts, and I can't put my finger on exactly why. I blow out a little breath. Oh, screw this. I do know why. He's hot as hell, and I keep picturing him having his way with me. And I have to stop. Just seeing my dad reinforces the fact that Ryker is dangerous.

Yet...

I can't help this pull I feel toward him, as if I'm the moon and he's the Earth.

"Hey, I have a question for you," I say. "Do you really think I smell like rainbows, or was that all part of the bet?"

He smirks. "Been wondering, huh?"

"Just curious."

"You smell amazing."

You do too, I want to say, but I don't.

"So, just out of curiosity and for no other reason, when you said that part about us having a connection..." My voice drifts off when my phone pings with a text. I pull it out and read the message.

"Who is it?" he asks.

"Connor. He wants to have lunch tomorrow in between classes at the student center—the pizza place." I stare down at the message for a beat then look up at Ryker. "Should I go?"

A muscle pops in his jaw. "If you want."

"Should I say no and play hard to get?"

He frowns. "If you want to go then go. Whatever."

I scowl. Why is he being so touchy? "Isn't this how normal people do dating, by asking their friends about how to respond to a text?"

"I do what I want and nothing else. You haven't dated much, have you?"

I shrug.

His gaze brushes over my lips, lingering. "Have you ever had a serious boyfriend, Red?"

"No. Have you?"

"No, I've never had a serious boyfriend."

I laugh and he grins. "You know what I mean," I say.

He nods. "I've never dated a girl longer than a month."

A month? Holy cow. "You really are a player."

He shrugs. "I've just never been in love."

"Ditto," I say.

He arches a brow. "Connor?"

I frown. "That isn't love. I-I'm just curious about him. He seems like he'd be a good fit for me."

"A good fit?" He shakes his head. "Red, come on. It's not an arranged marriage. You need chemistry and sexual attraction. You should be thinking about him all the time, and when he walks in the room, your entire body should get hot. Is that happening?"

No. I swallow. But I can't tell him that. I just can't. It would be revealing and would make me vulnerable.

My phone pings again and I look down. "It's him again." And even though Ryker hasn't asked what he said, I tell him anyway. "He says if I'm busy tomorrow, I can come over to his place tonight and watch a movie. Oh, that sounds... interesting."

Ryker shakes his head. "Do *not* do that. That is code for sex. It's past seven and that's a booty call."

I rear back. "Really? Seven is the magic hour for a booty call? I thought that was more like midnight."

"Nope. Think about it. It will take you a while to get over there—I'm assuming you still have an hour or so left on your shift—then you watch the movie. Voila, it's midnight and he's getting all handsy."

I narrow my eyes. He's exaggerating, but I play along. "Handsy. Damn. He seems so nice."

"You never know."

Another text. "He says he knows how to cook spaghetti and will make it for me if I come over. How sweet." I glance up at Ryker, who isn't smiling back. "I told him I like Italian."

His eyes glitter. "Everybody knows how to open a jar of Prego, pour it over noodles, and sprinkle Parmesan on top. It's a trick to get you to his place."

Hmmm. I cock my hip. "I've already eaten, but I do love food. It'd be a good trick if he'd asked me for another time. Do you know how to make spaghetti?"

"Of course. And mine isn't out of a jar. I did most of the cooking at my house growing up."

Fascinating. "Why?"

He shrugs. "My mom took off when I was three. It was just my dad and me."

I absorb that information. I always imagined him living in a white-picket-fence type of family with parents as athletic and beautiful as he is. Everything I know about him realigns. We've both lost our mothers, in a way. Then it dawns on me that I don't think many people know this about him. "And you'd make me spaghetti? Not as a trick, but as a friend because I love it?"

His eyes meet mine. "Right now?"

I shake my head. "No, in your dorm room sometime. You make spaghetti and I'll bring dessert. You do have a kitchen right?"

He looks bemused, as if this conversation hasn't gone the way he expected. "I've never cooked for a girl before."

"But you would for me?"

He cocks an eyebrow. "What's for dessert?"

My body flushes, picturing us in a small kitchen. Pots and pans are everywhere. My ass is planted on the bar, and I'm reclining back with my knees up and my panties pushed to the side. He's got his jeans shoved down to his hips, grinding into me—

My phone goes off again. Bless. I exhale. "It's Connor again." I type out a response.

Ryker's lips tighten, and I think I see his fists curl. "What did you tell him?"

"Thank you for the offer but I'm working."

"What about lunch tomorrow in the student center?"

"You're nosy."

He shrugs. "I did help you get his interest. I want to know how my investment is going."

"I'm still thinking."

His lips compress, but his expression doesn't change. "I see."

There's a lot of meaning in those words, but before I can explore the complexities, the hostess waves at me, indicating a table of five she just sat in my section. I sigh. "Dang it. I have customers." I bite my lip. "I'm looking forward to my spaghetti soon. Just let me know when you're ready. I did pretty much invite myself over." Perhaps I shouldn't have.

He scrubs at his face and gives me a tired look. "Okay, I need to go. Good night, Red. See you later."

And he's gone, heading for the exit with long strides.

CHAPTER 14

PENELOPE

My car has a flat.

"Damn you," I mutter up at the gods who've seen fit to not only punish me with a shift where my dad came in, but now have left me stuck in a parking lot with a busted streetlight. Plus, Sugar's is already locked down and dark, the manager long gone.

I'm screwed.

I sigh and lean against the car, pulling out my phone and staring at it. Possibilities fly at me. Charisma mentioned how tired she was…and she did take care of Vampire Bill tonight. There's always my dad. I mean, that's what a normal father-daughter relationship would be like, right? I consider Connor, but I just turned him down for dinner. There's Ryker, but…

No. *I can do this.* I pop the trunk and lug out the small spare.

"You all right?" comes a slow drawl from behind me.

My heart drops at the voice. I mutter a curse as I flip around and squint into the darkness. Using my phone, I turn on the flashlight mode and shine it into the person's face. "Who's there?"

It's a man. He puts a hand up to shield himself from the brightness, squinting at the glare. "Whoa there. No need to put a spotlight on me. It's Archer."

"Oh, hey." I lower the light, keeping it on his chest, not quite at ease with him. My heart is still pounding as I run my eyes over him, taking in the vivid tattoos up his arms, most of them skulls and roses intertwined.

Doesn't make him a bad person, I remind myself. I adore tattoos but have never had the balls to get one.

"You've got a flat. You need some help?"

"Uh, no. I've got it. Thank you." I'm tense as I survey the parking lot, wondering where his car is. My eyes lands on a lone Range Rover, parked several spots away. I nod my head at it, playing it cool when inside I'm shaking. "That yours?"

He nods and sticks his hands in his pockets as he comes closer. "*C'est tout*, that's it. Parked it and went to a bar with friends after Sugar's."

His accent is thicker tonight, and I know why when the scent of whiskey wafts from him to me.

My danger radar climbs to high alert.

I take a step backward, and he holds his hands up in a placating manner, probably reading my face. "*Cher*, now, now, I'm just a good ol' boy. Don't fret."

Fear trickles through me, and I suck in air, feeling lightheaded. I don't like being alone with a drunk guy in a dark parking lot.

He sends me an oily grin and takes a step closer.

I hold my hands up, my voice high and thin. "Don't come

any closer, please."

He gives me a haughty glare. "You think I'm going to eat you up like a *cocodril?*"

I lick my lips. He means crocodile or alligator—I think.

The imagery in my head encourages the hair on my arms to rise. I'm picturing him knocking me over the head, stuffing me in the back of his vehicle, taking me out to the swamp, and murdering me. I still have my phone in my hand, and I clench it tight, cursing myself for not calling someone right away. My hand that isn't holding the phone shifts my keys and pushes them between my fingers in case I have to use them as a weapon. I lick my lips. "I already called someone."

"You did?" He takes another step closer.

"Ryker's coming to help me." I don't know why I say his name, but the change in Archer's face is instantaneous.

His expression hardens. "I thought you was with Connor."

"I can call who I want," I snap.

He takes another step until we're close enough that I can count the eyelashes around his eyes. His breath is sharp and pungent as he peers down at me. "You're a pretty thing. I like how you talk back," he says, his gaze on my mouth.

Terror jumps inside me, adrenaline fueling me as I shove at his chest. He stumbles back but hardly loses his balance. "I said stay back."

He looks pissed at first but then switches gears and laughs. Sticking his hands in his pockets, he glances down the empty street. "You sure you called him? If you was mine, I'd be here by now."

Look him straight in the eye. I nod. "He's probably worried right now that I haven't called him back because he told me to call him once I checked my trunk for a spare, and I already did that." I hold up my phone and wave it at him to show him I have it out and could have called him. "He worries about me and we're friends—good friends."

Archer's lips curl up, a smile without teeth, yet I feel the sharpness of it. His head lowers, his eyes at half-mast. "Ah, he's not your friend and you shouldn't trust him. You know why?"

"Why?" I don't like the know-it-all sneer on his face, and my hands tighten.

He thinks about his answer and points a finger at me, waving it all over the place. "See, *cher*, I'm itching to tell you, but if I do, it won't be fair."

My nerves are stretched too thin to piece together his drunken words. He walks forward and puts heavily muscled forearms on either side of my car, caging me in.

Shit. My hand clutches my keys. *Just stab him in the eyeball. Do it.*

But my arms feel like lead. I'm too scared to move.

His words are slurred. "You don't need him. I'll show you a real man."

A loud voice from behind him startles us both. "Dude! Archer? What's going on?"

Sweet baby Jesus. I'm saved. Relief washes over me and I crane my neck to see who it is.

Archer pushes off from my car and whips around.

Blaze is in his truck, idling by the road. He pulls to the side, turns the ignition off, and gets out then run-walks over to us. I recall tutoring him last year and how after each of our sessions in the library, he'd insist on walking me to my car.

"You okay?" Blaze asks me as I lean against my car, palms flat on the cool metal. My legs are noodles.

"I am now." I put my hand to my chest. "Just need my heart to slow down."

"Was he bothering you?" Blaze sends a narrowed, angry glance over at Archer, who's taken a few steps away from me.

"He's drunk," I tell him. "I don't know what would have happened if you hadn't come along."

"I didn't do nothing but ask her if she wanted some help," Archer calls out belligerently.

Blaze looks back at me, grimacing. "Did he touch you?"

"She shoved *me*," Archer shouts, but we both ignore him.

I shake my head. "He was leaning over me…" I shake my head. "He said stuff about Ryker I didn't get."

Blaze lets out a string of curse words and sends a menacing look at Archer. "You're an asshole, Archer. Why did you scare her?"

His jaw juts out. "I was just kidding."

Blaze's gaze comes back to me. "Do you want me to call the cops?"

I consider it, but in reality nothing happened. Yes, he showed up in the dark and said some odd things and came close to assaulting me…but he never technically laid a hand on me. My jaw clenches. Plus, he's a football player. I knew exactly what would happen if I called the cops. Nothing. He's too important of a player. Magnolia lives and breathes Waylon football.

"I didn't do anything!" Archer says.

"Just get him out of here," I say.

Archer kicks at a pebble on the concrete as he makes his way to his Range Rover. "Everyone believes the worst about me. Bunch of assholes." He pushes his hand out at us, as if he's done with us. "Fuck y'all."

He gets in his car, cranks it up, and peels out of the parking lot. As soon as he's gone, I let out a sigh of relief.

I send up a prayer that he doesn't hurt himself or anyone else.

"I told him I called Ryker, but I didn't," I tell Blaze as we watch Archer's taillights disappear.

"He would have helped you." He rubs his brow, looking at me contemplatively as if he's not sure what to say. He frowns, seeming to be mulling something over.

"What?"

Blaze looks at me. "I don't think we should tell Ryker about Archer being here. It will only make things worse with them."

I frown. "There's tension between them?"

"They have a history." He looks as if he might say more—as if he knows something I don't—but then he settles for walking over to my tire and studying it. His gaze is rueful when our eyes meet. "I guess you need some help with this?"

CHAPTER 15

PENELOPE

The Duke of Waylon enters my dressing room at the church, and I flip around to face him.

My eyes take in the thickness of his thighs in his beige breeches, the white linen shirt that's wet from the storm that rages outside. He stands with his feet apart. "You're not marrying him."

"Go to hell," I say.

He pops off his shirt with a swift movement and I gasp. He's built like a Greek god, rippling with power, an alpha male to the core. Droplets of water run in small rivulets across his muscles, tracing over his pecs and soft curls, dancing across his abdomen then disappearing inside his tight pants.

He cocks an eyebrow. "You're looking at me like you want me, Lady Penelope."

"The sentiment seems to be returned, my lord." I flick my eyes to the bulging tent in his crotch.

With two steps he's at my side and his hand tangles in my auburn tresses, tilting my chin back until our gazes are locked. He trails a finger down the curve of my face, and a flood of heat washes over me.

"Of course it is. You're mine and no one else's." He kisses me deeply, his lips like wine, dark and intoxicating.

My arms curl around his neck.

"Beautiful," he murmurs as he shoves my bodice down, freeing my heavy breasts.

"We can't do this," I breathe. But there's no truth in my words.

His glittering gaze spears me. "Indeed, my lady, we can. I'm going to fuck you until you forget all about your fiancé, Viscount Connor."

I slam my notebook shut, my chest heaving just like the heroine's. Why do I keep writing these ridiculous fantasies about *him*?

I flip on the TV where I find *Twilight* on Netflix and hit play. If I can't write fiction without Ryker as the hero, then I'll just veg out. I send a glare at my notebook. "You will not be opened again tonight," I announce.

"Shit!" Vampire Bill squawks.

I head to the kitchen, blaming my lapse in writing judgment on the fact that the handsome quarterback has been in my dreams at night more times than I care to count.

The doorbell rings as I'm popping popcorn in the kitchen. With a brief look at my clock—it's after ten—I clutch my around-the-house cardigan at the neck and grab my pepper spray. I will not be taken unaware again like last night with Archer.

I walk into the den and approach the door. "Who is it?" I call out.

"Ryker."

"Ryker?" I say back.

"Ryker!" Vampire Bill squawks, and I turn around to hush him.

"Yes," replies the deep male voice.

I stare at the door.

"You gonna let me in, Red?"

I frown at the door. "It's late. And stop calling me that. My hair is *auburn*."

I hear him laugh. "Late? It's Friday night, plus your lights were on when I drove past. And *Auburn* doesn't make a good nickname."

I cock my hip, already feeling rebellious. I'm not afraid to open my door—because Ryker—but I do want to mess with him. "Is this a booty call? It's past seven."

"No."

"Why are you driving past my house?"

I detect a long exhale through the door, and I picture him pushing his hand through his hair or just shaking his head at me. "Okay, that's fine. If you don't want my help in figuring out how to actually play pool before your date with Connor—"

"Wait!" I call out. "Don't leave! Give me a minute."

I *need* Ryker to help me.

I scan the room—it's a disaster—and like a Tasmanian devil, I tear through the den, straightening pillows and wiping crumbs off the end tables. I pause *Twilight* and warn Vampire Bill to watch his language. Perched inside his cage, he glares and gives me an *Are you kidding?* look.

He does and says what he wants.

"Are you going to let me in any time tonight?" comes Ryker's amused reply. "I don't care if you don't have any lipstick on..." His voice trails off, and when he speaks again, it's deeper. Huskier. "You *are* dressed, right?"

Dressed! Crap. I look down at my skimpy booty shorts and tank top under my sweater. Well, I am clothed, just not decent. I button the cardigan up from top to bottom, but when I look down, it looks as if all I'm wearing *is* the sweater.

"Okay, later then." I hear him scuffling on the porch and his voice is more distant, as if he's moving away.

Forget changing clothes. I fling the door open. "Wait! I'm here."

He turns back around and his eyes flare as they take me in, his electric blue gaze lingering on my legs before flying back to my face. He seems to get caught up on my hair and I touch it, knowing it's a mess, the curls everywhere.

"I take it you aren't going out?"

I shake my head. "Where would I go?"

He leans against my doorjamb and gives me a cocky grin. "I thought you might be headed to the Tau party. We won our game tonight."

"I heard."

He tosses an eyebrow up. "You weren't there?"

"Charisma told me before she left. She went to the party."

"Ah," he says, his eyes steady on my face. "So you're alone? No hot date?"

Only with my notebook.

"Nope. Just doing some writing. How was the game?"

A boyish grin crosses his face, a brightness in his eyes that makes me take in a sharp breath. He's so hot I can't breathe. "We beat Ole Miss 23 to 3. Twelve of those points were passes I threw straight to Blaze in the end zone."

"Nice."

He shakes his head at me. "We beat one of the best teams in the conference and you say *nice.*"

I shrug.

"You probably prefer playing pool?" He smirks.

I roll my eyes. "Why on earth did I lie to him? It was like my mouth was saying stuff, and I couldn't stop it."

He straightens up from his nonchalant pose and shrugs. "You wanted to impress him—because you like him."

There's a brisk quality to his voice.

"Yeah."

He gives me a short nod, his gaze moving inside the house. "May I come in?"

I open the door wider. "Please."

He eases past me, and I catch a whiff of freshly showered man, spicy and dark.

"You gonna spray me with that?" His eyes are on my hand, and I follow them to the pepper spray.

Oh! I forgot I was holding it.

I set it on the foyer table. "Sorry. You can never be too sure these days." I consider telling him about Archer, but I don't want to cause trouble between Ryker and his teammate.

"What were you writing?" he says nonchalantly as he stalks into my den, and while his back is to me, my eyes run over him, taking in the broad shoulders that taper to his trim waist. I picture the six-pack that is probably under that shirt. I briefly wonder if I'll ever see his abs. Probably not unless I sneak into the locker room someday. Tonight he's wearing a fitted black T-shirt and a pair of low-slung jeans that fit his ass like a glove. I smile to myself. I almost miss his button-down, but this isn't a bad look on him.

His well-toned athletic butt really is a thing of magnificence, the taut muscles shaped by good genes and working out constantly. I imagine him in shorts and a muscle tank, lifting weights in a gym, sweat dripping as he lifts, curling his bicep—

"Penelope. Are you listening?"

I start, realizing he's facing me and asked a question.

I blink rapidly.

What did he ask me? Writing! "Uh, nothing. Just toying with some creative writing ideas."

His gaze is intense and I think I see a glimmer of…heat in his eyes as he considers me. He sees my notebook on the coffee table and picks it up, thumbs through it. I can't tell if he's actually reading the pages, but my life flashes before me.

In an instant, I'm pressed against him, my hands tugging my journal out of his hands. I hug it to my chest like it's the Holy Grail.

He cocks an eyebrow. "Personal?"

I huff and show him the cover. "Did you not see where it plainly says DO NOT OPEN?"

He looks at me.

"What?" I snap.

He shrugs. "I'm just wondering what kind of things you write about. Is there sexy stuff in there, Red?"

"Absolutely not."

"You sure? Your face is flushed and you're breathing pretty fast. I might have to defibrillate you if you pass out."

I suck in a cleansing breath as I clutch my notebook. "You didn't read anything, did you?"

"I didn't read anything tonight," he says softly.

I harrumph and tuck my notebook into the desk that sits next to the media cabinet.

"So why aren't *you* at the Tau party?" I ask, straightening up to face him, determined to change the subject. "You should be in the middle of a fan-girl sandwich by now, Ryker. You should at least be 'doing laundry' with someone."

He shrugs. "I was on my way home from getting dinner when I saw your lights on."

Technically, my house is not on the main drag. He'd have to purposely make a few turns to get here, and I'm about to comment on this point—

"Shit! Ryker! Shit!" It's Vampire Bill, and I send him a *be quiet* look, but he just blinks back at me, his yellow eyes bouncing from me to the football player.

Ryker appears startled until he sees Vampire Bill, who is perched inside his cage on a narrow table in the den. Ryker glances back at me, a quizzical expression on his face. "I never took you for a bird girl. Maybe a cat or a small dog."

I huff out a laugh. "I inherited him when my neighbors moved."

"Oh?"

I nod. "Yeah, on moving day, they were going to leave him and let him live in the wild, but he can barely fly, and when he does get off the ground, it's just for short spurts." My lips tighten, and I'm feeling indignant all over again remembering the renters next door, a pair of young college girls who graduated two years ago. I came outside when they were debating about which side of the street to leave him on. Of course, I was horrified. I immediately took him in and did my best to be a good bird owner. I even took a class at the humane shelter, which I figure had to be better than what they did for him. I walk over to his cage and give Vampire Bill's head a little scratch, and he allows it for half a second—until he hops away and glares death daggers at me. "He's an African Grey and supposedly has the intelligence of a four-year-old. Sadly, he has a personality disorder. He hates everyone."

"Jock! Shit! Ryker!" Vampire Bill squawks, and I stifle down my giggle.

"But he is funny." I look back at Ryker, who's now standing next to me at the cage.

"Did you teach him that?"

I blink innocently. "Maybe."

"Uh-huh. You talk about me to your bird. Fascinating."

"Not really. We do a word of the day sometimes," I say as he stalks around my den, his eyes checking out my small but well-built house. His gaze takes in the decor in shades of gray and soft ecru. An elegant but rustic farmhouse-style chandelier illuminates the beige leather sofa and two baby blue plaid chairs across from it. The baseboard trim is thick and was recently painted a vanilla color by me this summer when I needed something to keep my mind busy and writing wasn't cutting it.

"Oh, what was today's word?"

I pause.

"Red?"

"Quarterback."

He grins.

And we do that staring thing.

"Nice place," he says, breaking our gaze as his eyes drift over the furnishings. "Homey. I like it."

"I grew up here," I tell him, my fingers touching one of the lime green pillows on the chairs. "My mom decorated. She was…pretty awesome." I pause. "I guess you don't get back to Austin much?"

"Nah, it's just me and my dad, and he's always busy with work. Hey, I'm sorry about your mom." He pauses. "You mentioned it in the bookstore…"

I nod.

"What happened?"

I rarely tell anyone the details of my mother's death. "She…she had a pulmonary embolism, a blood clot in her lungs. It was completely out of the blue and happened while she was riding her bicycle to work."

"Shit. I'm so sorry. That must have been awful."

Since her death, I've learned to harden myself to the events, but the sincerity in his voice gets to me. Tears tug at my eyes, and I push them down, adjusting my glasses. "It was a shock. What about your family? You said your mom left when you were three?"

"I rarely see her," he says. "My dad works all the time. He runs a small real estate company in Austin." His eyes land on the TV. "So, is this the movie you love so much?"

My gaze follows his. "Wanna watch with me? I just made some popcorn."

"I'm more of an action and adventure guy."

I sniff, feeling offended. "I bet if you watch the rest of this with me, you'll like it."

A smile tugs at his lips. "You're making a bet with me?" He shakes his head. "Oh, Red. You're on dangerous ground."

I nod, feeling confident. "There's some action in this one—scary killer dude."

"What are the stakes?"

"If you like my sparkly vampires, you'll have to make me spaghetti tonight." I'm giddy at the thought of watching him cook.

He considers me, his gaze thoughtful. "Done. And if I think *Twilight* is stupid, I get to read your notebook."

Oh…shit.

I lick my lips, and his gaze traces the movement. "How will I know if you're being honest when you say if you liked it or not?"

"You'll just have to trust me." His sea-green gaze glitters. "Why do you like it so much anyway? The way I understand it, Edward's not even a badass. He's more of a touchy-feely bloodsucker."

I huff. "How do you know so much about it?" I put my hands on my hips as he plops down on my couch and proceeds to make himself comfortable by arranging pillows and propping his feet up on the ottoman next to him.

"I may have googled it after you mentioned he was on your

pillow. Can I see the pillow?"

"Nope. You're getting nowhere near my bed."

He laughs.

As I watch, he leans back and raises his arms to stretch before grabbing the remote and starting the movie back up.

I'm still staring down at him, trying to wrap my head around the fact that Ryker Voss is sitting on my couch, acting casual—and is going to watch a movie with me.

He pats the spot next to him. "Come on, Red. We've got a vampire to ogle."

CHAPTER 16

PENELOPE

Ryker Voss is the most annoying football player alive.

Twilight is over. It's after midnight, and I should be dead tired, but instead, I'm debating the merits of my favorite book.

"That movie just plain sucked," he announces smugly.

I sit cross-legged, facing him, blue in the face from trying to explain the plot points.

He's shaking his head at me.

I'm feeling petulant and grumpy. I wanted him to love it as much as I do. "Don't you have a heart?"

He laughs. "Where were the gore and fangs? Not to mention the questionable hairstyles, creeping on her when she sleeps—and the sparkling in the sun thing? Toss in the no sex and it's two stars at best."

His eyes are lit with amusement as he watches me sputter. I wave my hands around, trying to find the right words to bring him over to my side.

"You're telling the truth?"

He nods.

My shoulders slump. It's like eating the best piece of

chocolate ever and giving a piece to your friend only to have them spit it out.

"I think the no sex is part of the appeal," I say. "Saving yourself for the one person you truly love—that means something."

He scoffs but then sobers when he reads the look on my face.

His lips part, and I see a dawning on his face. "Are you a virgin, Penelope?"

Panic at being so transparent rises for half a second until it ebbs away. I don't know why, but I feel like I can be myself with him. "Yes."

His face changes, the humor softening into amazement. "A twenty-one-year-old virgin...at Waylon? Impossible."

I stare down at my hands.

"Are you sure?" He's leaning in closer to me now, the heat from his body radiating to mine.

I roll my eyes. "I can assure you I've never had my cherry popped, hooked up, yada, yada, yada..."

I glance back up, and he's staring at me, his gaze swirling with an indecipherable emotion.

"How far have you gone with a guy?"

I cock my head. "Seriously? You're asking for specifics?"

"It's just so rare. I'm fascinated."

I chew on my lips. "Good. I'm glad you're not prejudiced against virgins."

His lips quirk. "You've been kissed. Obviously."

I nod.

His gaze lingers on my chest. "And second base?"

I nod.

His face grows still. "Third base?"

The air grows heavy. "What is third base?" I murmur.

"You want me to describe it?" he asks. There's a flush on his cheeks as we stare at each other.

Heat rises in my face. Yes. I want him to spell it out in excruciating detail, so I can replay it over and over when he's gone.

"Third base is when a guy—or a girl..." He stops and looks at me.

"Guy."

"Puts their hands..." He glances down at my legs and clears his throat. "Inside your underwear and touches you."

Fire licks at me. It feels as if he's touching me now, sliding his hands under my panties, his fingers dipping inside—

I suck in a breath. "Hmmmm, I see. And the purpose of this is to..."

His chest rises. "Fuck, Red. To get you off. Make you come. Have you ever had an orgasm?"

My eyes lower. "Oh, definitely. I'm just waiting for a special person to give myself to completely."

With scarcely a movement, he leans in and brushes my lips with his.

"What was that for?" I whisper as he stares down at me.

"Because...shit...I don't know. I wanted to." He sighs.

I twist my hands in my lap, my mouth saying something I don't intend it to. "A guy has never given me an orgasm. I mean...I have had one, but not caused by an actual human male."

His chest rises up and down in quick succession and he swallows. His eyes darken. "I see."

I pick at one of the loose threads on my cardigan. He watches me. "Sometimes I wonder if the feeling itself is different, you know, with a guy. If it's still that intense burst that goes off in your head and makes you warm and tingly." I let out a ragged breath I didn't know I was holding. "I think about it a lot. Who I want it to be…"

He stands abruptly.

"Ryker?"

He opens his mouth to say something but then shuts it and takes off for the kitchen. I'm not even sure he knows where he's going, so I hop up and follow him.

"What's going on?"

"I need some water. With ice, preferably."

From behind him, I watch as he flings cabinets open and shuts them.

"Glasses are on the right side, next to the fridge." I move in closer in case he needs help.

He opens the right one, grabs a glass, and fills it up with ice from the dispenser. Then he turns to the sink and starts filling up the glass. It overflows.

He doesn't notice.

"It's overflowing," I say.

He curses and pours out some of the water then lifts the glass and drinks it down.

"Um, I have some Gatorade if you're really thirsty."

His shoulders are tense, and he hasn't turned around, and my heart beats double time at the sparks in the air.

He sets the glass down on the counter and takes three huge breaths before facing me.

His expression is conflicted, a range of emotions flitting across his chiseled features. I can't read them, and I suspect he doesn't want me to.

I'm not sure what's going on. I shake my head. "I'm sorry if I went too far. I'm just comfortable with you. It's like we have this easiness when we're together—"

"No, stop. This isn't your fault." His voice is husky.

I ease over to my sucker drawer and pull one out. I'm so fast, I have the wrapper off and the candy in my mouth in three seconds. I ignore the fact that my hands are shaking. "Want to tell me what's going on then?"

He dips his head and rakes his hands through his hair. "Fuck. *Red.*" He says my nickname like it's torturing him.

"What's wrong?" I'm a little shrill now.

He sticks his hands in his pockets, looking unsure as he glances around the room. Anywhere except at me. "I shouldn't be here."

My jaw tightens. I enjoy him being here.

He scrubs at his jaw. "I just—don't need a distraction right now. I have to keep my head in the game."

"Why is me being a virgin a distraction to you?"

He groans. "It's not—*you* are." He waves his hands at me. "The whole vibe you have."

"Me?" I walk closer, being tentative because he looks like he might bolt at any moment. "What do you mean?"

He tugs on the ends of his hair, as if he's debating. "I'm into you, okay? I think about you a lot. Something about that kiss..." He groans. "I think about kissing you, fucking you—then fucking you some more."

My heart roars like a jet plane ready for takeoff. It's so loud I'm sure he can hear it. I swallow. "Me? A girl who's never seen an actual peen except on Tumbler?"

He nods, his eyes finding mine. His are low and heavy. "*You*. And you're into me, Red. I already know you are. I see it when we have our little stare-offs. I sure as hell saw it out there when we talked about third base." He looks down at me. "Your pupils are fucking dilated, babe. You're hot for me. Put that with how I feel...and it's dangerous."

I sputter. He isn't wrong, but...

He gives me a hard look. "Tell me, did you go to lunch with Connor?"

I recall our conversation at Sugar's when Connor texted me. "No, I had too much to do. Why? What are you saying?"

He glares at me. "You know what I'm saying. Do you really want him?"

I don't say a word. I'm afraid of revealing too much.

He lets out a heavy exhale. "I haven't had sex with anyone since last semester—since all that shit happened. It's the biggest dry spell I've ever had since I was a teenager."

Oh.

"Four months," he tells me.

"Is it because you can't get it up?"

He throws back his head and laughs and then sobers. "Fuck no. I'm hard as nails right now. For you."

I toss a glance down at his pants, and yep, there it is. My body gets hot.

"I just...I've been trying to focus on doing everything right with football...until you." His ocean-colored eyes swirl with emotion. "And, dammit, I don't want to hurt you. You're a nice girl—a virgin, even—and I don't know how the hell to deal with—"

"I don't want to be hurt either, Ryker." My chest feels heavy, as if someone has poured concrete on it.

"I won't let it get that far, Red. We're friends, and that's something." I watch as he seems to gather himself, shutting the cabinet door he left open and pushing his glass back from the edge of the counter. His eyes find mine. "It's late. I need to go."

I frown. "You're leaving after that little bomb? *Now*?"

He gives me a curt nod, his jaw grinding as if he's keeping words from coming out. "Goodbye, Red."

And then he's walking down the hall and opening my door and slipping into the night.

I'm rooted to the floor. I realize he didn't even ask to see my journal when he won the bet.

But that doesn't matter.

My breath catches as the truth hits me.

Ryker Voss hasn't been with a girl in months, and *I'm* the one he wants.

But he's afraid.

I am too.

I don't need a quarterback fucking up my life.

Tangled emotions rise up, and I suck in a shuddering breath. No matter what I tell myself, he's stealing my heart, bit by bit, and it's going to take everything I have to resist falling.

• • •

The next day is Saturday. I hop in my car and cruise to the Chi Omega house. Now that I have Ryker and Connor coming to the party, I signed up via email to help with the planning committee.

I park by the curb and waltz inside, putting my purse on the pink high-backed Queen Anne style armchair next to the door. My eyes take in the oak paneling, medallion wallpaper, and Victorian furnishings.

This place needs a *Property Brothers* makeover, but it's the same one my mom pledged. My gaze lingers on the chair where I just dumped my purse. I've seen pictures of that very piece of furniture in my mom's albums, and it makes me feel close to her. She was here…just like I am.

I hear crying as I walk down the hall. The sound comes from the common area where we have our meetings. Usually those doors are open, but today they're closed.

I tap lightly on the wood. "Hello?"

When I don't get a reply, I try the door, but it's locked.

I chalk it up to sorority house drama when Keri, one of the pledges, appears next to me.

"It's Margo," she whispers furtively.

I frown. "Our president?"

She nods. "She's been in there for half an hour. We were talking about the theme for the party, and she just ran out of the meeting."

I scratch my head. Margo's the kind of girl who eats metal shavings for breakfast and spits them at girls she doesn't like afterward. She *never* cries.

Keri shrugs. "The planning committee chairperson said we'd just proceed without her."

"I wouldn't count her out yet," I say then nod my head toward the room past the kitchen, a sunroom where we have a copy machine, a couple of laptops, and a bulletin board. "Why don't you head back to the meeting, and I'll meet you there."

Keri wavers. "They sent me back here to report on how she is—"

"Tell them she's fine and will be there in a minute."

Pledges. Margo and I may not be best friends, but we've been together for three years, and no freshman pledge is going to be talking about her and why she's crying. She hasn't been here long enough.

She reads my face and scurries off.

I tap on the door again. "Margo. It's me, Penelope. Let me in."

"Go away."

Her voice is wobbly, and I sigh. "As soon as you open the door."

I hear sniffling and guilt brushes over me.

"Open the door or I'm going to go get a hairpin and pick the lock, and you know, it might just mess up these old antique doors. I know how much pride you take in our house—"

The door flings open, and my mouth gapes at what I see. The normally coiffed and cool Margo is a mess with smudged mascara and stray hairs poking out from under her headband. Even her clothes are askew, as if she's been lying down. My eyes take in a fuzzy blanket draped over the couch in the back along with a pile of potato chip bags and candy bar wrappers.

"Why do you care?" she snaps.

"You're a person, Margo. I care."

She shrugs and flips around then takes a seat on one of the couches in the room. I follow her inside and shut the door, taking the seat next to her as I reach over and grab a wad of tissues off the cherry coffee table. I pass them over.

"Is this because I invited Ryker?"

She takes my offered Kleenex and dabs at her hazel eyes, the green in them more prominent when they're wet.

She tugs her navy cardigan around her shoulders. "You stole him from me."

I snort. "You embarrassed me in front of our whole sorority. Like you *really* liked him anyway?"

"God, no." She holds a hand to her chest as if the idea will give her a heart attack.

I smirk. "Exactly. I know your type. Wasn't your ex some kind of uppity Mayflower descendent?"

"His name was Kyle. And yes." She clams up, a stoniness taking over her expression.

I nod, recalling the details. "And you caught him with a Theta. Sasha? She's their president, right? And you wanted Ryker on your arm so everyone will see him and it will get back to your ex..." My words drift off. "Am I close?"

She wipes her nose. "Guess you really are the genius your dad says you are." Her words are brittle.

I frown. "You're jealous of me and my dad?"

She shrugs. "You have everything, Penelope."

I give her an incredulous look. "My mom is dead. I'm separated from her forever." My voice grows louder. "Your mom is alive and well—and married to my dad."

Margo swallows and looks away from me, shaking her head. "You're right. I'm sorry." She looks down. "You're all he talks about, you know. How smart and talented you are."

I blink. *Oh.*

She bites her lip. "My dad can barely stand me."

I shake my head. "Mine is just trying to make up for being shitty before."

"Well, don't we make a fine pair then." She picks at the green fabric on one of the pillows and continues. "Love sucks and doesn't last. Don't our parents know that?"

"Maybe when you find the right one, it changes things."

She tries to tuck her flyaway hairs back into her headband, and I reach over and help her. "I'm sorry…for causing a scene. I got so worked up when I came to the meeting, and it hit home that I don't have a date." She chews at her lipstick. "And I'm sorry about embarrassing you. It was a shitty thing to do. I'm not myself since Kyle."

I nod, accepting her apology.

She blinks away more tears, clearly still thinking about something…

The soft side of me can't take it. She *is* my stepsister, and perhaps there's a thread of something between us that can pull us closer.

"You're one of the smartest women I know."

A tiny smile flashes. "You really mean that?"

I adjust my glasses. "You took our academic standing to the top last year, and you weren't even president. And Kyle is a douche."

"An asshat with a stupid Rolex," she says, her voice gathering strength. "And that Porsche he bought—trust me, he is totally compensating."

I smile. This is the closest we've ever come to having a real conversation.

I stand. "We can sit here and cry or..." I nod toward the door. "Suck it up and get to work. Keri looks like butter wouldn't melt in her mouth, and odds are she's planning on making SpongeBob SquarePants the theme of this party."

Margo's brows hit the roof. "Indeed."

Of course, I'm exaggerating, but if that's what it takes to get her claws back out...

I look at my nails. "Hmmm. Sometimes those pledges need to see who's boss. This might be one of those times."

She straightens her shoulders. "They have no idea what kind of hissy fit I can throw."

Amen, sister.

She stands and we walk out of the room together.

We aren't exactly friends, but my gut says we definitely aren't enemies either.

CHAPTER 17

PENELOPE

The following week, I'm late for the library as usual and practically running as I juggle my backpack and a few extra books. I've just turned the corner around a big oak tree when I run into Ryker. We've seen each other in class this week, but either Connor has been talking to me or Ryker's been surrounded by other players or jersey chasers. Sure, I could bust through the crowd and talk to him, but my heart knows the truth: we're avoiding each other since his visit to my house.

We collide and several of my books fall to the ground.

Great. I inwardly groan at my penchant for always looking my worst—in other words, a shirt that says *Mother of Dragons*, orange skinny jeans with holes in them, and a pair of leopard flats. At least I have lipstick and mascara on and my hair is down and tame for once.

"Whoa!" he says as we stumble back, and he reaches out to steady me. "Slow down."

"Sorry," I murmur as I bend down to pick up the books.

He leans down to help, holding one of them up as he pops an eyebrow at me. "*Dark Lover* by JR Ward? Now that sounds like a literary gem." He turns it over and skims the back.

"It is."

He flips it over and studies the shirtless guy on the front. "I've got him beat, Red."

I take it out of his hands. "This happens to be a fantastic series. You might even like it. Lots of blood and gore and fangs." I smile.

"Really?" He stands as I do, helping me up as I open my backpack and cram the books inside. He shrugs nonchalantly and looks off in the distance. "I meant to ask you—how did the pool date go? Wasn't it supposed to be this week?"

"It's been delayed. We're going out soon." I managed to put Connor off for a while with the excuse that I had to work.

He sticks his hands in his pockets. "So you didn't go out with him yet? Interesting."

I shrug, playing it off. "Well, you never showed me how to play pool."

"Oh," he says, a thoughtful look on his face. "I can do that. How about tonight?"

Excitement curls at the thought of him leaning over me and showing me how to hit a cue ball.

But...

I point to myself. "Distraction, remember?"

He exhales, his gaze intense. "We haven't hung out in a while. Or talked. If you can handle the proximity, I can."

I mull it over. I don't have to work, and Charisma already mentioned she has plans to go to a Tau party tonight.

"There's a Tau party, but I'm not really in the mood to go," he adds.

"Okay," I say, coming to a decision without really thinking it through.

He smiles and we begin to walk. "Where are you headed?"

"Library. I do a study group there when needed."

"Oh?"

I nod. "Usually for lower level geometry classes."

"You're some kind of genius, aren't you?"

I grin. "Your GPA isn't too shabby either."

"How do you know?"

I roll my eyes. "I did my research, quarterback. Also, you're in an upper level math class when your major is psychology, so you must like numbers. Am I right?"

A dimple pops out. "Maybe I took it because I knew it was likely you'd be in there."

I laugh as we walk across the quad. "You're such a liar."

"Well, then I guess it was fate that we both ended up in it. I'm shocked we never had a class together before. I wonder if we would have been friends sooner." He gets a contemplative expression on his face and halts.

I stop with him. "What?"

He shakes his head. "I just realized we might not have met if I hadn't been part of the scandal last year." His eyes find mine. "You wouldn't have written your editorial, and Archer never would have bet me I couldn't get you to go out with me. You never would have dumped water on me." He laughs. "Crazy, right, that something good came out of it?"

Indeed. I nod, my gaze lingering on the curve of his face, the way his hair curls up at the ends.

He flashes a grin. "Plus you opened my eyes about how

sucky *Twilight* really is—but I'd watch all of them with you if you wanted. That's a true friend."

I laugh. "Thank you...I think?"

Someone squeals his name, and we both turn to see a skinny, pretty, blonde girl in a miniskirt and a low-cut green shirt. Her giant boobs bounce as she runs toward us and grabs him in a bear hug, throwing her arms around his waist. "Ryker!"

He's motionless, standing with his arms at his sides as she coos over him, brushing her lips over his cheek, her hand squeezing his bicep.

Of course, it's none other than Sasha, the Theta who hooked up with Margo's Kyle. I grimace, imagining what it would be like to walk in and see your boyfriend banging this Playboy lookalike. Not pretty.

She bats her eyes up at him. "I haven't seen you at any of the parties. We need to get together soon." She rakes her hand across his shoulders, wiping at a nonexistent piece of lint. "You looked amazing at last week's game, by the way. Remember that time we went to the basement after we beat LSU and I—"

"Uh, yeah." His face is carefully blank, and I suspect—am almost certain—she was about to recall some tryst they had.

It says a lot about a girl that she will talk about her sexual exploits in front of another girl. But then Sasha's not exactly a nun.

My gut says he's slept with her.

My heart tightens.

I have *no* claim to him at all, as I remind myself.

We. Are. Just. Friends.

I BET YOU | 149

"So how are you?" she says, easing in closer to him.

"I've been busy with practice," he replies, but his eyes are on me.

I swallow and break our gaze, thinking about these confusing feelings I have for him. Because I can say all day long that I just want to be friends, but the truth is I'm so fucking hot for him that it hurts. I can't stop writing about him. I can't stop looking at him. And I want to pull out every blonde hair on Sasha's head.

What if I fall all the way for him? Is this the kind of thing I'd have to put up with?

How can one girl ever be enough for him? My mom wasn't enough for my dad.

He looks down at her, a polite smile on his face. "Hey, Sasha. I'm talking to someone. Do you mind?"

"Oh!" Sasha looks over at me as if just noticing I'm here. She smiles. "Have we met?" Her long lashes flutter against her porcelain complexion.

Several times. "Yes."

She squints. "Wait. You're a Chi O, right?"

I nod. "I'm Margo's stepsister." Never in my life have I been proud to own that one. But the thing is, when you screw over a Chi Omega, the girls will line up behind her to get you back.

"Oh." She laughs, the sound grating on my nerves. "I suppose she doesn't like me very much." She leans in conspiratorially. "Just tell her Kyle was a one-time thing, will ya? No harm, no foul. She can have him back."

My eyes narrow, but my voice is sugary sweet and oh so

Southern. "Sweetie, she doesn't even know who you are."

She cocks her head. "Oh. Really? That can't be right. I'm sure she knows—"

"Mmmm, oh yeah, she's moved on to bigger and better. But how *nice* for you to tell me it was just a one-time thing." I smile brightly. "Take care now. Use condoms."

I hitch my backpack up on my shoulder, give Ryker a smoldering glare, and walk off.

If that's the kind of girl he goes for—my fists clench—then what on earth does he see in *me*?

Ugh. Why does it even matter? Neither of us is going to act on it.

Ryker calls my name, but I don't stop.

I hear footsteps behind me. It's him. "Hey, why did you run off like that? We were in the middle of making plans."

My jaw tenses.

"Red. Come on. I told her to buzz off."

My voice is sharp. "Like that makes it better? How many girls on this campus have you been with?"

He flushes. "I never claimed to be a saint. I'm not the same person I was last year."

I snort. "I didn't see you in a rush to get away from her."

"I was being polite!"

I halt and look at him. "You shouldn't have been!"

His mouth parts at my vehemence, but I take off walking again and he keeps up with me.

"Why are you so upset?" he asks. "Are you jealous?"

"Get over yourself." I'm breathing hard as I walk-jog.

He takes my arm and pulls me to a stop. "You are. You can

go on and on about Connor and how perfect he is, but if a girl stops and says hi to me, you storm off. Why is that?" He studies me intently. "Don't you think that means something?"

We stare at each for several seconds. My chest is rising and so is his, and I almost feel that if I took one tiny step toward him he would wrap me in his arms and kiss me so fucking hard.

"Red. Say something."

No. He's the one who left my house; he's the one who said he didn't want to hurt *me*.

"What are you thinking, Penelope?" His voice is layered with emotion.

It's as if he needs me to tell him something, to pour my heart out to him.

But I can't. I won't.

I inhale a sharp breath. "This distraction needs to get to the library."

I pull my arm away and take off in a full-on run. I probably look ridiculous running in flats and juggling a backpack, but it is what it is.

My eyes close briefly as I hurry toward the library.

God help me. I can't fall for him.

I just can't.

CHAPTER 18

RYKER

A few hours later, I'm in my dorm room, stewing after seeing Penelope. I clench my fists and pace around my bedroom. Fuck, I'm antsy, and all I can think about is how pissed she was about Sasha and how amped up I am that I can't get her to admit she wants me just as much as I want her. It doesn't matter that she's a distraction right now. It doesn't matter that I've sworn I won't get involved with anyone.

She's just…different.

My eyes land on a framed picture of my dad and me at my last high school football game, and my lips twist. If I had a solid relationship with him, maybe I could call him up and talk about this pressure I feel to be the best, to be a top pick in the draft. But my dad isn't the kind of guy you open up to. Plus, he's still disappointed in me after the fighting scandal.

My chest is heavy and I scrub my jaw. There's no one to talk to, really, about Penelope. Blaze is too immature, and Maverick lives with Delaney now so I barely see him. And Dad? Ha. He thinks women are for sex only. Guess I can't blame him considering how my mom left us.

I get a text and grab my phone.

It's from Blaze. **Dude. Your girl is here at the Tau house.**

My girl?

Penelope, asswipe.

I exhale.

On my way.

I hop in the shower, and twenty minutes later I'm out the door and headed to my truck.

The frat house is thumping with the strains of Post Malone as I walk in the door. It's a full-scale party with people everywhere, open pizza boxes on the counter, and a keg in the kitchen. I grab a red plastic cup of beer and head to the basement where most of the people like to congregate.

Penelope is the first person I see, and I pause mid-step on the stairs and nearly spit out my drink when I get a gander at what she's wearing: a plaid miniskirt with a fitted white collared shirt. The buttons are done all the way to the top and a little scarf thing is tied around her neck. Schoolgirl. At first glance, it's demure, but then I look down and see her high-heeled black boots. *Good God.* My teeth snap together. Her auburn hair is curled and in pigtails, and she's not wearing her glasses—a clear sign she's on a mission.

Is it Connor she's trying to ensnare? I run my eyes over the crowd, but I don't see his familiar tall frame and dark hair. My fists unclench. Good. Sure, he's decent, but a kernel of anger rushes through me every time I see the nerdy asshole.

I watch Penelope and Charisma—and is that Margo? Yep. The three of them, along with several other sisters, are laughing as they dance together at the edge of the space. No dudes around them.

I don't even know Blaze is next to me until he speaks, his gaze on the group. "You got here fast. I see you're watching the Chi Os," he murmurs.

"Nope."

He chuckles, and I turn to give him a sharp look.

"Something you want to say?"

He scratches at his head. "Dude, you've got a thing for her, for Penelope. Like bad."

"No, I don't."

He shakes his head and gives me this look like he knows shit. "I'm your go-to guy with the ball, man, and I read you like a book. You can't keep your eyes off her. Even that day at Sugar's..." He shakes his head.

I swallow and rub at my jaw.

Blaze muses. "You'd have pretty babies together."

My eyes flare. "Are you drunk?"

He shrugs. "I've had a few, but just because I'm a football player doesn't mean I'm not romantic and shit." A grin flashes across his face. "Plus, you deserve some good in your life. I say go for it. Win that bet and get the girl at the same time."

He's babbling. I squint at him, taking him in. "Question. Ever watch *Twilight*?"

"Team Jacob all the way."

I shake my head. "I don't even know you."

He shrugs. "I have sisters. Girls love that shit."

A slow song comes on, one of Ed Sheeran's, and I see a group of frat boys eyeing the girls.

Hell no.

With a muttered farewell, I leave Blaze behind and head toward Penelope. The closer I get, the tighter my chest feels.

What's it going to take to make her see I'm not the person she thinks I am?

Why does her opinion matter to me?

I watch her toss her head back and laugh, her hair curving around her shoulders, lying in copper coils.

"What's up? Enjoying the party?" I say as I stop in front of them, giving them my signature cocky grin.

"Oh. Hey." It's Penelope and she's staring at me—like she does—as she takes a sip of her drink.

I don't even pretend to do small talk. She isn't one for it, and I don't want to give her the opportunity to run away from me.

"Let's dance." It isn't a question.

I take her hand, clasp it in mine, and tug her forward. She follows.

"Brute. She didn't say yes," Charisma calls out after us.

"She would have," I say over my shoulder.

Penelope hasn't said anything as we reach the middle of the makeshift dance floor. She curls her arms around my neck and looks up at me. My hands linger on her lower waist, so fucking tempted to press myself completely against her, but I don't because my dick is a steel rod.

My gaze wanders over her auburn hair. She's so gorgeous it makes my teeth hurt. "Nice outfit," I say. "Did you wear it for me?" I can't stop the bullshit coming out of my mouth. Fuck—the truth is, I don't know how to talk to her. Sure, I know how to flirt and fuck, but I don't know how to really like a girl. I recall the fact that I asked her to do laundry with me. I really suck.

"I dress for myself." She shrugs. "I didn't know you'd be here."

I nod, staring down at her. "You ran off today before we could finish our conversation."

"Captain Obvious."

"It wasn't cool. I was trying to explain to you that I don't give a shit about Sasha."

Her eyes fly to mine. "Really? I figured you were into her...all big boobs and bunny-like. That isn't me."

"I know you're not like that. It's what I like about you."

She bites her lip, and my eyes linger there, wondering how it would feel if I kissed her again, this time hard and intense and with so much feeling...

She exhales. "Look, can we forget about everything and just dance?"

"Hi. My name is Ryker. I play football. I love piña coladas and getting caught in the rain. I like making love at midnight, and...I can't remember the rest of it. What's your name?"

She giggles, and I know I've won her over. "Piña coladas?"

I pop an eyebrow. "Just going with the flow here. Don't dis coconut and rum until you've tasted it."

She laughs. "Okay. I'm Penelope, and I also love getting caught in the rain...and yoga?" She smiles. "Sorry. I can't remember that song either."

"I'm the football player you've looked for..."

"Come with me and escape."

We both laugh.

"See, this is easy," I say as I pull her closer, until her breasts are pressed against my chest. "I like getting to know you," I murmur in her ear.

She tilts her head back, gray eyes glinting up at me. "Is that so?"

"Mmhmmm."

Her lashes flutter down as if she's hiding her emotions, and my hands tighten around her, my fingers trailing over the soft fabric of her skirt. I'm itching to run my hand over her ass and claim it as mine.

"I have a question for you," I say.

"Yeah?"

"Did you come hoping to see Connor?"

She shrugs.

"Did you come hoping to see me?"

Those long lashes lie against her cheeks.

"Penelope?"

"Hmm?"

I want to say *Let's get out of here.*

Let me get to know you...let me unwrap that skirt and show you exactly what it feels like when a man gives you an orgasm.

The air in the room changes, and I look up and see Archer coming down the stairs with a few other defensive players. Our eyes meet across the floor, and his lips tighten as he rakes his gaze over Penelope.

He turns back to one of the guys and points at us. They laugh and sneer.

My gut churns. Dammit. I don't want him watching us together, wondering if I'm dancing with her just to win the bet.

"What is it?" she says, looking up at me. "You got quiet."

I smile down at her. "Nothing, Red. Look, I'm sorry about today. I shouldn't have let Sasha say some of that shit in front of you."

"She was staking her claim. She wanted me to know she'd had you." Her lips compress.

"Well, she won't have me again."

She doesn't look sure as she watches me, and there's a thoughtful look on her face like she's going to say more, but she settles on, "Okay."

As soon as the song is over, I walk with her back to her group and say my goodbyes. She watches me with a frown and perhaps disappointment. Maybe.

I imagine I feel her gaze on me as I walk across the basement and head to the stairs.

I pass by Archer on the way out, and he can't help but make a comment. "Leaving so soon, golden boy?"

I shrug. "Nothing for me here."

His eyes drift over to Penelope, a hardness there. "Got turned down, huh?"

"Fuck off."

And before he can reply, I'm out the door.

CHAPTER 19

RYKER

The Sunday after our next win, I make plans to meet up with Maverick at the Waverly Hotel, our usual place. We don't have any classes together this year and now that he's living off campus with Delaney and his sister, it's like he's on another planet. I'm stoked today because there's only one game left on his suspension. Pretty soon, we'll be back in the saddle and running things like we used to.

It's about to storm outside as I waltz in the door of the hotel, a rather swanky place for a small college town like Magnolia.

The maroon-clad doorman greets me with a slap on my back. "Ryker! Hot damn! Badass game Friday night," he tells me with a broad grin. "I couldn't get a ticket, but I watched it on ESPN. You think you'll be a first-round draft pick in April?" Looking flushed and excited, he's probably still in high school.

"One can hope," I say as I autograph a piece of paper he has tucked in his pocket.

"I can't wait, man. Wherever you go, I'll be following."

He gives me a fist bump. He's a true fan, and I dig that.

I stride across the room, and Maverick waves at me from a table near the bar. He's a tall guy with brownish blond hair and a handsome face, and people sometimes confuse us for brothers —except I'm more handsome. I smirk as he tilts his head toward the big screen behind the bar that's showing the highlight reel from Friday.

I grin and head his way.

When I arrive at the table, he's got a Guinness waiting for me.

I take a seat, get a full view of his body, and feel the blood drain from my face. "What the fuck happened to you?" I'm staring at the dark-colored arm sling he's wearing.

He gives me a *don't freak out* look. "Broke my collarbone running yesterday." He grimaces. "Might have been a rock on the sidewalk."

No. Just *no*. I shake my head. "What kind of athlete breaks his collarbone *running*?"

"The kind who runs in the dark."

I rub my forehead. "How many weeks will you be out? Does Coach know?"

He gets a tight look on his face. "He knows. I saw him yesterday. It's a minor fracture, and I won't be out long, just three weeks."

Grimness blankets me. "Your suspension was almost up."

He sighs, a look of resignation on his face. "I'll be back with half a season left."

My teeth grind. With our bye week coming up, that will give me a small break, but I'll still have two additional games with Archer as captain. I give him a steely look. "You know those late-night jogs are shitty. I've told you a million times not to do it."

He huffs out a laugh.

"Why?" I hold my hands up in the air.

"Okay, Mom, stop your bitching." He smirks. "Delaney's already given me a good talking to."

I sigh. "I'm glad you're happy, man, and I'm glad everything's worked out, but I wish you were on the field." I think about Archer. "At least when you were captain of the defense, Archer kept his mouth in check. And this betting thing…" I drift off.

He chuckles. "Remember that time I bet Blaze he couldn't eat all those corndogs at the county fair? Dude puked for an hour." A sigh comes from him.

"Those were the good ol' days," I say. "Things are different now."

We move on and talk about Friday's game, picking it apart and discussing strategy for next week. Even though he isn't on the team right now, I depend on him.

After we order and finish our burgers, Maverick's phone pings with a text, and when I see him smile down at his cell, I figure it's Delaney—and probably time for me to head out.

For some reason, Penelope comes to mind. I pick at the label on my beer.

"Dude. Where's your head tonight?" Maverick's voice brings me back. He's off the phone and watching me.

"Nowhere," I say.

Maverick smirks. "You need a girl."

"I'm sick of jersey chasers," I mutter.

"Been there." He nods and laughs. "Let Delaney set you up with one of her friends."

I shake my head. "No."

Maverick asks for the check, and when the server leaves, I watch him walk away, my gaze looking around and stopping on a hot girl with auburn hair.

Penelope? I squint, my eyes narrowed in on a couple at a small round table tucked away in a dim alcove with a candle in the middle.

Is she on a date?

It's not Connor she's with and it's not her dad, so who the hell is it? He's older, maybe mid-30s, with thinning sandy hair and glasses. As I watch, he leans in over the table, and their discussion appears intense.

My eyes go back to her face. *Where are her glasses?*

My lips flatten. Fucking date.

"Who's that?" Maverick asks, following my gaze.

"Penelope." I tilt my head toward their table. "You know her—or him?" I ask.

He furtively checks them out. "Nah, but I don't get out much."

I tell him about the piece she wrote for the *Wildcat Weekly* last year, not really surprised he doesn't remember her or the article. He's from Magnolia too, but he went to public school while Penelope attended the private school. As far as the article, Delaney kept him isolated from most of the bad press, and Penelope's was just a tiny ripple.

I mention the bet, and he raises an eyebrow.

"You into her?" he asks ruefully. "That makes the bet easier."

"That's not my style, man."

I look away from him when Penelope stands up from the table. My eyes widen. She's wearing a white dress with splashes of roses on it, and her auburn hair is twisted up in some kind of fancy knot. The dress clings to her curves, accentuating her hips, her long legs. She's wearing more makeup than usual, her eyes thickly lashed, her lips a deep red.

The man stands as well, his hand on her shoulder. She says something, picks up a portfolio off the table, and hugs it to her chest. I watch as she flips around and darts to the exit. I think I see a tear running down her face.

Oh, hell no.

Before I know it, I'm throwing cash at Maverick to pay for dinner and saying goodbye.

I stand up.

"It's interesting that I've never seen you jump up to chase a girl so fast," he murmurs as I walk briskly away. I wave him off and catch up with the asshole she was with, easing up next to him as he's hot on her tail. I nudge him with my shoulder.

"What the heck?" He catches himself, his eyes darting to me and then widening. "Oh, excuse me."

"Yeah. Excuse you. By the way, don't follow her. I insist."

He blinks and follows my gaze. "Penelope?"

"You catch on fast."

He stutters and mumbles something about "agent", but I'm already gone and rushing to catch up with her.

The doorman greets me with a grin and pops out an

umbrella since it's started to rain. Big drops fall steadily on the hot concrete as I look up and down the street.

"Where did the girl in the white dress go?" I ask.

He points to the alley next to the hotel. "She darted down that way. There's a free parking lot in the back."

I know the one. With a sharp turn, I take off after her and see a flash of her skirt as she turns behind another building.

I call out her name, but the steady rain has morphed into a downpour and thunder rumbles in the sky.

I run down the alley and take the same right she did. Finally, she's stopped next to her car.

"Penelope!" I call out and jog over to her, sidestepping puddles.

I reach her and she looks up at me, a frown on her face as she huddles in the rain that's drenched her dress. I do my best to keep my eyes off the lace bra she has on underneath.

"What's wrong?" I ask just as a strong wind blows. I take a step closer to her. Mississippi is known for its thunderstorms and sometimes a tornado or two, even in the fall.

"I'm soaked, for one, and I have a flat tire. Again!" Her lips compress as she glares down at the slumping car. "It was just a spare, and I kept meaning to get a new one, but I never had the time. Just a great ending to an already crappy day."

With a brief look down, I see the dismal-looking spare. "Come on," I say. "My car's this way." I nod my head toward the other side of the street where the covered parking is. I reach for her hand and clasp it firmly. "We'll worry about your car later."

A flash of indecision flicks across her face for half a second before she nods. She clutches her portfolio to her chest, and we take off running.

She nearly trips and I pause as she bends over and tries to adjust her heels.

Fuck that.

We're only about twenty feet away from the covered parking lot, so I sweep her up and take off.

"What on earth are you doing?" she calls out over the downpour as I adjust her, cradling her in my arms. She isn't a lightweight, but she's light enough for me to run with. Her free hand that isn't clutching her folder curls around my neck.

"Trying to keep you from breaking your neck," I say back gruffly.

I look down at her, and I'm feeling...protective. *Again.* I'm a caveman when she's around.

I dodge a mud puddle, and she slips a little until I hitch her up closer. "You're going to kill us," she yells out, and I laugh.

Hell, this is more fun than I've had in weeks.

We enter the parking garage, and I set her down on her feet. She sways back and forth a bit, and I steady her as she huffs out a little laugh. "That was exciting. No one's ever run with me in their arms before. I'm not a small person."

"You're welcome." I smirk, doing a futile job of trying to get the rain off my clothes.

We're both soaked, and I watch as she uses her free hand to wipe the dampness from her face. She pushes her hair back off her forehead.

I take in her plastered hair and smeared mascara. I grin. "You look like a drowned raccoon."

Her eyes drift over my damp clothes, lingering on the V-neck of my button-down. "You look like a wet...football player."

I laugh and step closer, tilting her chin up. "Hey, who was that guy?"

Her lashes flutter against pale cheeks. "No one important."

Uh-huh.

I open the passenger side of my truck and shove over books and a few practice jerseys. She gets inside and I help her with the seat belt even when she insists she can do it. "Just let me do it. This one gets stuck."

"Okay." She sighs, her hands folded in her lap.

I get the buckle done and look at her.

"Was it a date?" I ask, circling back to the mystery dude.

She smirks. "Hardly. He's at least ten years older than me."

A few ticks of silence stretch between us and I sigh. Her door is open and I'm standing in front of her. "I'm not starting this truck until I know who he is and why you were upset."

Her eyes flash up at me. "Has anyone ever told you how stubborn you are?"

"So are you, babe."

She stares down at her hands. "He's a literary agent."

I straighten my shoulders, coming to attention. "You're writing a book?"

She nods. "I write about everything."

"Well, if it's anything like football, to even get an agent to meet with you is a big deal."

Her shoulders slump. "My dad set up the meeting for me." She shrugs. "I sent him some samples to read, and he called and asked to talk with me. I thought he was going to offer me a big deal with a signing bonus…" She pauses, and her hands twist in her lap. "He only came because he's friends with my dad." She swallows and shoots a rueful look at me. "He said my work has promise but isn't for him. I want to write romance."

My cock twitches, recalling her *romance*.

"I'm sorry." I hold my hands out. "Not sorry that you want to write romance—that sounds great—but sorry he didn't work out."

She nods.

"There are other agents," I tell her. "You just have to find the right one." I lean over and my lips touch hers, an indulgent graze where my tongue licks her bottom lip. I straighten back up, taking in her scent, lemony and sweet.

We stare at each other until a horn blast makes us both start.

She swallows. "Thank you for the pep talk."

Right. Back to business.

I shut her door and run around to my side, crawling in and cranking up the engine. I turn right out onto the main drag.

"My house is the other way," she says.

I shoot her a long look. "I know. We're going to Cadillac's so I can teach you how to play pool."

Her eyes flare. "Okay."

I reach over and toss her two of my jerseys. "Here, these are clean. You can use one to dry off and put the other one on over your dress. I can see your nipples."

She flushes.

"They're pink," I say tightly.

"Oh."

I clear my throat. "As opposed to being, you know, another color."

God. I'm an idiot.

She's silent as she moves around in the cab, drying off. She takes a makeup mirror out of her purse and reapplies her lipstick then dabs at her eyes. From the depths of her bag, she finds a brush and lets her hair down. My senses tingle as she brushes it out, the smell of her permeating the small space. Finally, she's satisfied with her appearance and takes the bigger jersey, puts her arms in, and slips it over her head.

"How's this?" she asks, her voice uncertain.

I flick my eyes over at her and my heart stops. I swallow. Her hair is down and curling up around her face. A soft bloom tints her cheeks, and her lips are deep red.

I'd like to pull this truck over and fuck her long and hard—

"You'll do," I mutter.

CHAPTER 20

PENELOPE

Cadillac's is a tradition with Waylon students. A dimly lit laid-back place, the walls are lined with photographic memorabilia from old cars and Marilyn Monroe and James Dean headshots. There's even a signed photo of Elvis on the wall, and it makes me laugh, recalling my ridiculous conversation with Connor. Some claim the original owner was a onetime movie agent who retired to Magnolia in his 60s. That was years ago and I don't know who owns it now, but it's a fun place to hang out in, a diner with a long bar and eating area, pool tables, and an arcade in the back with video games and bowling. The diner section is my favorite with its 50s-style car-shaped booths and jukebox.

Tonight's crowd is starting to gather, lined up at the bar for the Sunday five-dollar steak and potato deal.

"I look ridiculous," I say with a pout as I follow Ryker to the pool tables.

He also changed clothes, pulling from a gym bag he keeps in the car. As soon as we walked in, he hit the restroom and changed into athletic shorts, a Waylon shirt, and a ball cap. I admit, I'm a bit fascinated by the way his hair curls around his hat. It makes me want to whip it off and run my fingers through it.

"You look great," he says rather grimly and then mumbles something else, but I can't make it out.

"I can't hear you," I say, double-stepping to keep up with him in my heels. "Why are you being so surly?" He's been this way since we walked in the place, and my gut tells me it's because the first person we ran into at the door was Archer.

My eyes drift over to the section of seats where he is now, and sure enough, the asshole is watching us. Anger returns as I recall how scared he made me the other night. Our eyes meet and his are beady and watchful. I frown. I don't know what his and Ryker's deal is, but it makes the hair on my arms rise.

Ryker keeps trucking, his long legs stalking to the wall where the pool sticks are. He's standing there, studying our choices, and I take the moment to appreciate his broad shoulders and the way they taper down to his perfect ass.

He tosses a look at me over his shoulder. "See something you like?"

"No," I huff.

"Right. I forgot." He grabs two sticks. "You don't like football players."

I exhale.

"Come on," he says, and I follow him across Cadillac's until he stops at a table in the far corner.

"I'm starting to feel like a little puppy following you around," I say as he puts the balls in the rack, arranging them by solids and stripes.

He grunts.

I sigh.

"Nice table," I comment. "It's very green."

I get no comment, so I try again, determined to get him in a good mood.

"Is it actually called a pool table? Or should I say billiards table?"

He looks at me. "Either."

I put my hand on my hip. "I'm going to call it The Table of Very Green Fabric."

I see a ghost of a smile cross his face, and I'm giddy. Success.

He walks back around and stands next to me. He looks down at me, and I see when his eyes go to my chest and linger. Yeah, he mentioned my nipple color earlier, and it got me excited, but then we come in here and he's a stone wall, all brusque and businesslike.

Isn't that what you want? Distance?

I'm not sure anymore. Maybe I *want* to be his distraction. I chew on my lip.

"You listening, Red?"

I start, realizing he's been going on for a couple of seconds.

"Right here with ya." *When I'm not daydreaming...*

"In a standard game, you put the eight ball in the middle of the rack." He points to said item.

I follow his finger. "Huh. The rack is an equilateral triangle." I glance over at him, and he's got that damn eyebrow cocked. His dimple flashes.

"I suppose so."

"Okay." I nod. "This is good. Math is good."

He chuckles. "I never met a writer who loved math so much."

I tap my head. "Smart women are the best. Have you ever dated a girl who even knew what an equilateral triangle is?"

"I never asked them."

"Because y'all were so busy having sex?"

He shakes his head at me. "You don't have a very high opinion of football players, do you?"

A long exhale comes from me.

"What?"

I glance up and he's studying me intently.

"The truth is my mom got pregnant with me when she was dating my dad. Instead of sticking around, he went off to the NFL."

He thinks. "Could she have gone with him?"

I shake my head. "I don't think she wanted to. She never said she did. I guess they just didn't love each other enough." I sigh. "She loved it here. She was devoted to her students. She was smart and beautiful and kind…"

"Like you." His gaze finds mine.

I nod.

"I'm not your dad, Red. You have to give people a chance. We're not the same."

"Of course not."

"But I'm a douchebag because of him?"

"No," I say softly. "Never in a million years."

He leans in closer to me and I feel the heat of his body. He touches my cheek. "Good. Then that's progress."

My heart skips a beat at the intensity of his gaze, at the electric current that stretches from him to me. The string between us is tight, an undercurrent of fire and ice mixed together. I wonder what it would look like if he were mine. If he loved *me*…

Someone walks past us to get to the jukebox, and the moment is broken.

He takes in a big breath, looks down at the pool table, and continues. "Er, I guess we need to finish this."

I nod.

He looks back at the table. "Whatever ball you get in a pocket, that's what you are, solids or stripes. If you make one of each variation, you get to choose. If you shoot the eight ball in a pocket, and it's not the last ball, you lose. I'll show you." He steps around me and leans over with his cue stick, his shoulders taut with athletic grace. The muscles in his forearms ripple as he aims and strikes a red ball hard, sending a solid into a pocket on the right.

"You look good doing that," I murmur.

He takes a swig of the beer he ordered when we walked in and sets it down on the table next to us. "Just point and shoot. We can work on technique—enough to get you through a few shots with Connor."

His jaw seems to grind at the thought.

"Ryker." I'm tired of this. Of him helping me get Connor.

But his profile is hard. Implacable. "Come on, Red. Let's do this thing." He tilts his head toward the table.

"Maybe we should just forget it." I toy with the weight of the stick.

"No. I want to show you how to impress him," he says.

"I don't want to impress him anymore."

There, I said it. I mean it, but Ryker isn't having it.

He scowls. "That was the objective since the kiss at the bookstore. For you to go out with him. You need to do it. So you *know*." He studies my face.

Know what?

I don't ask. I'm scared of the answer. Because once I say it aloud—*I want you, Ryker*—then it's real, and I have to deal with it.

I take a step closer to the balls and chew on my lip as I concentrate. Since I'm right-handed, I hold the base of the stick with my right hand and attempt to line it up for a shot that will put a striped ball into a left pocket.

"You look like you're going spearfishing." He sets his beer down. "Let me show you."

He walks back to where I am and stands behind me as I'm bending over the table, his hands covering mine. My body tenses and my knees go weak at the feel of him, and my ass may have twitched a little to get closer to him. I'll never own up to it if he asks though.

"Everything okay?" I ask as he just stands there.

"Yeah." He clears his throat, and in a slow movement, he demonstrates the correct way to line up the shot with the stick. "A good basic technique is to put your index finger on the top of the stick and curve it." His hand strokes my pointer finger, arranging it in the correct form. "Like this," he says. "Hold it tight. You have total control of the stick."

But my body is out of control. The heat from Ryker sears

my skin, and he smells like a tree I want to climb. "Okay." My voice is mangled.

He eases back and his hand lingers on my left side. "This arm will never move. Use your back and shoulders."

"Back and shoulders," I repeat, but my mind is hardly on pool. It's on the way his hand glides to my waist and rests there. "Spread your legs as wide as your hips and keep your feet at a 45-degree angle. You need a good stance if you want to get in a good shot."

"Good shot…got it," I manage to say as he leans into me. I can't see his face and I'm dying. I want to see what he looks like when he looks down at me.

My hand trembles.

"You okay?" he asks.

"Mmhmm. Just getting stiff from being bent over."

"I assure you…being stiff is totally worth it when you get the stroke right."

I blink. Stiff…stroke…*oh God.*

He continues talking in that very deliberate way of his, seemingly unaware that his words are like sex on a stick. *Shit— sex on a stick…pool stick.* I'm losing it.

"All right. Next, line up the tip with the cue ball, aim for one of your balls, and shoot." He takes a step back to give me room, but I pause. "Just hit it, Red. Aim for that blue stripe and get it in the pocket."

I close my eyes and put everything I have into the shot, shoving the pool stick straight at the cue ball.

In retrospect, I guess I shouldn't have closed my eyes.

When my eyes open, it's as if everything slows down—you

know, the kind of moment that happens in a flash yet it seems to take tiny steps to get there? I see Connor coming from the arcade part of Cadillac's with a group of guys, mostly chess club types. He's laughing at something as he tosses back his beer.

He never sees the ball coming for him.

I want to yell for him to duck, and I guess I could have, but it wouldn't have mattered because it happened so fast.

Please don't hit him in the head is my mantra as the scene plays out.

First, it hits a retro Lucille Ball sign functioning as a fancy-looking light above the pool table next to us, and for half a second, I think it's going to miss Connor—but then it ricochets off the light and slams into his crotch.

He goes down like a sack of bricks, and his beer flies through the air before shattering on the concrete floor. Shards of glass shoot everywhere, and beer splatters on the wall behind Connor.

My stick falls out of my hand. "He'll never have babies." Ryker is next to me in an instant, and I look up at him. My mouth opens and closes. "Holy shit. You think he's okay?"

"I don't know. Let's go see," he says, a grim look on his face.

We walk over to them and dread fills me.

Connor's friends are bending down, and there's a flurry of activity from the staff as they walk over to where he's still on the floor. A girl in a 50s-style pink dress and apron is carrying a broom and a dustpan and focuses on getting the glass swept up while a managerial-looking lady is bent over Connor.

It's not until we're right in front of the scene of the crime that I realize I've grabbed Ryker's hand at some point. He glances down and then looks at me, his eyes questioning. He lets my hand go.

Connor is pulled up by one of his buddies and the manager. His hat is cocked sideways and there's a red spot on his cheek, and I wonder if he landed on it.

He maneuvers to stand, his face pale as he winces.

"You okay, man?" someone calls out from a neighboring table.

"Hit me in the upper leg," he mutters, looking around at the circle of people who've gathered. "Damn. Hurts like hell." He cranes his neck toward the pool tables. "Who shot it?"

My eyes flare and I barely keep myself from squeaking.

"Not sure," his buddy says.

The manager pulls up a chair for him and says something about getting some ice and an accident report.

I lean over to Ryker and whisper, "At least his manly bits are okay."

He nods.

Connor eases down in the chair then looks up and sees us, his eyes bouncing back and forth.

I wave at him.

"You should go check on him," Ryker says, and I nod and take the few steps to Connor's side.

I pat him on the shoulder. "Hey…you. Are you okay?" He blinks as if confused, and his eyes go from me to Ryker, who's behind me in the background. Connor comes back to me and takes in the jersey and high heels I'm wearing. "You're wearing Ryker's jersey."

I nod. "Yeah."

"I didn't know you were here." He pauses. "You told me you were busy all week."

I nod, choosing to not comment on that. "Are you going to be able to walk?"

"Yeah, yeah, just…it got the drop on me, ya know?" He laughs as one of his friends claps him on the back.

He grimaces and rubs his inner thigh. "I'm fine. Probably just a bruise. Where did that ball come from anyway? Did you see?"

Great. We're back to that again. I bite my lip.

One of his friends points to the far back table where we were playing. "I think it came from that direction."

I laugh. "But you're okay, so that's good, right?"

He nods. "So, you guys came together?"

"Just as friends," Ryker says as he takes a step forward to join us. "I found her in the rain with a flat tire."

"Oh." Connor's head turns back. "That sucks."

I nod.

Ryker continues. "As a matter of fact, I need to run, but I think Penelope wants to stay."

I scowl and turn around to stare at him. "What? No, I should go too."

"I can take you home," Connor says. I turn back to him, and he's got a hopeful look in his eyes. He pauses as I frown. "Only if you want to stay…maybe we can play a game after I sit here a bit?" He chuckles in a good-natured way, and I feel horrible all over again for being the shooter.

"I think I'm done playing pool," I say.

"Oh," Connor says, his voice unsure. "We can grab some beers?"

"No, I really think I should go—"

"Yes, she'll stay," Ryker interjects, cutting me off.

Color rises in my cheeks, and I turn to him as Connor is distracted by one of his buddies who's come over to hand him an ice pack.

"I can answer for myself, Ryker," I hiss.

"Don't be stubborn," he says.

"You're the stubborn one."

His teeth grit as we stand there and look at each other. "You should stay."

"Why?"

"Because you need to be with Connor." There's an uncertain look on his face as he takes his eyes off mine and looks at him.

I'm distracted as Connor seems to catch his breath and stands up. He talks to a waitress and points over at me.

"I'm going, Penelope," Ryker says adamantly.

"Wait—"

Connor joins us, his gaze on me. "Come on, the waitress said she'd get us a table before they're all gone. You staying?"

Before I can say yay or nay, Ryker has pivoted around and stalked away from us.

He pauses near the door when Archer calls his name and says something. Ryker says something back and the crowd that hears him goes silent, their glances bouncing between the two football players. I inch closer to see what's going on, part of me wanting to see if Ryker is okay, but before I can, he's gone, slamming the door so hard behind him that the glass wobbles.

Archer turns back around, his eyes shifting from me to Connor, an expression of satisfaction on his sharp face. He lifts his drink in my direction; I give him the middle finger.

CHAPTER 21

PENELOPE

Connor takes me home later in his sparkling silver Mercedes-Benz G-class SUV, which is as solid and practical as he is. I hadn't realized he was rich, but after a few questions I discovered he comes from a long line of wealthy cotton farmers in Tennessee—who also happen to own pool halls. Weird, but then admittedly I hadn't known much about him at all except for what I'd observed from afar. He also informed me that he wants to be a video game designer, which didn't fit at all with my image of him as a doctor or lawyer, but I guess you never really know someone until you spend a couple of hours with them at Cadillac's.

The sleek leather interior inside the luxury car is spotless, without books or football jerseys or the scent of sexy man. A collection of chess pieces hangs from his rear-view mirror. The inside smells just like him, that sharp twang of cologne I remember from prep school. I glance over and half expect him to be wearing a pink Polo shirt with the collar popped, but instead, he's sporting his usual jeans and a Waylon shirt. He's taken his cap off though.

I'm quiet on the ride. I can't keep my mind from turning to Ryker and how he left me with Connor.

We're destined to never be anything but friends.

"Your mind is a million miles away," Connor says as he turns down the street to my house.

I look over at him and study the curve of his face. He really is handsome.

"Ever heard of *Twilight*, Connor?"

He grimaces and huffs out a derisive laugh. "Who hasn't? I dated a girl who was huge into romance books. Pretty much a waste of time."

I cock my head. "Why's that?"

"Skews your view of love. Everybody knows that. There's no perfect hero. And the sex is not even close to how it really is."

"Romance doesn't skew. It broadens your horizons."

"Seriously?" He laughs but then sobers when he sees the expression on my face.

"I want to be a romance writer someday. No, I take that back—I *will* be a writer."

He eyes me warily. "Oh, shit. Sorry."

"Yeah. Out of curiosity, if I asked you to watch *Twilight*, would you?"

He smirks. "Truth?"

"Of course."

He throws me an eyebrow waggle. "Only if I knew I was getting something at the end."

"I don't think I know you at all," I say musingly.

"But I'm looking forward to getting to know you,

Penelope." His voice is soft, and his eyes leave the road briefly to drift over to my face. "I mean, the night's still young if you want to watch that movie of yours…" He grins at me.

I don't smile back.

Instead, I look down and study my clasped hands. By now, I'm sure my lipstick has faded, so I pull out my tube and reapply. I inhale a deep breath, gearing up. "There's something I have to tell you."

He glances at me. "What's that?"

"I lied about playing pool. I don't know a pool cue from a fishing rod. In fact, I'm probably a much better fisherman. I wouldn't know what an eight ball was if I didn't have the big one that tells your future when you shake it. I lied because I was nervous, and I wanted you to like me. In retrospect, it was stupid, and I'm sorry I misled you." I let out a huge breath I didn't even know I was holding. "Damn that feels good."

His eyes flare, and he's silent as he pulls up to my house and puts the car in park. The vehicle idles at the curb as the silence between us swells. I can tell he's gathering himself.

"I've shocked you."

He stares out the front windshield and rakes a hand through his hair. "That's a lot to take in."

"I don't advocate lying. I didn't plan to do it, but when you asked me about pool, I wanted to impress you. I've always thought you were studious and just my type…" I stop. I'm rambling.

He turns the car off and turns to face me. "Okay."

I take another breath. "And I hit you with that ball tonight. Actually, it was the first time I've even picked up a pool stick, so it's no wonder I nearly killed you. God, you should have seen that white ball flying through the air...it just zeroed in on you, like fate was trying to tell me something. I really thought it was going to hit you in your man parts."

He pales.

"I mean, thank God it didn't." A small laugh comes out of me. "Ryker really wanted me to learn how to play..." I bite my lip.

Connor shakes his head and adjusts his glasses, looking befuddled. He pauses. "Do you even like Elvis?"

"Not particularly."

He grimaces.

"Yeah. I suck." I exhale, my fingers undoing my seat belt. "Anyway, I'm really sorry, and I completely understand if you never speak to me again. We do have class together, but I won't be offended if you just ignore me and keep on walking." I smile wryly at him.

He frowns. "I would have liked you anyway."

"Again, I'm sorry." I put my hand on the door handle. "Thank you for the ride." I take a deep breath and get out of the car, shutting the door.

"Wait." He gets out and comes over to where I'm waiting at the curb. "You did all that just to go out with me?"

"Not my most shining moment."

"It is flattering though." A sheepish grin grows on his face. "I'm not a hot jock, ya know, so I'm surprised you went that far."

I smile, feeling a teensy bit better. "You're a unicorn. Any girl would love to be with you."

He studies my face. "So do you still want to go out? With no pool playing involved?"

"Ah…you're very nice, Connor, but…"

The silence grows as we look at each other.

I shake my head. "You really *aren't* my type."

He shakes his head and points a finger at me knowingly. "Ah. Ryker. I knew it. It's been him since the beginning." His eyes widen. "Wait—was that kiss in the bookstore real?"

I sigh and shrug.

"Interesting," he says, sticking his hands in his pockets. "You know I saw the whole thing, right? I also recall your arms were around *him*, so—"

"I was there," I say.

"Mmhmm." He laughs and looks down at his feet. "Look, I should have noticed you sooner and asked you out a long time ago, and maybe this would have all gone down a lot differently —"

"Let's try something," I say, interrupting him and taking a step closer. "Kiss me."

He laughs and shakes his head. "What? Why?"

"Let's call it an experiment," I answer. I need to know if I'm just such a hard-up virgin, any kind of male attention gets me going.

He studies me for a moment. "You're not going to slap me?"

I smile. "Nope. I promise."

"Okay."

I straighten as if preparing for battle as he cups my shoulders and leans in. His head lowers, and his lips touch mine, the pressure gentle.

He eases back a few second later. "Anything?"

"No," I murmur. Not even a twitch. "But you're great," I add brightly.

"Damn." He grins. "Friends?"

I nod. "Yeah. For sure."

"Good luck," he calls out to me as he walks back around to his side of the car.

He pulls away and I watch him go.

And there you go. Welcome to the end of an era. Maybe he was always built up in my head anyway, a way to keep myself occupied and distracted from other things.

Like my mom.

Like Ryker.

I take the sidewalk up to the front porch and see a white piece of paper tucked between my door and the frame.

I rip it open, remembering the last time I found a note on my porch.

I bought you a tire and changed it. You shouldn't be driving on a spare. Call me in the morning, and I'll take you to the Waverly to get it before class.

Ryker.

PS. Don't worry about that agent dude. You got this.

My fingers trace the llama he drew at the bottom.

God. My heart dips. Ryker Voss is one complicated man. He did all this—yet he pushes me as far away from him as he can.

I go inside, and I'm a little giddy from not having the hassle of messing with my car. Part of it, too, is that I told

Connor everything. Acceptance is a beautiful thing, and I want to revel in it.

"Pen! Shit!" Vampire Bill's squawk makes me smile as I walk past him. I give him a cracker from the box next to his cage.

"Good boy!"

I grab my phone and a glass of prosecco then head to my bedroom, where I change into a camisole and a pair of lace shorts. After that, I get Vampire Bill situated on the desk in my room, tell him good night, and crawl into bed.

I'm right in the middle of reading when my phone pings and I dive on it, expecting Ryker.

It's my dad. I quickly scan the messages he sent earlier that I didn't see. I skim past them to read the most recent one.

When I didn't hear from you, I called Walter. He gave me the rundown. I'm sorry things didn't work out.

I sigh and respond. **It's okay. I appreciate the help. I didn't expect you to do that. Thank you.**

Good night, he sends, and I respond likewise.

On a whim, before I can change my mind, I type out, **I'll come over for lasagna soon.**

I set my phone down, moving on and thinking about Ryker. My fingers pluck at the edges of my sheets.

Forget waiting until morning to talk to him.

I drain my drink and dig deep for the nerve to initiate a text. It's easier than talking to him face to face anyway. Perhaps it's because when we text, we don't worry about the repercussions of our words. We just talk and there's no pressure.

Thank you for everything, I send to Ryker. **I owe you.**

His reply is immediate.

You're home?

Yeah.

Alone?

Of course, I reply.

Are you in bed?

Yes. My heart kicks up, and my chest rises.

Is your head against Edward's face?

I laugh out loud and Vampire Bill glares at me. "What?" I say to him. "Ryker's funny."

The sparkly vampire is on my pillow, I reply.

So, if I shave my chest hair off and toss on some glitter lotion, you'll be into me?

I burst out laughing. **Maybe.**

Done.

OMG. Stop teasing me. I'm giggling.

Who said I was teasing?

I smirk. **Okay, so the next time we watch a movie, you get to pick.**

I'll pick the Avengers.

I can get down with Thor.

On second thought, I'll go with Texas Chain Saw Massacre.

I sigh, a smile on my face.

I need to go, he types a few minutes later after we've been texting for a while and I've lost track of time. We make plans for him to pick me up at eight in the morning the next day to take me to get my car.

I wanted to say something first. My heart thunders as I

nibble on the inside of my cheek. **I told Connor the truth. He knows.**

There's a long pause, and I'm holding my breath as I wait for his reply. The tension builds inside me, and my mind races, trying to figure out what Ryker is thinking.

Smart move. You're never going to be a pool shark. When's your next date with him?

I smirk. Ryker has assumed Connor wouldn't care that I lied. Men. **There isn't one.**

Why? he sends back immediately.

I open my nightstand drawer that houses my collection of lip balm. I swipe on some mango and stare at my phone. God. What do I say? This feels like a significant moment.

I'll have to tell you in person.

Tell me now, he sends.

I picture him in his bed sending the message, his face intense.

Why?

You know why, Red.

Even though he's not here in the room, I sense the alpha male in him coming through the phone, the command in his tone. Heat pools in my lower body, and I squirm on the bed.

Several moments have gone by and I think maybe he's done texting me—but then a new one comes through…and I die.

You were meant for me, he sends.

I can't breathe. Looking down at his words, I read them over and over, my heart pounding.

Something has changed. I feel the shift in my heart,

opening up.

I toss my phone across the room, and it scares Vampire Bill.

"Shit! Ryker!" he squawks.

CHAPTER 22

PENELOPE

The sound of knocking on my front door comes about fifteen minutes later.

Vampire Bill is squawking like crazy as I jump up, grab my long cardigan, and slip it on over my shoulders. I run to Charisma's room and open the door. She isn't there, and I exhale, recalling a message saying she was staying over with someone.

A knock comes again, and I fly into the den with my pepper spray in hand.

"Who is it?" I shout, once again cursing the fact that I don't have a peephole. I really need to get one installed.

"Ryker. You didn't reply to my text. Did you really think I was just going to let that go?" His voice is dry.

I dash the few steps over to the hall mirror and check my appearance. I look…insane. My hair is poking out in crazy places everywhere, and I do my best to smooth it down. One side of my face has a bit of drool from where I had just fallen asleep, and I scrub at it frantically.

"Penelope. Open the door." I hear a quietness in his tone

that makes me work even faster.

I jerk open the hall drawer, pull out a tube of lip balm, and slap it on. It's not my preferred color tint, but what's a girl to do when she has a six-foot-four sexy man outside her door? You gotta take what you can get.

And my boobs. Shit! I have no padding. Nothing but a lace camisole. I tug the sweater around me.

"Give me a minute," I call out and turn toward my bedroom. Maybe I have time to put on a bra—

"Nope, Red. Now." *Oh.* There's that teeny bit of command in his tone, and I like it.

Squaring my shoulders, I turn back around and fling open the door.

Wearing black gym shorts and a button-up white shirt— very confusing—his broad shoulders shift as he slouches against my doorframe. His hair is brilliantly mussed and his eyes gleam.

Crazy outfit or not, he is gorgeous. "Kinda late for a visit. I'd definitely classify this as booty call category."

He straightens up and rakes stormy eyes over me, lingering on my lips. "You put on lipstick."

"It's tinted lip balm."

He grins. "You only put that stuff on when you're nervous."

"Not true."

"Don't even try with me."

A smirk plays around his full lips, and I let out an exhale. "Did you drive all the way over here to discuss my makeup routine?"

His eyes glitter. "Invite me in. Isn't that what you have to do for vampires?"

I give him a quizzical look. "No, not all vampires. It's different depending on who wrote the book. Twilight's vamps can enter any door they want, but Stephen King's scary vampires in *Salem's Lot* have to be invited inside." I wrinkle my nose. "His version is particularly scary. Razor sharp teeth, black eyeballs." I take a big breath. I'm rambling.

"I'll let you tell me all about it if you want." His eyes flash to the inside of my house. "I want to come inside." The silky sound of his voice vibrates every atom inside me.

Come inside…

I'm thinking bad thoughts.

"Why?" My voice is wobbly with nerves. I grip the door. "There's only one reason a guy shows up at a girl's house at one in the morning."

"But you aren't that kind of girl," he says softly, his gaze lingering on my chest and working its way down to my legs. His eyes come back to mine and I falter, seeing the way his have darkened. "Goddamn, you're beautiful."

I suck in a breath.

He huffs out a laugh and props a muscled bicep against the doorframe then leans down until our faces are inches apart. "You ignored my text, Red. You ignored a text where I said some pretty revealing shit. I'm not sure how I feel about that." He lifts an eyebrow. "Should I be pissed off? Should I pretend it never happened? Or better yet, should I just come over here and prove to you that I meant every word?" He pauses and pretends to think. "But you know, in a way, I've been doing that already. I feel like I'm always proving shit to you. Hell, I spent two hours fixing your car tonight. What else do you need to see that I'm the one you want?"

"You left me at Cadillac's with another guy!"

"So you could see you didn't really want him."

My mouth is open, and I quickly shut it. My body, which has a mind of its own, leans toward him until I'm standing on the threshold, our bodies an inch from touching. "I want you," I say.

He cups my face, his blue-green eyes at half-mast. "Do you have any idea how long I've wanted you?"

"How long?" I ask on an exhalation, our breaths mingling. He smells like toothpaste and it makes me smile. He prepared before coming here.

"Maybe since the moment you wrote that article, and I saw you on campus and made the connection. You don't care who I am. You're the most honest person I know."

"So before I spilled water on you?"

He laughs.

Butterflies flip in my stomach. I tug on his shirt until his lips are a breath away from mine. "Then shut up and kiss me."

He captures my mouth and murmurs my name as his hands go to my lower back, pressing me against him. Forget that bookstore kiss. Forget every kiss I've ever had. This one is *real*. This one is fire and ice and burns so good. His tongue tangles with mine, going deeper, searching and tasting me. His lips consume me and I give it back just as good, our mouths battling for dominance. He pushes his hands into my hair and I moan as his teeth nip at me, his tongue insistent. Need and desire build momentum within me, and I think I might combust from a kiss alone. This. *Him.* I've wanted him forever. Maybe back to the first time I saw him come out of that bathroom at the Tau house with only a towel wrapped around him.

He stops to breathe, his forehead resting against mine as our chests heave. "Fuck me, Red. You're on fire." He presses his mouth against my neck and sucks hard, and I groan at the flashes of electricity it sends straight to my core.

"I'm so glad you came for me," I whisper.

He pauses, and I look up to see his throat working. "I like those words on your lips."

I take his hand in mine, and we walk inside. He shuts the door and turns back to face me.

My chest is heaving. His is too. My eyes flick down to the bulge in his gym shorts. God. He's probably huge.

My eyes fly up to his face, and he's wearing a smirk, as if he knows exactly what I'm thinking. His eyes go to my notebook on the desk. "You been writing in your notebook about me?" he asks, and it's such a non sequitur that I shake my head.

Realization dawns and I gape. *"You read the Holy Grail?"*

He holds his hands out. "At Sugar's, but before you freak out, I didn't mean to."

"What part did you see?"

"Where the Duke of Waylon ravishes the virgin with his big cock."

I blink, adjusting to the knowledge. "Well, you seem to have gotten the gist of it."

He trails a finger down to my sweater and unbuttons the

first button. His lips brush my collarbone. "I can make it come true."

"Big appendage and all?"

He undoes another button, eyes like fire as they brush over me. "Oh, Red, you have no idea."

I don't. I really don't. "I'm a virgin. I know I told you already, but I feel the need to point it out again."

"I haven't forgotten." He undoes the next button and parts the sweater until the lace bodice of my camisole appears. "Beautiful," he murmurs.

"Well, don't get your hopes up." I wave my hands around my chest. "This is all smoke and mirrors. My bras are all padded."

"Is that so?" He gives me a hot look as he unbuttons the last one and pushes the cardigan off my arms. It drops to the floor, forgotten. With a slight brush of his fingers, he cups my breast through the camisole, his fingers tweaking my nipple. "You couldn't be any more perfect."

His eyes hold mine and the air is electric.

I'm going to die if he doesn't do something soon.

I must have spoken aloud because he chuckles and pushes the top of my camisole down, easing the delicate straps lower until the garment slides down and my breasts are free. My nipples rise to meet him as his head lowers and he kisses them. He cups me in his palms and massages, tugging until I clasp his head in my hands, gripping his scalp as his tongue toys with my peaks, taking them in his mouth and sucking. He's gentle then rough and hard.

I can't breathe. Delicious sensation wraps around me.

"Ryker."

"Hmmm," he moans as he kisses up my neck to my ear. "Where's your bed?" he whispers.

I point him in the right direction as he sweeps me up in his arms and carries me to my room.

"Shit! Jock!" Vampire Bill squawks.

Ryker laughs and sets me down on my feet. I reach down to pull up my camisole, but he stops me. "No, don't hide your body," he murmurs as he trails a hand through my hair.

I reach for him, and we kiss, the intensity rising. I tear at his shirt, but the buttons are tiny, and I can't get it open fast enough. He rips at it until they fly around the room, landing with little pings on the hardwood floor. He whips his arms out and tosses it away as if it offends him.

He stands there, his sculpted chest rippling with muscles, the deep V of his hips disappearing into his shorts. I touch the golden curls on his chest.

"You wore the white shirt...for me?"

He smirks. "I know you like it."

A long sigh escapes my lips, and I curl my hand around his shoulder then tug him close until we're pressed together. I lean down and tease his nipple with my mouth.

"Red," he moans, tightening his arms around me.

I lean my head down to listen to his heartbeat. It's as erratic as mine, and I know, I know...

"You're perfect," I say, my voice bemused. Happy.

"Don't stop kissing me," he groans before taking my mouth again. We kiss and kiss until I can't think. His lips skate down my neck to my chest. He falls to his knees, his hands cupping my ass. He moves slowly and deliberately as his tongue finds my navel and explores while I arch my back to get closer. I call out his name, my hands twining in his hair. His touch is masterful.

With a deft motion, he pushes my lace shorts down to my ankles and his mouth kisses my hipbone, sucking there.

"What are you doing to me?" I breathe.

"Whatever you want," Ryker replies, looking at me with dark, heavy-lidded eyes.

I want it all, my heart thunders.

"We don't have to take this all the way," he says softly. "But I'm going to make you come. Hard. You're going to be begging me to fuck you. You're going to be begging me to fuck you every single day you're alive…"

I nearly orgasm right then. "You're the cockiest sonofabitch I know," I murmur.

"Is that a yes?" he growls, his hand sliding in between my legs and sawing back and forth over my clit.

There's a boldness in his gaze as he watches me. Rapt attention. He quivers, a full body tremor as I spread my legs apart, and he eases me down on the bed. I'm half on and half off as he kisses the top of my foot, the inside of my knee, the birthmark I have on my thigh, lavishing attention. His fingers pinch my nipples lightly, as if I'm a fine piece of porcelain and he's exploring it. His mouth trails hot kisses over my stomach and he's murmuring my name and saying how good I am, how beautiful—

He licks my center, and my back arches, writhing in sensation as he plays me. The pleasure is exquisite and excruciating at the same time. I want to bend space and time so that we never leave this bed, his mouth always torturing me.

I throw my hands behind my head and scoot to be closer to his hot mouth. He props my legs open wider and devours me, his fingers working my core, his mouth skyrocketing me straight to the heavens.

"Ryker," I moan, my head thrashing. I feel disoriented, a taut string between him and my body and a fire that's gathering at the base of my spine. I'm going to spin out of control.

"Come," he says, his scruffy jaw brushing against my inner thigh. "Come, Red." His finger slides inside me, catalyzing a storm. "You're mine," he says against my pussy with a hard suck of his lips, and the vibration combined with his tongue sends me over the edge. I detonate and shatter into a million pieces, falling and falling until I'm nothing but sensation and need and desire. Tears spring to my eyes.

The aftershocks vibrate my body, and he rides it out with me, taking me further with his mouth, pushing me until I scream out his name.

"Hell yes," he says as he makes his way up to my face.

He kisses me hard, and he tastes sweet and hot. I'm spent, a limp puddle of nothing, but my hands eagerly curl around his shoulders.

In a smooth motion, he picks me up, slides underneath, and places me on top of him.

He holds me tight to his chest. As if he'll never let me go. "That, babe, is third base first class."

• • •

A quick glance at the clock on my nightstand tells me it's two in the morning, but neither of us is asleep. We talk about everything. He tells me about always striving to be the best in football, hoping it's enough for his dad, hoping his mom will hear about how talented he is. Emotion clogs my throat when he tells me he only talks to his dad once every few weeks. My mom is gone, but she always had time for me. I guess I was lucky that way, and not everyone is. He's never seen a good relationship. I guess I haven't either, but with him, I'm starting to think there's hope.

Hope is a dangerous thing, though, because the more you hope for something, the more painful it is when it all comes crashing down.

But I don't think about that. Not now. Not while he's in my bed and he's looking at me like I'm the only thing in the world.

"What would you do if you didn't have football?" I ask. Snuggled in his arms, I play idly with one of his chest hairs.

"I'd take over Chris Pratt's role in *Guardians of the Galaxy*." He grins.

I tug at one of the hairs, making him yelp.

"What's that for?" His tone is indignant.

"Because you're not giving me a serious answer."

He laughs, looking over at me. "Okay, serious answer: football is it. I love the game and the high I get from being on the field. If I lost it...I don't know. Maybe coach. What about you?"

"I'm the same. It's writing or nothing for me. Like you said, Walter isn't the only agent around."

He nods, playing with a strand of my hair, twisting it

around his fingers. "You know, your dad has given me some pretty good advice about the NFL."

"Yeah?"

He thinks for a moment, his eyes holding mine. "And I've been thinking…if I got you pregnant, I would never leave you."

He delivers the words softly, and I suck in a sharp breath.

We both lie there and stare up at the ceiling, the dim light from the den, which I never turned off, softly illuminating the room.

It's an easy silence, the kind where barriers are let down and there's hope and promise. Ryker takes my hand in his and laces our fingers together.

I prop my head up on my arm. My hand rests on his chest, still amazed that his heart is racing because of *me*.

"Make love to me, Ryker."

He freezes, his hand tightening in my hair. He tugs me down until we're nose to nose. There's earnestness in his eyes. "I mean, I'm dying to make this official, but are you sure?"

I nod.

His face is undecided, and I pop him on the arm. "What? You came over here for the booty call, remember?"

"This isn't a booty call," he says.

"Are you going to ravish me or not, Lord Ryker?"

He bursts out laughing, and before long, we're both chuckling, but soon his hands are on my skin, brushing against my face as he stares into my eyes. He kisses me languidly and long, his tongue toying with me, teasing me.

"There are condoms in the nightstand," I tell him as I push

down his shorts and take in his cock as it bounces against his abdomen. It *is* magnificent and better than I ever imagined, long and deliciously hard. I curl my fingers around the mushroom-shaped bulbous head and stroke.

He closes his eyes and moans. "Fuck."

Emotion and desire guide me as I take him in my mouth and lavish attention on him, my fingers holding him steady. He calls my name, asking me to stop, but his voice is needy, and I don't. I feel a heady sense of power over him. He's intoxicating. Or the feeling is. I don't know because I can't even define it. I'm a vast vortex of sensation, and he's the only thing I want to fill me up.

His hands are everywhere, on my breasts, my ass, my hips, my core. Stroking. Caressing. Making me moan. I don't know where he ends and I begin. I do what he indicates and touch him wherever my fingers decide to go. It's mind-altering, and when I tell him to, he maneuvers me underneath him.

His hands tremble as he slides the condom onto his shaft. "You okay?" Sweat beads on his forehead as he hovers above me.

"Yes."

There's a look of hesitation on his face, and for a moment, I think he might jump out of bed and leave.

"What's wrong?"

"I don't want to hurt you," he says. "Ever."

"You won't."

His body cages me in as he props himself up and gets in position. Guiding his cock, he slides in slowly, pushing with an easy pump. He stops and watches me.

"More," I say, and he goes in farther. I wince at the bite of pain that vibrates in my center. We're truly one. Connected.

"Fuck, you feel so good. I want to go slow, but..." His voice is jagged.

I nod because I can't speak.

He eases out and then back in, his thickness stretching me, and I feel every hard inch as he glides back and forth. I move against him, wanting the friction, wanting *him*. With his free hand, he tilts my chin up so we're face to face. He's panting and his arm quivers from holding himself taut.

I'm bombarded by intense sensations, by a million blots of fire that are currently coursing through my skin.

Why did I wait so long? I was waiting on *him*.

Guided by instinct, I lift my leg and crook it around his back while his hips thrust inside me. His tempo speeds up, his chest heaving with exertion. I twitch from the primal pleasure of it and writhe underneath him, pain turned to pleasure as I urge him on with my hands. I lick his nipple and suck, and he tosses his head back, his cock velvet steel as he makes me his.

I reach up and run my tongue up his neck, tasting his sweat. He bites his lip and gives me a searching look that defies explanation and emotion.

I'm lost in heady desire. Him. All *him*. I stand at the edge of a cliff, tall above a beautiful blue-green ocean, and with one little step I'm diving in headfirst until I shatter upon hitting the warm waters. Pleasure blooms over my skin, taking me deeper.

"Ryker," I say as I come and my body clenches around him, milking his.

I've never been so alive; yet, I'm dying at the same time.

My orgasm sends him into a tailspin. His breathing quickens, his eyelashes fluttering as he strokes inside me, fast and hard, my name a litany on his lips. Cupping my ass in his hands, he lifts me to get deeper. We're up against the headboard, and it bangs against the wall. His shoulder hits the nightstand and my wine glass and book fall. The sound of our sex, the smell of him in my nose...this is everything.

Drenched in sweat, he looks down at me. "I could stare at you for a hundred years."

"Ryker," I whisper as he throws his head back and increases his tempo, his hands adjusting me for deeper friction.

"Red, yes. Fuck yes." His cocks thickens, and I groan as he roars his release, his body clenching and shaking as he strokes inside me.

He collapses on top of me as if he's just sprinted a thousand yards.

His beautiful, hard body is the best thing I've ever felt. I cling to him as we wrap our arms around each other, and for the first time since my mom passed, it feels like everything really does have meaning. A purpose. There really is fate. There really is emotion that transcends sorrow and sadness, those pains merely preparing you to accept the sweetness in life. Love.

• • •

"That was better than any chocolate I've ever eaten," I say to him a few minutes later as I lay propped up on his bicep with my leg thrown over his thigh.

He chuckles and looks down at me with a gleam in his

gaze. "It's not always like this."

I come to attention. "Is it because we have…something?"

"Hmmm." He plays with a strand of my hair, twisting and twining it around his fingers.

It's not the answer I want, but I can tell he's teasing me by the little smirk that plays around his mouth.

I pluck at one of the springy hairs on his chest. Laughing, he shoots up and pins me beneath him. "Woman, if you're going to pull my beautiful chest hairs out, I'm going to make you pay."

"How?"

He leans down and takes my nipple in his mouth, and I groan.

A few breathless moments pass and the need between my legs returns, longing to be extinguished. I feel his cock hardening next to my thigh, so I wrap my fingers around it and stroke. I'm not sure I'll ever get enough of him. "I love what you do to me." My voice is rough.

He raises his head and looks at me, his gaze glittering. His chest heaves and a slight flush makes his color high. "I have so much to show you…"

I stroke his length, my thumb brushing over the wetness of his cock now that he's taken the condom off.

"Like what?"

He moves until he's sitting up propped against the bedframe with his hands on my hips. He grabs another condom and slides it on then shifts me until I'm straddling him. He guides his cock inside me, taking me by the waist and leading me until I get the rhythm.

He tangles his hands in my hair as I ride him, sliding him in and out, moving my pelvis until the friction rubs against my clit. I moan.

"Everything, Red," he says breathlessly against my neck. "I'm going to show you the whole fucking world."

• • •

The next day I'm awake by six and running on nothing. Both of us have shadows under our eyes as we hop in the shower. Together.

Afterward, while he's styling his hair—it's a process, he says—I go through my closet carefully for the perfect outfit. I'm not a virgin anymore, and for some reason that requires something a little extra. Maybe a scarlet A? I laugh under my breath.

With my best bra on, I pick a fitted pink Chi Omega T-shirt and a navy plaid skirt that's the shortest thing I own. I pair it with some booties and we walk out of the house together. I feel high from the possessive way he looks at me.

He opens the door for me, and I blush and drift past him, catching a whiff of his male scent. *Mmmm. Not Polo.* I smile at him and he laughs.

"Sleep well?" he asks as he slides in the cab and shuts the door.

"Excellent."

He grins over at me as he pulls away from the curb. "Nice dreams?"

"Pirate dreams."

A slow grin works its way up Ryker's face.

We're quiet most of the drive, because hello, we just had sex. Spectacular, mind-blowing sexy times.

"Why are you giggling?" he asks, tossing a glance at me.

I bite my lip. "Just thinking about last night."

"About how awesome it was?"

I scoot over to his side. "Meh, it was okay."

He flashes his gaze over at me. "Liar, but I forgive you. Just promise me you'll sit this close to me every time you get in my truck." His arm goes around my shoulders, and I slide in closer. His thigh is pressed against mine and my insides melt at our proximity. How it is possible that I want him…again?

Once we pull up to the parking lot, I see my car and can't help the smile that comes to my face. He did that. He went out and bought a tire and lugged it back to the Waverly and used his own tools to fix my car—and I didn't even ask him to. It makes me horny.

My eyes jump to him, and he's grinning at me. Still wearing last night's shirt and shorts, he looks deliciously rumpled and sexy. "We're here," he says softly.

"I see."

He rushes around to open my door and I slide out, gazing up at him. He towers over me, and I put my hand on his chest. His ocean-colored gaze is intense as it brushes over the features of my face.

"Thank you for fixing my car."

"Thank you for last night," he says then kisses me gently. My arms go around him and we go from zero to a thousand in a heartbeat. I'm squirming against him, pressing myself against his hard cock. He murmurs my name as his hand slips around my lower back and slides under my skirt. Precisely why I wore it.

His mouth moves down my neck as his fingers dance over the silk of my underwear. He hitches my leg up and wraps it around his waist, his hand gliding up my thigh to my panties—

A car horn blows in the distance and we both laugh under our breaths as we separate.

He smirks down at me. "I guess it's not a good idea to make out right in the middle of town."

"No," I agree, clearing my throat. Then I see his neck on the left side, the side that was facing away from me during the drive, and I bite back a smile.

"What is it?" he says when I let out a giggle.

"I gave you a hickey last night." His eyes flare as I lean forward and touch the purple bruise near the base of his throat. "It's barely noticeable," I say.

I reach for my purse and pop out my compact mirror to let him see it.

He laughs and looks back at me. "Your mark."

I wiggle my eyebrows. "That's right."

"So...when can I see you again?" His voice is husky. He rests his forehead against mine when I don't answer right away. "Well?"

"Why?"

He looks down at me. "I want you. You want me. There's nothing complicated about that."

I want you. It does sound simple, and I may have given him my V-card, but if this *is* just a let's-fuck-a-while kind of thing then I want to play it cool. I have my pride. "What is it about me specifically you want?"

He looks at me. Arches a brow. "Really? Did I not just make you orgasm three times?"

I feel tension building in my chest, and I battle it down. I'm not going to be sucked into my insecurities right now. "I'm not a jersey chaser and I want things clarified."

"Oh." He stills, a line forming on his forehead as his brow pulls down.

"Are you planning on...*doing laundry* with anyone else soon?"

"No. I've been waiting on you to figure out that I'm the hot piece you want—not Connor."

I grin. "Then you can see me soon."

"Soon?" There's a hint of impatience in his voice, but I ignore it.

I nod. "Text me later?"

He agrees.

"Now kiss me," he says, pulling me back into his arms. My hands are already curling around his neck, missing the feel of his, the hardness of his muscles, the scent of him that lingers on his shirt. He leans down and brushes his lips against mine, our tongues tangling, and when he pulls back to end the kiss, my mouth chases after his, wanting more.

He tells me he'll text me later, and with a kiss goodbye, I walk to my car, crank it, and drive away.

I glance in the rear-view mirror and he's still standing there, watching me.

CHAPTER 23

RYKER

Blaze is adjusting his shoes when I walk into the locker room. The place is mostly empty since most of the team is already on the field. I've just come from working on the sidelines with the quarterback coach and popped in to grab a new jersey.

"Is that a hickey?" he says, laughing.

I touch my neck and grin at the memory.

"You look radiant as shit," he comments with an eye waggle. "Get lucky last night?"

I smile. I'm already jonesing to see her. To slide between those perfect legs and feel like I'm home.

I just shrug.

He walks in closer. "Oh, you're being tightlipped. Nice." He grins. "You know I can't stand that shit. Who was she?"

"Hmmmm."

"You didn't come back to the dorm," he continues. "And you never do that. I even texted you this morning to check on you."

It's true. If I'm with a girl, it's at my place and on my

terms. But she's different.

"Well?" he presses. "Who's the girl?"

"Ah..." My eyes go to the bet board on the wall. The bet isn't there, but it may as well be. Every guy on the team knows about it.

I scratch my jaw, not sure what to say.

I decide to play it off.

"I helped Penelope with her car. Flat tire. It was late..." My words linger off.

I turn back to my locker, hoping like hell he doesn't ask more questions.

"Her tire? Again?"

Again? I toss a look at him over my shoulder. "Yeah. Why?"

He darts his gaze away but doesn't say anything.

I frown. "What is it?"

He scratches his head. "Nothing. Just...she had a flat last week outside of Sugar's."

A spark of jealousy flashes through me at realizing he knew something about her that I didn't. "I got her a new tire, so it won't be flat again."

"Cool."

I study his closed-off face—which is weird. Blaze is an open book. In fact, usually he never shuts up.

I face him, giving him my full attention. Something is off. "So when was this? Did you help her?"

He fidgets, moving from one foot to the other. "A while back. I was just driving by after hanging out at Cadillac's and her car was in the parking lot and..." He stops.

"And?"

"It was late so I pulled over. Archer was with her." He shrugs. "Not a big deal."

My spine straightens. He's buried the important part in the middle of that. "Archer? What was he doing there? Was he changing her tire?"

He chews on his lip. "He was drunk…" His voice trails off and my hands clench.

"Spit it out, Blaze. What happened?" I've taken a step toward him and he holds up his hands. "I know exactly how Archer is when he's drunk. He's belligerent as shit. Did he hurt her? Threaten her?"

"Hang on, dude. She was fine. Archer was just messing around and left as soon as I showed up."

I picture Penelope alone with Archer in a parking lot at night and anger simmers. My jaw tightens. "Why didn't you tell me?"

"Look at you—you're jonesing to rip his head off right now." He shakes his head.

I rub my jaw, scrubbing at my unshaven face. I look at the bet trophy, and my teeth snap together. I'm so sick of this shit.

He shrugs. "Just let it go, man. We have a big game this week to focus on. It's homecoming. Put everything else aside. Nothing else matters."

Whatever.

A few minutes later I'm on the field with the rest of the team as we run through some scrimmages. The offense gets in the huddle, and I call a play, a new one we've only used a couple of times. We clap and line up, getting into formation.

Archer reads the line and calls his defensive play. There's a bit of indecision in his voice as he yells out a change, and they move around, adjusting to what they think we're going to do.

The ball is snapped and I do a fake pump then hand it off to Blaze, who runs past the defense and straight in for a fifty-yard touchdown.

Fuck yeah.

We celebrate and I'm pumped.

Coach yells out his approval and tells us to run another one.

We get in a huddle, and I call the play—the same one, but we line up differently. My eyes are on Archer, watching as he reads us and calls his formation then changes his mind and runs back and forth along the line of scrimmage, telling his guys what to do.

"Get your shit together, Archer," I call out.

He sends me a glare. "Just snap the goddamn ball."

My fucking pleasure.

The ball is snapped and I catch it, smooth and easy. I fake a throw and although the play calls for me to pass it off, I see an opening in the defense and take off running. Typically, I don't run a lot even though I'm fast. If a defensive guy tackles me or lands on me wrong, it can hurt like hell—or worse.

But I didn't get to be number one in the country for nothing. I take my chances when I see them—*and* I want to rub it in Archer's face.

My offense catches on and tackles the line that comes for me.

With a quick sidestep, I dodge the slower guys and dart to the right. The field is wide open and adrenaline pumps as my feet smack against the green turf. Out of the corner of my eye, I see a shadow behind me, looming fast. Archer. He's one of the fastest guys on defense, plus he never took his eyes off me. Makes sense he'd be tailing me.

I see the goal line. *Must get there.*

I've gone at least thirty yards, enough for a first down, and I realize I'm not going to make the touchdown, so I aim for the sideline to get out of bounds.

Just as my feet cross the white line and the play is done, my shoulders are shoved and a foot is kicked in my lower back. I can't stop the momentum as I plummet down on the turf. My head bangs inside my helmet as it hits the ground. *Fuck.* I'm jarred for a full five seconds. Blinking, I turn over and stare up at the sky.

Archer's face blots out the sun. "I beat your ass, quarterback."

I swallow, mentally taking inventory of my body. I'm okay, although my head is rattled. I didn't lose consciousness, so odds are it's not a concussion.

I whip my helmet off and toss it over to the side, gasping in air. I hear running and, in my periphery, see Blaze up in Archer's face.

A couple of the other defensive players jog over, and they join the shouting match. The offensive guys are next, and pretty soon it's a shoving match. I push myself to standing, swaying a bit. Coach blows his whistle for us to settle down. I shake myself off, blinking as I focus on Archer, who's danced off toward the other sideline.

Anger ignites as rage sweeps every cell in my body. I

march toward him.

Blaze is next to me, gesticulating wildly as he tries to talk me down. Dillon is with him, repeating everything Blaze says. "Dude, don't freak out. He's just showing off. You shouldn't be running anyway…"

I ignore them. My fists curl as my equilibrium returns. I'm so goddamn sick of him. I was fine and dealing with his shit until Blaze said he was *flirting* with Penelope.

He's never getting near her again.

Stalking, I reach the sideline and grab Archer's shoulder, spinning him around. "Take your helmet off," I bite out.

He smirks. "You gonna cry about the late hit? Maybe if you could win a bet then your game might improve." He laughs and looks around at the other players. "Oh wait a minute—word is your girl is dating some other guy. She left you at Cadillac's. Saw it with my own eyes." He pouts. "Does that make poor little Ryker sad?"

Rage boils. "Take. It. Off."

He shrugs and looks around the field nervously, his gaze landing where Coach Alvarez is, but I already know Coach is watching. The man knows when someone has taken down his quarterback. My guess is he's letting us vent for a few. He knows how tense we've been.

Archer twitches, his head fidgeting as he looks back at me. "Get over yourself," he hisses. "It's just a game. Penelope Graham is just a game."

"That he can't win," one of the defensive players says under his breath.

Enough. I put my hands on Archer's helmet and tug it off

his head.

"Get off me, man!" he shouts as I throw it on the ground. "You ran the play. What did you expect?"

I rear back and hit him square in the face, splitting his lip. Pain shoots through my hand and arm and I flex my fingers to shake it off.

He backs up with his hands out, and I give him a grim smile. He's not getting away from me this time. Everything rushes at me like a tsunami—the shit from last year, my Heisman snub, the fact that he harassed Penelope. He's pushed me past the point of caring. "Isn't this what you want, Archer? You mess with me over and over and want a reaction. You got it." I hit my chest with my fist and his eyes flare. "Come on, take your shot. Or are you scared?" I grin at him, feeling that rush of power that comes when you know you have the upper hand with someone.

Archer's face reddens and his lips make a thin line. "Fuck you."

A sardonic laugh comes out of me. "You're a pussy. All you want is to ride me about some stupid bet. Look around, asshole. We're playing football. Not schoolyard pranks. I can't fucking wait until Maverick is back on the team and you go back to the little nobody you always were," I say. "And Penelope *is* mine. She's always been mine. That bet is won, paid in full."

The words rush out and part of me wants to tug them back because I know what it means, but I'm running on pure adrenaline. I've cracked wide open and everything is spilling out.

Some of the guys from the team edge closer.

"…did he say he won…"

"…yeah, he did…"

My guys whoop and fist-bump each other.

I block it all out and focus on Archer. "You're the loser. Now take your hit. I'll even let you."

His entire team is watching and murmuring as he dives for me and gets in a tiny pop to my face, but I'm back and on him in an instant. I've got him up by the collar of his jersey, and I'm aiming for his face again when three of my offensive guys pull me off.

I struggle and fight as they drag me across the field.

"Stop, man. Enough already! We fucking won! Let it go." It's Blaze's voice and he's tugging at my arms. "Think about your hands, dude! Protect the arm."

They push me to the other sideline and form a wall so I can't get to Archer. I fume and pace the field as they murmur at me to settle down.

But I've reached a point where they can't talk to me. I shove them all away.

It dawns on me that I've cracked, that I've messed up somehow, but I push those thoughts away. Not now. Not now.

The quarterback coach is up in my face, checking my hands, and I grimace as he barks out an order for an ice pack. I don't even care if I'm hurt.

On the other side of the field, support staff checks on Archer. I see him running his mouth and pointing at me.

Blaze hits me on the back. "It's cool. It's over. Slow your breathing, man. Take a breath."

I ease back as one of the staff puts an ice pack on my hand and then dabs at what I assume is blood around my eye.

Coach Alvarez has gotten Archer's side of the story, and I watch as he marches across the field to where I am. I'm still pacing when he gets up in my face. "Do you think that solved anything, Voss?"

I glare at him.

"Well?"

My teeth grit and I spit out the words. "It made me feel better."

He bites down hard on the pen in his mouth. "You got a lot of nerve, son. Is it out of your system?"

My gaze bounces over to Archer. "Not by a long shot."

"Then get your ass to the showers. I expect to see you in my office in half an hour. Understood?"

I nod.

He gives me a grim look. "You're dismissed."

I straighten my shoulders and shove everyone off me then stomp across the field.

After I shower, I plop myself down in Coach's office and wait for him to show up. My left hand rubs at the part of my fist that hit Archer's face.

Coach walks in and takes a seat on the edge of his desk. His eyes are hard as nails as he rakes them over me. "That was the stupidest thing I've ever seen you do."

I straighten my posture and lean forward in the chair. "Sir —"

He holds his hand up. "No excuses. I know it was a late hit. I know you guys have your differences, but that's what makes being number one so goddamn elusive. You have to want it enough to let that shit go. Do you want it? Do you want to be the first pick in the draft? Do you want to have the world at your fingertips when you leave this shithole of a town?"

I swallow. "Yes sir."

He gives me a short nod. "Then show some leadership and coolness out there. You looked like a high school kid who's pissed off that someone's dating his girl. Get over this...rift you have with Archer."

But...

Archer doesn't respect me. He's the one who should be sitting in here. Not me.

"Life isn't fair, Voss," he says, as if he's reading my mind.

My fists curl. "I didn't start the shit—"

"No excuses."

"Or what?" I say.

His eyes harden. "Don't make me have to decide."

Oh, I know what he's insinuating. That he'll replace me with the backup, Dillon.

Screw that. I respect the hell out of him, but I won't be forced into a corner to behave when I'm not the one who needs an attitude adjustment.

"I hope it doesn't come to that, sir." I stand up and stalk out the door even though he hasn't dismissed me.

CHAPTER 24

PENELOPE

"Sine, cosine, and tangent are the main functions used in trig," I explain to the small study group I meet with each week in the library, pretty much my favorite place on earth. In fact, I make sure my study section always meets on the floor right smack next to the romance section. Sometimes I even think if the whole writing gig doesn't work out, I can always be a librarian and live around books forever.

My phone buzzes for the third time, and I set down my notebook. "Guys, my phone keeps going off. It must be important." I smile at them. "Let's take five then meet back here."

They nod and stand up to stretch as I grab my purse to retrieve my phone. I read the text.

Want me to rescue you?

I grin. Ryker. I didn't see him last night, and he missed class this morning, but he hasn't been far from my thoughts.

Being apart from him has given me a chance to catch my breath. Our night together, the memories of it, still swirl in my head. I can't wait to see him.

From what? I say.

You look bored as hell. I can make that look go away.

I look around the library, but all I see are tall stacks of books and a few study tables. He isn't at any of them. **Where are you?**

Next to some books.

I shake my head and smile. **There are books everywhere.**

Just know that I'm watching you. 😌

Are you a stalker?

Maybe. You look pretty by the way.

I blush.

Nice shirt, he sends.

I look down at his practice jersey. I wore it on purpose.

I'll give it back to you.

Keep it. It looks better on you. I have a surprise for you.

A couple of the students are tapping their pencils against the table, and I send a quick look at them. One of them gives me a questioning look. "You ready?"

Time to get to work. **I have to go**, I text then tuck my phone away.

Half an hour later, most of the students have left, and I'm packing up my things.

I push the chairs up to the table and lean over to wipe it off.

"Hey," comes Ryker's voice from behind me.

I flip around, and there he stands, his broad shoulders leaning against a tall bookcase, half of his face in shadow.

It doesn't lessen the impact of him.

I wonder if he's been waiting for me this entire time.

"Hey," I reply softly. I've replayed our conversation from when he dropped me off at my car a hundred different ways, trying to decipher where we stand.

"I missed you in class," I say. "We covered differential equations."

"Nice. Did you take notes for me?"

"Not a jersey chaser or your secretary."

He laughs. "The claws are out. I didn't expect you to. We can plan a study session at your place if I get behind."

I toy with the straps of my backpack. "Yes, we could." I'm already picturing him in my bedroom, spreading me out naked on my bed while I recite math facts.

"No more work tonight?"

"All done." I walk over to him, and he steps forward out of the dimness of the shadow. "Ryker! What happened to your face?" I scan his features, taking in the purple bruise around his right eye. Moving closer, I wince at the puffiness and the worn look on his face. "A fight?"

He sighs, looking away from me. "You could say that. Archer and I..." He shakes his head. "There's some bad blood between us."

I inhale sharply. Ah.

He rakes a hand through his hair. "It's nothing you have to worry about."

I frown. "Was it on the field?"

"Yes." His lips tighten and he rubs his jaw. "Blaze told me about him showing up when your tire was flat. But that wasn't the main reason we got into it. There's...a history there." He gets a weird expression on his face, one I can't read. "There's something I need to tell you. Something that happened at practice..." His voice trails off as I lean in and brush a kiss across his cheek. I'm not quite sure how to maneuver this new...thing we have.

"Is it that you missed me?" I smile.

He stares at me and opens his mouth but then closes it, a shuttered expression on his face.

"Ryker? What's wrong?"

He swallows and looks down. "Nothing. It can wait."

"I see." But, I don't. He's being very tightlipped, which means he isn't ready to talk about what's on his mind. "Is everything with Archer okay now?" From covering the games, I know tensions run high among players. Sometimes a good old-fashioned fight can settle things down.

A muscle flexes in his jaw. "No." He tilts my chin up. "I've missed you, Red."

A blush steals up my cheeks.

"And there's somewhere I want to take you tonight. A surprise."

"Are you asking me or telling me?"

He arches a brow, and I'm glad to see his mood seems to be improving. "You'll want to go. You've wanted to see me all day—"

My eyes flare.

He continues. "And I know that because you wore that shirt to get my attention. You can't tell me no—"

I cock my hip. "I *can* tell you no, and—"

"Because I suspect you've missed seeing my handsome face—"

"I wear what I want to—"

"Maybe I can't tell *you* no, Red."

I stop what was about to come out of my mouth. God. He sure knows how to shut me up. "Good," I say softly.

He takes my backpack from me and hitches it over his shoulder then tosses an arm around me. "Come on, let's get out of here."

"I hate surprises," I tell him as we walk down the aisle.

"Is that so? Even the good ones?"

"Mmhmm. On my tenth birthday, my mom surprised me with a clown, which terrified me. Not to mention I was too old for clowns by then and didn't give a flip about balloon animals. I really wanted a Justin Bieber birthday, but alas, he was on tour."

He smirks. "Most people are scared of clowns."

I nod in agreement. "I barfed on his big yellow shoes. Pretty soon the other kids started puking. Of course, it didn't help that I'd been reading *It*—when I was clearly too young for it."

He chuckles. "I bet you were a handful."

"I was an angel." I throw a glance over at him. "What's the big quarterback afraid of? Spiders? Snakes? Big linebackers?"

He tosses his head back and laughs as we head down the stairs, and I'm glad he's in a better mood. "You'd never believe it if I told you. And I'd have to swear you to secrecy."

"Is it creepy?"

"Hmmm, you'll probably laugh." He pauses. "I really shouldn't tell you."

"You can't do the old bait and switch with me. Tell me!"

He laughs. "Fine. It's *alektorophobia*." He gives me a questioning look. "Know what that is?"

My mouth curls up. "Come on, you're asking the girl who's had a word of the day since she was five. Of course I know what it is. You're afraid of chickens—but not birds, I suppose, since Vampire Bill didn't freak you out."

He smirks. "And it's not really a phobia. I just wanted to impress you with my vocabulary. It's more of an irrational fear of roosters."

I smirk. "Childhood trauma?"

He nods. "At the petting zoo."

"I'm picturing you running amuck and a mean old rooster chasing you across a field."

"You must be psychic. Pretty much nailed it. FYI, they run fast."

We laugh and all at once, I feel...giddy. My heart stutters in my chest, and I stare at him.

"We should get going," he says, and only then do I realize we've been looking at each other for several seconds.

We walk out the door and into the cool October air. The sun is low on the horizon, a few hours from setting, and the smell of fall is in the air, crisp and sharp. Ryker stops and sets my backpack down to take off his blue and orange varsity jacket. With a small smirk on his face, he arranges it around my shoulders.

"I didn't say I was cold," I murmur, but I've already stuck my hands in the pockets. It falls past my waist and two of me could fit inside it, but I'm in no hurry to take it off.

A smile works his face, and he pushes a strand of hair

behind my ear. "Let's go."

• • •

It feels like a date.

He opens the passenger side door of his truck for me, and once I'm tucked in, he gets in and pulls out of the parking lot next to the student center. I sit on my side, but it doesn't stop my eyes from watching the roped muscles in his forearms. I begged him to tell me where we're going, but he's not budging.

"Are you hungry?" he asks as we turn onto the main drag that will take you through Magnolia. We pass a few restaurants, even Sugar's, but I had a late lunch with Charisma before I went to the study group, so I tell him I'm not hungry. He nods his head toward the back seat. "I grabbed some wine from the store before I came to see you. There's chocolate back there too. I had an early dinner in the cafeteria, but I didn't know if you'd eaten anything."

Chocolate? Wine? Oh, this is so a date.

"I'm fine," I say. "Are we celebrating?"

He sends me a heated look. "Yes."

Hmmmm.

"What kind of wine did you get?"

"The girly kind with bubbles. I know you like it. But, don't think I'm too fancy. Where we're going, we won't really use glasses, so it's just a little six-pack with twist-offs." A gruff laugh comes from him and I almost think he's embarrassed. "Classy, right?"

I imagine him waltzing into the liquor store and purchasing girly wine. I smile. "Twist-off wine is totally redneck, but I'm not complaining."

He nods and looks back at the road. "Great."

Leaving the lights of town, he turns down a secondary road that's mostly deserted with the exception of a few houses every mile or so.

"Are we going to the boonies?"

"Almost there."

"Should I be scared that you're taking me out here to ravish me?" I ask.

"Mmmm." He throws me a look, and I see his gaze sweep over my body, lingering with heat.

Damn him. He's so vague. I slide over to his side, curl my hand around his thigh, and whisper in his ear. "Where are we going, Ryker?"

He gives me a grin and turns sharply onto a gravel road.

We drive up a hill, bouncing around in the cab over the bumps and holes in the road.

He grabs a couple of blankets from the back seat and then hands me a small wicker basket that looks new. I peek inside and see the six-pack of wine with the chocolate.

"Where did you get this basket?"

"The store."

"You bought all this just for us?" I pick up a small jar of fancy olives and look at him. I'm picturing him at Target or Walmart, wandering the aisles. "What else is in here?"

He grins sheepishly. "Some strawberries are on the bottom. Hopefully they didn't get squashed by the wine."

"Wow." My eyes blink. I'm speechless.

"It's been a while since I had a real date, Red. I was just

trying to cover all the bases."

"You did well, grasshopper."

He chuckles as we walk down a stone path toward a large ranch-style log cabin. A red barn sits off to the right. The sound of cicadas buzzing surrounds us, the sun low and orange, close to the horizon. The smell of fresh hay bales reaches my nose, and I inhale a deep breath. "I love being out in the middle of nowhere." I look back at him and see he's watching me. "Have I been to a toga party here?"

"Probably. It's an old farm one of the former players owns. He donated it to the team, and we help maintain it. It keeps us in shape during the offseason." He points at the log cabin. "The team has retreats out here every spring, and every fall we have a big bonfire party."

"What are we doing here? Are we going into the cabin?"

He shakes his head. "No. Come on, I want to show you something." He grabs my hand, and we take off up the hill to the left on a small trail. He adjusts his steps so we're walking in sync.

We meander along the path for a while, passing tall trees and utter silence.

"What is this secret place?" I ask. "You're not a serial killer, are you?"

He grins. "There's a waterfall a few hundred feet down the trail, and a meadow that's full of sunflowers in the fall. It's pretty amazing. I found it when I was running out here with Maverick last year."

"Oh."

"Is this stupid?" he asks suddenly, looking more

discombobulated than I've ever seen him. "This is so stupid. Maybe we should head back to town and just get a beer at Cadillac's."

I reach out and take his hand in mine.

"It's a meadow?"

He nods.

"With pretty flowers and trees around it?"

He shrugs nonchalantly.

And I watch him. *Seeing him.* He has such a soft side. My heart flutters. Does he even remember that Edward and Bella found a meadow in *Twilight*?

I exhale slowly.

"I love it, Ryker. It's the perfect date. Let's stay."

We make our way down the path and stand in the middle of a small clearing that's banked on either side by bright yellow sunflowers. We lie down on the blanket and talk. I tell him my favorite movies and songs and books; he tells me his. He describes a sailboat he wants to buy some day, and I describe in intricate detail my pirate fantasy. I end up drinking most of the wine because he can't stomach the taste of it. When the stars come out, we hold each other, our breaths mingling as we kiss. He undresses me under the dark sky with a tenderness that burns into an uncontrollable fire. Eventually, he takes me from behind, his hand on my hips, my name on his lips. His hand curls around my shoulder and runs through my hair as he tells me I'm his.

Afterward, we hold each other, and I don't speak at the wonder that is *us*. I want to tell him how I feel...but instead, I send a silent prayer up to the heavens, begging them to watch over us.

CHAPTER 25

PENELOPE

"Is the DJ booked?" Charisma asks as we sit next to each other in the library. "I hope he's bringing some kickass lights and maybe a karaoke machine. I want this 80s theme to be OTC."

I grin. "Over the top cool?"

She smirks. "Off the chain."

I pull out the to-do list I've been working on. "Yes, I confirmed with him and also with the catering company. The pledges are decorating tonight."

It's a few days before our homecoming party, and I'm scrambling to get everything done. I've been waiting here for a few girls from the planning committee to meet. Normally, we gather at the Chi Omega house, but the pledges are having a sleepover, so Margo decided we would forgo the craziness of the house to finalize the details at the library. I check my watch, and she's late. Everyone is. I send her a quick text to see where she is.

"Is that Ryker?" Charisma murmurs as she waggles her eyebrows at me.

"No."

"Got any juicy bits for me? Is the package in proportion to the frame?" Her eyes gleam with curiosity. Yes, I told her about Ryker.

"All you need to know is the deed is done."

"Dammit. Why are you so tightlipped? I need to know!" She flops down in her seat and glares at me.

"What about Blaze? What's the scoop on him?"

She shrugs, her face flaming, which is unusual for her. "Meh. Nothing to tell."

"Aha. See. You're not telling me everything."

I tap my pen against my pad and think about Ryker. We spent the last two nights together, and each day, he meets me at the student center in the morning to walk me to my first class.

"You're beet red," she exclaims as she pulls out a bag of chips and starts munching. "You're thinking about him, aren't you?"

I look pointedly at her snack. "You're not supposed to eat in here."

"I'm a rule-breaker." Her eyes go past my shoulder and flare. With hurried movements, she straightens her hair over her shoulder and checks her lipstick in the reflection of her phone.

I follow the direction of her gaze and see Blaze coming in the entrance of the library.

"Oooo, here he comes," I tease her.

She grunts. "He's just so…rambunctious. And who names their kid Blaze? I mean, it's bound to give him some kind of ego…" Her voice tapers off at his arrival on the staircase from the lower floor.

I watch as the brown-haired hottie takes the steps two at a time, a gleam in his eyes as he reaches our table. He gives me a nod then focuses on Charisma. "Hey babe. Whatcha doin?"

She tucks a chip in her mouth, chewing loudly. "NOT A BABE." Her voice carries over to several tables.

"Shhh."

She ignores me and looks at Blaze, who's sat down next to her. "I told you last night—"

I interrupt. "You said you were helping the pledges."

She blinks at me. "Uh, I *was* going to do that, but when I drove past the athletic dorm, Blaze was—"

Blaze's eyes widen. "She texted *me* and asked to see me under the pretext of studying. Then she took advantage of me." He sighs. "It wasn't the first time."

She throws her hands up. "You both need to back off—"

"Hello, *cher*," a low voice says from behind me.

Our table goes silent, and we turn to see Archer with Sasha on his arm. Her blonde hair is swept up on either side with sparkly lion clips, the mascot for the Thetas, and her pink-tipped nails are curled around Archer's bicep. A couple of the defensive players I don't know linger around them, and I suppose it's Archer's posse.

I'm relieved Margo isn't here yet to see Sasha.

"Hello," I say with a brief dismissive nod, only because Southern social etiquette demands a response.

"You guys studying?" Sasha asks.

Charisma glares at her as if she's an idiot. "We're planning our massive homecoming party—which is going to be way better than yours."

Sasha's eyes harden. "Is that so?"

"I'll be at the Theta house," Archer says, giving me a smile, his teeth sharp, the light from the overhead florescent bulbs glinting off the diamond studs in his ears. I grimace. If he were a vampire, he'd be one of the creepy, unsexy Stephen King ones.

"Perfect," I say sweetly. "Please carry on then. There are plenty of open tables tonight." I wave my hand at the entire empty section in the area to our right. I don't have time to deal with Archer and his machinations.

But the duo lingers. "Haven't seen you around in a while," he says to me, and I look up from my to-do list.

"Good," I say.

He snaps his fingers. "Oh, yeah, that's because you're doing Ryker on the regular now. How's that going?" He smirks at me. "You finally caved and gave it up. I really thought you hated him. Turns out, you're just like all the rest." His lip curls. "Come see me when he's done with you. I'll hook you up with something better." He grabs his crotch.

My first reaction is horror. Awful, mind-numbing horror. Then rage makes me go white-faced. My fists curl, and before I know it, I'm standing. "Go to hell, asshole."

Archer laughs and Sasha's eyes widen.

Blaze jumps to his feet and stalks over to where Archer stands. "Hey now, watch yourself. Nobody wants to hear your bullshit. Leave."

"I don't want to leave," Archer says.

"Come on, girls, let's move downstairs." Blaze's hand is on

my shoulder, but I shake him off.

"No." Out of my peripheral vision I see indecision on his face as he gives me space. With one step, I'm in Archer's personal space. I take in the bruise under his eye, the split lip. "Looks like someone beat the shit out of you," I say.

His hands clench. "Your boyfriend got in a sucker punch."

"You better run along before Ryker shows up," Blaze says from behind me.

"I don't give a shit about Ryker," he mutters, narrowing his beady eyes. "But maybe she needs to know the truth."

"Stop fucking with our team," Blaze tells him quietly. "You're the problem. Not Ryker."

Archer smirks. "You're just his little lapdog."

Blaze takes a menacing step forward. "I said leave."

My chest is rising rapidly. How does he know about me and Ryker? It's possible he's just throwing out guesses. "Wait a minute," I say. "I want him to explain himself."

An expression of glee flits across Archer's face.

And I feel trapped, as if I've reacted exactly the way he wanted me to. I straighten my glasses. Charisma is next to me, bristling like a mother hen. "Yeah. Speak, jerk face," she says.

Archer sighs, a pleased smirk on his face. "By the look on your face, I guess it's true then."

"What?" I bite out.

"Ah, *cher*, did you think Ryker was into you?"

Blaze lets out a groan. "Fuck."

I don't say a word. But my face is on fire. My hand clings to the back of my chair. Whatever he's going to say...I think my heart already *knows*.

He tsks. "See, you'd think you would have figured it out after the bet at Sugar's. I was counting on you holding a grudge, but you went and gave it up anyway."

My lips are numb. "Stop beating around the bush and say what you came to say, Archer." My words are controlled, tight, and surprising cool, considering I'm flopping around like a dying fish on the inside.

"Well, it wasn't a bet we put on the board, but every player knew the stakes. Offense against defense."

"A bet. I see. What were the stakes?" I hold my breath.

He looks at his nails. "I bet Ryker he couldn't screw you by homecoming—and the bastard went and did it early."

"And how do you know he accomplished the task?" My words are cold.

Archer's eyes gleam. "Why, he told everyone at practice this week. That's why we got in this little fight. I was offended for you. Ask Blaze. He was there."

I look at Blaze's face and it's white.

An anvil lands on my chest. A small breath of air escapes my mouth and all the air in the library is gone. The spacious room feels tiny and tight and...

I blink and swallow. *Get yourself straight, Penelope.*

But I can't. It's too much, and all my mistrust and insecurities come roaring back to the surface. I take a step back and collapse down into the chair.

Blaze is up in his face now, his fingers pushing at Archer's chest.

Nausea washes over me but I hold on. My head tries to process everything I thought was real between Ryker and me.

Sasha laughs and looks around, confused. "Like, it's not even a big deal. At least you got to sleep with Ryker, right?"

It's doubtful she knew anything by the surprised look she gives me, and I throw my gaze around the library, searching faces, wondering if others know the intimate details of my sex life.

Charisma is next to me, gathering my things together and tucking them inside my backpack. I let her, my gaze on the table. I stare down at my list. Feeling frozen. Sick. I want to scream. I want to puke. I want to die.

But it's a library and I can't do any of those things here.

Blaze is arguing with Archer when one of the librarians comes over and asks them to be quiet. I feel disassociated, as if I'm floating up at the ceiling above the scene, watching everything play out.

My hand holds my chest as I swallow down emotion and focus my attention on Charisma. "Get me out of here."

She nods and takes my arm then we leave the group behind. She escorts me down the staircase, and I feel her eyes look over at me, gentleness there. "You're white as a sheet, Pen."

Before I know it, we're in the parking lot and at my car. She gets in the driver's seat and cranks it up as I get in.

With a squeal, she pulls out of the student parking lot and heads to our house.

"What about the party?" I ask, my mind blank. "We didn't finish…" My words choke off, and I hitch in a breath, one I think I was holding since the moment we walked out of the library.

Tears stream down my face, and I reach up and touch them.

Charisma grinds her teeth next to me, her eyes darting over my way before looking back at the road. "I'm going to kill that sonofabitch. Where is he right now?"

My mouth feels like cotton, but I push through it to get the words out. "He went to Maverick's place tonight. It was his sister's birthday. He asked me to go…but I wanted to wrap up the party stuff." I sound like a robot.

OhmygodRykertoldthefootballteamwehadsex.

I heard the ring of truth in his voice when Archer said it. I clutch my stomach. The nausea that was bubbling in the library is imminent. "I'm going to be sick."

She jerks the car over, and I jump out and hurl, my body spasming. There's nothing there except a soda I had earlier.

She rubs my back. "I'm so sorry. If it's any consolation, I haven't heard a word anywhere about this—even from Blaze. You know I would have told you."

"Do you think it's true?" I say.

She chews her lip. "I know I'm not great with advice, but in this case, you need to talk to Ryker. Get the story from him, not some loser football player who creepily hit on you once."

I feel fresh tears prick my eyes, and I stuff them down, determined not to let them win. "Those bets mean something to them." I use a stash of napkins from the glove compartment to wipe my face. "And if it's some kind of misunderstanding, why didn't he tell me about it?"

She shakes her head. "Do you care about him?"

I nod and bite my lip. "I never should have trusted him. He's ruined…everything."

CHAPTER 26

PENELOPE

"I don't want to go home," I say to Charisma as we get closer to the house. My chest aches at the thought. It's where he and I hang out. Make love.

She shifts her eyes toward me. "You wanna go find Ryker and kick him in the nuts?"

I clench my hands. "No. I-I can't talk to him yet."

She sighs and bangs her hand on the steering wheel. "I really want to punch him."

"No."

"It might make you feel better?" She sends me a wry grin.

"No."

She does a U-turn at the next intersection, tires squealing.

"What are you doing?" I say, hanging on to the side of the car.

"We're going to Cadillac's. I can't handle you being all quiet and monosyllabic."

"I can't face people," I say, hands fluttering.

"You can. People adore you, Pen. Adore. You're kind and sweet, and you didn't do anything wrong. He's the one who needs his dick cut off for spouting off about you at practice. Come on, let's go and just have a drink. I won't ask you to shoot pool." She grins, and I know she's just trying to make me feel better.

I sniff.

Because her comment just brings back memories of Ryker showing me how to play.

"I guess I don't really have a choice," I say on a small half-laugh, half-groan noise when she pulls into the packed parking lot.

"Nope."

She tugs a makeup bag out of her purse and gets to work on me. She helps me remove the dark mascara under my eyes and repair my red lipstick. I let my hair out of the messy bun and fluff it up, checking it in the visor mirror. I straighten my *Word Nerd* shirt and skinny jeans.

I frown. "I'm really not in the mood for this."

"Just come inside for ten minutes. You need to decompress, and this is the perfect place."

I don't tell her I don't need to decompress. I need to process. But when she gets something in her head, she's a dog with a bone, so I sigh and nod.

"You're gorgeous," she says. "Let's get you some tequila."

We walk into Cadillac's, and thank God, there isn't a football player in sight. We aim for the bar in the back, both of us settling on stools.

I've just slung back my shot when a text pops up on my phone.

Penelope. I can explain.

At first, I'm not going to reply, but I can't help myself. **Is it true?** My palms are clammy as I grip my phone.

Another pops up. **Let me tell you why. Please.**

My jaw flexes, and I suck in a breath.

"Don't respond," Charisma says, reading over my shoulder. "Let him worry."

Another text comes in after a few minutes. **Where are you? Blaze said you left the library to go home. I'm here, and you aren't.**

My lips tighten, and I turn my phone over so I don't see his texts.

Margo walks in and makes a beeline for us. Charisma texted her earlier and told her we were moving the meeting to Cadillac's. She's looking a little harried if her fast stride is anything to go by as she maneuvers her way through the crowd, clutching the navy cardigan around her neck and smiling tightly at the people she passes.

Some of them give her a surprised look.

Winding around the masses of co-eds, she finally reaches us, her pale pink lips tight. "This is where you want to have a meeting? This place reeks of stale beer and body odor." Her nose sniffs.

And it's so Margo...that I have to flash a small smile. At least *she* hasn't changed.

"Get down off your high horse, MP. We had a crisis at the library. And have you seriously never been inside Cadillac's? WTF is wrong with you?" Charisma says.

"MP?"

"Madam President," I say, deciphering Charisma's

acronym.

She frowns. "And what crisis?"

I recount the incident, my tone cool. Hard. I'm holding it all in right now. Barely functioning in a tequila-fueled haze.

"Holy shit." A frown burrows in her forehead. "That type of bet doesn't sound like Ryker. I mean, everyone knows they do them, but they're usually harmless, stupid pranks." She gets a steely look in her gaze. "And you heard this from Archer? He's a first-class dickhead."

"The Chi Omega MP just said *dickhead*," Charisma calls out to the randoms surrounding us. "Everyone drink!"

"Here, here," comes from several patrons and they eagerly comply.

She signals the bartender. "Garçon, bring me a glass of wine for the lady, please." She looks over at Margo. "What kind, MP?"

"Champagne?" she answers. "Do they serve that *here*?"

I nod. "It's terrible, but it's my fav."

She looks down at my shot glass.

"For the pain."

She bites her lip and leans in. "Are you sure all of this is true?"

"He texted me and didn't deny it." A horrible thought hits me. "What if this is all over social media?" I recall the video from Sugar's that was supposedly deleted.

Charisma gets the champagne from the bartender and hands it over to Margo then pulls out her phone, her lips set. "I'm on it. I'll text Blaze and get the deets. He's got some explaining to do. I'm never going down on him again."

Margo's eyebrows hit the roof, and I bite back a giggle. Thank goodness for alcohol.

She takes a drink and stares at me over the rim of her glass. "I know one thing for sure—there'll be no football players allowed at our party. And I think we should tell Coach Alvarez. He doesn't put up with shenanigans."

Charisma studies Margo. "For an uptight bitch, I like how you operate. Honest to God, I think you're better since Kyle dumped you. That experience definitely brought you down a peg and made you one of us."

"Uh, thanks?" Margo says.

I'm feeling warm from the shots. I nod. I like Margo a hell of a lot more than I used to.

Charisma taps her chin. "I have some volleyball guys on speed dial. A couple of basketball players, too. I'll get them to come." She nods, as if warming up to the idea. "Yeah, we're revoking all the football invitations. Those chauvinistic assholes can all go hang out with the Thetas. I don't give a shit. We don't need them."

I'm tearing up and I laugh.

She laughs with me.

"If someone is doing shots, I'd like to get in on that." The voice is deep and familiar, and when I turn around on my bar stool, I see Connor.

He's wearing his ball cap and a grin. I'm definitely not crushing on him anymore because my heart doesn't even skip a beat.

"I'm game for a few if you ladies will let me join you? My treat." He smiles.

Margo takes him in, her gaze lingering on his broad shoulders. "I'll have another terrible champagne."

I nearly gasp in surprise.

He ends up ordering a beer for himself, a champagne for Margo, a screwdriver for Charisma, and another shot for me. His nicely defined bicep reaches between Margo and me to give the bartender a wad of cash.

"This is my stepsister, Margo," I tell him, and then I sit back to see how it all plays out. She's looking at him with wary yet interested eyes, and he's looking at her lips. It just might work. He's got the money she's drawn to. Although I do wonder how a video-game designer would stack up in her eyes.

He takes a swig of his drink. "Didn't know you had a stepsister."

"No one does. She likes girly drinks and little sweaters. She's also headed to NYU after gradation to get a graduate degree. Aren't you going there too?" I recall one of our conversations before class a few weeks back.

He gives Margo a considering look. "Yes, I am."

Margo draws little circles on the bar with her finger, her gaze bouncing from me to Connor, a bit of an accusation in her eyes that says, *Are you trying to fix me up with your one-time crush?*

"Yep," I say out loud before tossing back my shot.

They start chatting about their plans for next fall, and I look down at my phone and turn it over. Just to see.

I'm so fucking sorry. Please talk to me. Where are you?

My teeth grit and I clutch the phone, so tempted to type out a message, but I don't. Instead, I click my phone off for good and stuff it deep into my purse.

• • •

The sound of banging on the door wakes me up. I blink open my eyes and peer over at the clock on the nightstand. Almost one in the morning. *Shit.* I've only been asleep for thirty minutes. I rub my eyes and run a hand through my hair, patting it down. Blearily, I stumble out of bed, walking past the clothes I wore yesterday in a pile on the floor where I took them off when we got in from Cadillac's. Charisma, Margo, Connor, and I closed it down at midnight.

Vampire Bill squawks from his cage. "Shit! Door! I need a cigarette! Call the cops!"

"No need for that," I mutter. "I have a pretty good idea who it is."

And so…

I should just ignore him.

Instead, it's as if my soul is connected to his, as if I know he's out there waiting for me to open the door. And part of me wants to see him—even if it's only going to break my heart.

I grab my long cardigan and tug it around my shoulders then make my way out to the hallway.

"Who is it?" I ask.

"Ryker." His voice is husky, and I rub my arms.

Charisma pops her head out the door, her hair definitely looking decidedly worse than mine. "Need some help?" Obviously, she heard who's here. "I can hold him down while you pluck his chest hairs out?"

"No." I shake my head, so she goes back to her bedroom

and shuts the door.

I open the door and there he is. Wearing gym shorts and a Waylon hoodie, he looks rumpled and worn out. His gaze captures mine, his face lined and hard. The bruise around his eye brings everything that happened with Archer back into sharp focus.

"What do you want?" My hand clings to the doorjamb, and I block the entrance to my house.

"You didn't respond to my texts," are the first words out of his mouth. Accusatory.

"I know."

"I've been worried sick. I sat on your porch for an hour hoping you'd come home. I went back to the library. I drove all over campus." He exhales, pushing a hand through his hair. "Can we talk?"

"No." I shake my head.

"Why?"

"It's late, and I've been drinking, and I don't want to be around you." My voice is brittle. "You broke my trust, Ryker. You told the team we had sex."

A muscle in his cheek flexes. "Drinking?"

"At Cadillac's with my friends." Then I have to toss in, "Connor was there."

Anger flits over his features and his eyes sharpen. "Really?"

My arms cross. "I don't owe you any explanations."

His eyes laser in on mine. "But I owe you one. Let me come inside and we'll talk."

I rub at my forehead, already feeling the twinges of a

headache that's bound to morph into a full-blown jackhammer by morning.

"Red—"

"Stop calling me that."

He bites his lip. "It didn't happen the way you think it did. I didn't have sex with you and then just bust up in practice, high-fiving everyone. Did you really think that about me? After everything we've talked about?"

I frown. "Don't point fingers at *me*. This is not my fault. You fucked us up all on your own."

He swallows and looks away. "I know. I tried to tell you in the library the other day. I just couldn't."

My heart cracks at his admittance and pain ripples through me.

"I wasn't on board with that stupid bet, Penelope. I *never* accepted it. I told him no since the beginning. I'm not that guy. You know me."

Do I?

"You have to believe me." He leans in and I take a step back.

"Please. I don't want you inside my house right now."

He scrubs at the shadow on his face with both hands, a ragged look on his face. "Just…give me a chance."

"Why? I gave you something precious, and you told everyone about it. Did you tell them I was a virgin too?"

"*Fuck*…no. I didn't even mean to say what I did. It just came out. Blaze had just told me Archer harassed you then I went out on the field and he tackled me and we fought. My anger was out of control…I don't know…everything just fell apart. I just…snapped." He lets out a pent-up breath. "I hate that I said it, Red. I hate it so much. I wanted to take those words back—"

"Once you ring a bell, you can't un-ring it."

He closes his eyes briefly. "I'm sorry. So fucking sorry."

Emotion tugs at me, pulling at my chest.

But…I can't.

"Sometimes sorry isn't enough. Good night, Ryker."

I shut the door in his face.

CHAPTER 27

PENELOPE

Margo sits across from me at the student center. Her face is pale, and she looks like she might hurl.

"Hangover?" I ask as we eat lunch together.

"Ughhhh," comes from her as she sucks down her second glass of water.

"I should have told you to hydrate last night. Champagne headaches are the worst." I grimace. I was smart and took a Tylenol before I went to bed; plus, I guzzled a Gatorade.

She nods and looks down at her pizza. "I don't think I can eat this."

"It's barely edible anyway," I say as I munch on my slice that has pepperoni, sausage, and mushrooms.

"I ended up going back to Connor's place last night."

My ears perk up. "Oh yeah?"

"We had a few more drinks. We might have played strip chess." She gulps. "Then I woke up on his couch wearing his shirt and my underwear."

"And…did anything happen?"

She groans. "That's the bad part. I have no idea. I got up

before he did, grabbed my shit, and left."

She said shit. I bite back a grin.

"Well if you were on the couch, probably nothing happened."

She sighs. "I guess." Giving herself a shake, she tightens her sweater around her shoulders and crosses her arms. "So, what's the latest on the party? We all ready for tomorrow?"

I set down my pizza, flip my notebook page, and run my gaze over my list. I feel as if I'm moving in slow motion. All I can think about is Ryker and what he said. I shove it down and bury it deep. "Yes. We're meeting the pledges here and walking over to the game together. Then we'll head to the house. Everything's all set."

"And the players? Did Charisma take care of uninviting them?"

I nod. Charisma eagerly volunteered to be the one to text Blaze. Her message said, **If any football players show up, we will pull your nipples off. Really. We will.**

"She's got it covered."

Margo nods. "Good." Then she frowns and gives me an odd look.

"What's up?" I say.

"You recall the day I was with Ryker in the science building and you showed up?"

I nod.

Her chest leans in over the table, and there's a glint in her eyes. "I just remembered something Archer said to him. They didn't know I was standing there, and it was hard to hear, but I caught the gist of it."

"What?" My lips tighten.

"No, it's not bad. I recall Archer giving him grief about a bet and Ryker saying he *wasn't* doing any bets." She squints. "I really think Archer was referring to you, because you had just walked past us." Her teeth chew on her bottom lip. "Does that make you feel better?"

I shrug. The truth is he told them he *won*.

I sigh. "Are you saying you want Ryker at the party?"

She waves her hands. "No, no! I don't care about that anymore. That whole thing was stupid, and I never should have put my own issues with the Thetas over everything else..." She stops. "I'm just trying to be a good stepsister, I guess, and help you figure this out."

I smile. Something good has happened. We're friends.

Her eyes go past my shoulder and land on something. Her expression hardens. "There's Archer. Don't look, but holy moly, his face."

Of course I look. I turn around, and he's coming out of the bookstore. There's no Sasha next to him and no other players. He's wearing a black hoodie with the top up, but it doesn't hide that he now has two black eyes. His gaze darts around the student center and then he hurries down the steps and out to campus.

My hands clench around my notebook. *Shit.*

Margo grimaces. "He looks like someone beat the poop out of him."

"Again," I say.

Charisma has come in from getting her pizza and takes a seat across from me. "Yep. I heard about it in class this morning. Apparently Ryker showed up at his door, pulled him out in the hall, and pummeled him. Took four RAs and the house director to get him off Archer." She chews on a slice. "None of his buddies helped him either. Not one single player on the defense."

My face is grim. "What's everyone saying about me and Ryker? Does everyone know?"

She gives me a pat. "No one is saying anything, and I've been pressing. There's nothing on social media. Only assholes will talk it up anyway."

I nod.

"What did Ryker say last night? Maybe he's the one squashing this?"

I shrug.

I'm just so…done.

And broken.

Just talking about him makes my chest ache.

• • •

I'm walking out of my writing class when I pass by my dad's office. I see it two times a week as I walk this hallway and never once have I stopped to see if he's there.

Something's different today. I feel different. Raw. Emotional.

Hitching my backpack up on my shoulder, I ease over to the sign posted next to his door to check out his office hours. He doesn't have a class scheduled right now, and when I knock on the beveled glass door, his gruff voice says, "Come in."

I open the door and step inside. It's a spacious office with a big window, dusty potted plants, and a few shabby armchairs—typical professor. A large oak desk dominates the room with a line of heavy bookshelves behind it. My gaze lands there and stays.

"Have a seat, please. Got to get these grades in before I lose my place." He's got readers on and is staring down at his desktop.

"Okay." I settle into one of the roomy green armchairs across from him.

At the sound of my voice, his head pops up and he takes off his glasses, setting them on the papers in front of him. "Penelope! What a pleasure. I wasn't expecting you. How are you?"

"Good."

"Classes going well?"

I nod. "Of course."

He stands up and comes out from behind his desk to give me one of his hugs. He pats me gently on the back.

He looks down at me and smiles then frowns, giving me some space as he goes back to his desk. "How's the job at Sugar's?"

"Great."

It's our typical run-through of questions. Just like we always do.

"I'm still at the library too."

He nods, looking perhaps a little excited that I'm here but also uncertain. His voice is careful. "Is everything okay?"

Okay?

Not exactly. My heart's been crushed by a football player.

But I don't think that's why I'm really here. I'm here because this has been a while coming. He's worked here for three years, and I've never once visited.

My eyes rove over the room and I see pictures of me in various places. One of a piano recital, another of me on a horse at camp, one of me in choir. My high school graduation is front and center on his desk. Mom took them all, and they're copies I've never seen. I suppose she sent them to him. The only event he attended was my graduation. I take in the family photo of all of us this past 4th of July at his pool. He even had a special timed camera and arranged us altogether, me, Margo, Cora, him holding Cyan.

He follows my eyes. "Not sure you've ever been to see me here. I've got quite the collection." A sigh slips out of his mouth. "It was tough not being there for all your adventures."

But he'll be there for Cyan's.

I tamp that feeling down, and really, it doesn't have the bite it usually does.

"I'm proud of you, you know." He tilts his head toward my graduation picture. "I was never as smart as you." He chuckles. "You definitely got that from your mom. Remember how she got you doing the word of the day when you were little?"

"Yeah."

He leans on his desk, his eyes on my face, and I know he's trying to suss out why I'm here, what I could possibly want— but even I'm not sure of that.

There's a cross-stitched piece of art framed on his wall, and I stare at it, feeling my eyes water. Cora made it, I'm sure.

She's always working on things like that. It's big, about eight by ten, and has hearts on it with a stick family of five—and I guess it's all of us. In the middle is a caption. *Live love, breathe love, give love.*

I chew on my lip and hug my backpack.

"Penelope?"

A tear has made its way down my face, and I swipe at it. I take a breath, the words lingering at the periphery of my mind, the ones it takes having your heart broken to really understand.

"I miss Mom...so much..." I stop and take the Kleenex he gives me.

"I know, love."

I suck in a breath. "It hurts that you found someone so fast and then started a whole new family..."

"I understand." His voice is soft. "I didn't plan on it. I came back for you, and in the meantime, I met Cora. Love works like that sometimes, comes right out of the blue and you see that you didn't even realize everything you've been missing."

I nod and think of Ryker.

"She's my second chance, I suppose. I love her more than anything—just like I love you. Unconditionally."

I let out a shaky breath. "You're really trying. You got me a car, that interview with the book agent..." My voice drifts off.

"I'm sorry it didn't work out."

I wave him off. "No, it didn't, but it's good for me. I may get shot down a hundred times before I figure it out."

He agrees. "Whatever you do with your life, you're going to be amazing, Penelope. Vivien raised a kind, beautiful person." He pauses. "I want to be a good dad to you. I want to be better than I was when you were little."

I nod, my eyes watering again. "And I do want to be part of your family. I want it more than anything." I whisper the last bit, and he makes a noise in his throat as if he's overcome. He comes back around the desk to wrap me up in a hug, and I hang on to him—maybe for the first time ever.

And everything with Ryker and the bet…I hug my dad and let it all go.

CHAPTER 28

RYKER

Archer and I sit side by side in Coach Alvarez's office. Just the sight of him makes me want to jump up out of this chair and pounce on him again, like I did last night when I showed up at his door.

I smirk. I got some good hits in before the RAs and house manager managed to pull me off. I crack the knuckles on my right hand. I guess I shouldn't have hit him with my throwing arm, but I wasn't thinking straight. Not after Blaze showed up at Maverick's and told me everything that happened at the library.

The first thing I did was try to find Penelope. She was my first concern. Her. All her. I just wanted everything to be okay between us.

Coach lets out a heavy sigh and considers both of us.

He's angry, I'm fuming, and Archer's just pouting.

"Well, boys. That's quite a story you've both told." He leans in over his desk, arms folded. "Let me be sure I have it right." He levels his hard gaze at Archer. "Take your hoodie off, son. That's just disrespectful."

Archer's jaw grinds but he whips it off. He shoots a look at me. "With all due respect, sir, all you heard was Ryker's story when he came tattling to you this morning. I didn't make him take the bet or blab about his sexual exploits to the entire football team."

Coach jerks to his feet and points a finger at Archer. "Don't you give me any fucking lip, boy. You and I and everyone on this coaching staff know you've been wrangling to win that trophy any way you could. It doesn't take a genius to see your games. You wanted to be captain and you got it. You wanted to antagonize Ryker and you got it. And now you're messing with the daughter of one of my best friends. It's time to shut the fuck up and listen."

Archer pales as his mouth opens then shuts.

I nod. "Guess you didn't know that little tidbit, did you?"

"Shut up, Ryker," Coach snaps, but I don't even care. I've got the taste of victory in my mouth, have ever since I woke up this morning and knew I had to do something before this spun out of control and ruined Penelope's trust in me forever. I mean, I don't think she'll ever give me a shot again, but at least I can try to fix this mess for her.

I went to Coach's house at six in the morning when he was barely out of bed and hadn't even had a cup of coffee. I was haggard, exhausted from getting almost no sleep, and desperate. In the past three years, he's been more of father figure than my own dad, and maybe it was that thought that spurred me to sit down at his kitchen table and let it all out. Archer and his games, the flat tire, the bets—how I feel about Penelope.

Little did I know he was also Penelope's dad's coach years ago. Apparently, they still play golf together.

He listened, cursing a blue streak with each revelation.

And now here we sit.

Waiting for judgment.

He hitches up his pants and glares at both of us. "It ends today. We're going to put this behind us and never speak of it again. If there is even a breath of it anywhere on social media or as gossip, you will be suspended from the team," he growls. "This schoolyard nonsense is for babies. And not a fucking word will you speak to each other unless it's *you look nice today* or *may I buy you a sandwich* kind of shit. Do you get it?"

I nod. It's all I want. A real team. "Yes sir."

He looks at Archer, whose lips are tight.

"Speak!" Coach says, making him flinch.

Archer swallows. "Yes sir. I understand. Does this mean I can still be captain?"

Coach glares at him. "Neither of you are captains. Not until you prove me wrong by your conduct. Feel me?"

We nod.

"Good." He comes around the desk. "Now, let's go talk to the team." Coach stalks over to me. "I'm giving you point on this, Ryker. Say what you want to your teammates and get it all out."

I give him a brief nod, and we walk out. I know exactly what I'm going to do.

CHAPTER 29

PENELOPE

"You make a better Madonna than Madonna," Charisma tells me as I plop down in the student section of the stands. I preen and strike a pose for her, my big cross earring dangling against my neck.

"Do a turn so I can see," Margo calls out a few seats over.

I have a little room, so I do a pirouette in my black tutu and hot pink lace crop top, a consignment store find. The edges of the shirt are scalloped, and it comes to just below my titlets. A long black beaded necklace with a heavy cross pendant dangles to my navel, and a studded chain is wrapped around my waist and hangs down. On my feet are black booties with lacy socks.

It fits the rebel in me well.

Charisma gives me a fist bump. "Looking stellar."

"You look snazzy yourself. Indiana Jones, I presume." I check out her pants, hat, and the whip that's resting next to her.

She toys with it. "It's for Blaze. Later. I'm going to make him pay for not telling me everything."

Margo is in a pink business suit with shoulder pads, pumps, and bouffant hair. Connor is next to her and has on a Polo with the collar popped and penny loafers. Finally, it fits.

"And that's a touchdown, folks! First one of the game for the home team!" The announcer's voice blares as the Wildcats score. I put my eyes on the field to see what's going on. I was supposed to meet the Chi Omegas and walk over with them, but in the end, I needed some time alone to pump myself up before heading to the stadium. Part of me almost didn't come, but eventually, I threw my clothes on and drove over here.

It isn't long before my eyes find Ryker's jersey as he jogs off the field to let the defense go on.

Our seats are close enough that when he reaches the bench and stalks toward the quarterback coach, I feel as if I can't breathe. He's magnificent dressed in his uniform. Broad shoulders. Tapered waist. Tightly muscled arms.

He takes off his helmet and whips his hair out of his face. It feels like forever since we spoke though I know it was just yesterday in the early hours.

Time moves differently when we aren't together. Slugging along.

I grab my purse and put on lipstick, freshening up my cherry red. I contemplate sucking on a lollipop, but I forgot to bring any.

He looks up, his gaze searching the crowd, up and down the rows until finally he finds me. The air stands still and nothing seems to move as we look at each other.

I can't make out the details, but his face softens. He closes his eyes briefly and when he looks at me again, I imagine I see regret on his visage. Amid the screams of the crowd and over the heads of the cheerleaders, he mouths something at me.

I shake my head at him and hold my hands up. No clue.

Do I care what he's saying?

Part of me does. I want this anvil off my chest.

"What's he saying?" Charisma murmurs.

"I don't know."

She looks from him to me. "Uh, are you sure? Because it's pretty clear to me what that is."

"I don't know!"

He waves his hands and tries again, but another player comes along and gets his attention. He turns his head to look at the field then stares back at me. The other team has given up the ball, and it's his turn to head back out. He sends me a final look and takes off for the huddle.

I watch him.

"Seriously? You didn't see what he said?" She's looking at me like I have two heads.

"No."

She exhales, a thoughtful look on her face. "Let me ask you something: have you ever done or said something you really regretted like a second later?"

I nod.

"Have you done it recently?"

I think. "I manipulated Ryker into coming to the party. I made him feel like a commodity. His words."

"Right. Sometimes we do and say not so great things to get the thing we really want—even at the expense of others."

My lips tighten. "He bragged about having sex with me."

"He's a man. He reacted like a Neanderthal. Plus, dude, he's never been in a relationship. He doesn't know how to act.

You've got to train him up right." She gives her little whip a crack.

I nod. "So what was he saying?"

She gives me a little smile. "Pen, that's something you'll have to ask him yourself."

A couple of hours later, the game is over. We beat Georgia 7 to 35 and the fans are intense and excited. Without a loss yet, it looks like we might have a championship year.

I've left the field and am in the parking lot almost to my new Volkswagen—yes, I'm driving it—when I get a ping on my phone. I dive into my purse.

Part of me wants it to be Ryker.

I think about those words in my dad's office: *Live love, breathe love, give love.*

My phone pings again before I can find it, and I let out a groan of frustration. It's at the bottom of my purse. I let out an aggravated yell then finally snag it and yank it out.

It's him. My hands shake.

Hey.

The parking section I'm in is mostly deserted with no one around, so I drop my purse to the ground and hold my phone like it's a grenade.

What do I do? What do I say?

Hey, I send back. **Great game.**

Thanks. You busy?

Only about to host the party of the year. **No**, I type.

Really? Don't you have the party?

We're texting like nothing is wrong, but I feel the undercurrent, the reality that we are different now. Vulnerable.

Yeah.

I'm not coming. I just wanted you to know I got the message from Blaze.

Okay.

He sends another text. **There's something I've been wanting to say and I just haven't found the right way—**

The screen goes blank and I realize my phone has died.

"No!" I shout up at nothing in particular and let out a growl of frustration. I stomp my foot.

"Penelope." The voice is deep and husky.

I whip around and there he is.

His hair is damp from the shower, curling at the ends. He's wearing a button-up shirt and low-slung jeans. My gaze eats him up, missing him.

"What…were you there the whole time?"

He nods. "Coach let me skip out early and miss the celebratory talk. I showered fast and waited for you to leave and followed you." Uncertainty crosses his features. "I was nervous to say anything in person, and I thought maybe if I texted you…"

I nod, getting it. We tend to say more in texts.

I think back to the game where I watched him the entire time, unable to shift my gaze away. And here's what I realized. The Ryker of my heart would never participate in a bet that involved me. And I didn't need Margo to tell me that. Or Charisma to explain about how sometimes we say things we don't mean.

I know him.

I think maybe I've known him for a long time, or my soul

has. Since the moment I researched and wrote the article about him, he carved out a place in my brain, and now he owns my heart.

He comes in closer, a hesitant look on his face. "Did you see what I wrote?"

I hold my phone up. "Well, my phone died...so no."

He's reached me now and we're close, just a few inches between us. He smells like sandalwood and spices, and I want to lay my hand on his chest and feel his heart beat.

I do it. My hand trembles as I press it against his body. I gaze up at him and emotion swirls in his eyes. "Your heart is racing."

"I love you," he says quietly. He closes his eyes then opens them. "You're the best thing that's ever happened to me—even better than football. If I had to pick between the two, it would be you every single time."

My legs feel like jelly.

"The truth is, I wanted you that day at Sugar's and it had zilch to do with a bet. I wanted you in my bed and it had shit to do with a bet. You are all I want, and if you'll just forgive me for my big mouth..." He pauses and rakes a hand through his hair. "I can't go on knowing you hate me, Red."

"I could never hate you." Tears prick at my eyes.

"Yeah?"

I nod, need for him rising, the need to fix this growing gulf between us.

So many things are a mystery. The origin of the universe, if vampires are real—okay, probably not—but one thing is certain. *I love him.*

It's a connection I've felt since the beginning.

"I love you too, Ryker. So much. I've never felt this way…" My voice cracks.

His eyes gleam as he trails a hand through my hair. "Penelope, I don't deserve you, but fuck if life isn't better with you. I'm more of who I should be with you, and I promise you, I will never let you down like that again." He cups my face, his gaze intense. "You…are…everything."

I chew on my lip. "Is that what you were saying on the field? That you love me?"

He nods. "I was close to getting on the jumbotron and announcing it. Hell, the team already knows."

I arch my brows. "They do?"

He takes my hand and leads me over to his truck, which I parked right next to. On purpose? Maybe.

He continues. "Before the game, Coach let me speak to everyone. He pretty much gave me free rein—seems he has a soft spot for you."

Ah. "I barely know him, but he is friends with my dad. What happened with the team?"

"I took down the bet trophy and chucked it in the trash. I ripped the betting board apart. No more bets. It's a tradition that's over and done. My decision."

I've never been in the locker room, but I picture him in his football gear, ripping if off the wall and throwing it in the garbage.

"Was the team upset?"

He shakes his head. "Red, those guys were so fucking relieved to be rid of that thing. Even the defense and Archer's posse. It's caused so much shit."

"And Archer?"

"Quiet as a church mouse. Maverick's back next week anyway."

I suck in a breath. "So how does the team know you love me?"

He smiles softly. "I told them, Red. I made a big, touchy-feely announcement. I said you were the girl of my dreams and if any of them fucked it up and talked shit about us, I'd kick their ass." He gets a faraway look in his eyes. "Can you ever trust me…us…again?"

Not trusting has held me back long enough.

I nod, a tremulous smile on my face.

His hand curls around my midriff and lingers on my backside, cupping my ass. His gaze is smoldering as he looks down at my non-shirt. "Now, care to tell me where the rest of your clothes are?"

"I'm Madonna. I get to be slutty. There's no judgment."

"Fuck yeah, you do. But only with me," he growls. His lips take mine in a hard kiss, sucking on my tongue and devouring me, tasting me as if he's stranded in the desert and I'm a tall glass of water. He drinks me down, consuming me.

Holding him tight, I give it right back, my mouth clinging to his. His hands pull me close.

"Can we get frisky in your truck?" I ask a few minutes later.

He cocks a brow. "It's a hardship, but I'll do anything for you, Red."

CHAPTER 30

RYKER

We walk up to the Chi O house, and it's a wild scene. People are on the porch dancing and whooping, and music blares from around back as pink and white lights flash in the sky—Chi Omega colors.

I take Penelope's hand and gaze down at her. Her lips are swollen from my kisses and her hair is a little lopsided, but damn, she is fucking hot.

I give her a quick kiss on the cheek and straighten her pink shirt, which isn't really a shirt at all, basically just a bra. I'll let it slide because she's with me.

We reach the porch, and a few people come forward to slap me on the back and congratulate me on the game. I nod and tug Penelope closer. I don't want her getting away from me tonight. I want to take it all in. *Her*. The fact that she loves me. The realization that this year—it's going to be my best one yet.

Charisma comes barreling through the doors of the house.

"It's about time y'all got here. This party is OTC!" She's wearing some kind of wide-brimmed fedora and carries a whip. Blaze tags along next to her, his hand stuck in the back pocket of her khakis. Penelope texted her earlier and said we were back together and that the football boys were coming to the party. I guess word travels fast.

Which might explain Blaze's yellow parachute pants and tight red silky tank top.

"Nice shirt," I say to him as the girls talk to each other.

He rolls his eyes. "Charisma. She's taking this 80s theme seriously."

I pop an eyebrow.

"She's telling you what to do *and* dressing you?"

He shrugs. "You see her. She's a force. I have a hard time telling her no."

I laugh.

Margo joins us on the porch with Connor in tow and I pause, feeling my inner caveman getting riled up.

Penelope leans over and whispers, "He's with Margo." Her face breaks out in a smile, and she gives my hand a squeeze. She must have been watching my reaction. She does that a lot. We both do, I guess, each of us in tune with the other.

Margo comes forward and presses a wad of clothes into my hand. "No one enters without appropriate attire. Chi Omega rules."

Penelope giggles, and I think it's an inside joke.

I look down at the bundle. "You're telling me I can't come in unless I put this on?" I release Penelope's hand to hold up the outfit, a huge pair of lightweight black baggy pants with elastic on the bottom and a tiny blue tank top. "No fucking way." I check the label. "This shirt's an extra small...in women's!"

"We know," the girls say almost in unison, watching me with relish.

"But it's Wildcat blue and perfect for you." Penelope smiles. "We got the clothes on Amazon a while back, anticipating that some big growly football player might not want to dress up."

"You're welcome, QB1!" Charisma adds as she and Margo high-five each other.

"Clearly we did this because we had too much to drink at one of the planning meetings," Margo says with a little hiccup. "But I like it!" She grabs Connor's hand. "Come on, let's go get more champagne."

I look down at the MC Hammer pants and back at Red. She arches her brows. "Whatcha gonna do, Baby Llama?" Her accent is sweet and exaggerated, and I grin.

"Babe, I said I'd show you the world once, and if that means me dressing like this, I'm all in." My voice trails off as she blushes.

"Stop with the fuck-me eyes you two," Charisma says. "Off to the changing room with you, Ryker." She points inside to a bathroom right off the foyer.

Blaze tags along with me as we head into the house. "Dude. I can barely breathe in this thing. Do you think it's cutting off my circulation?" He tugs at his...blouse?...and I bark out a laugh.

"Red looks good on you, man."

He mumbles. "It better."

I head to the restroom.

"I'll grab us some beers," he calls out, and I give him a

nod.

I close the bathroom door and strip off my jeans and button-down. If this makes Red happy, I'm all about it. I'm picturing her face when she sees me in my outfit when the door opens.

"Dude! Wait outside!" I turn around expecting to see Blaze, but it's her.

She closes the door behind her, and her eyes are bright as she takes in my naked body. Of course I pose, tightening up my muscles.

"Couldn't stand to be without me, huh?" I grin.

She looks down at my cock, which jerked to attention as soon I saw her.

She pounces and gives me a kiss, her legs wrapping around my waist. *Fuck yes.* I'll never get enough of her. I enfold her in my embrace, holding her by the ass as our lips cling together. Heat roars through my veins. I feel like a rock star with her. Like I can take on the world and nothing bad will ever happen.

We get hot and heavy, and my fingers slip inside her panties from behind. I groan at the feel of her silky skin. "You're wet, babe."

"You've broken the seal and now I can't get enough." She gets a glint in her eyes. "How about third base right now, and later we can do the pirate thing?"

I kiss her hard. "I created a monster…but hell yeah."

A few minutes later we walk out to the party.

"Nice shirt!" Dillon calls out as we pass by him.

I pop the strap on my blue tank top. It's itty-bitty and my chest hair is poking out everywhere. "Yours too, man."

He's wearing the same parachute pants and a bright yellow tank. Looks like all the football guys were cornered. "You got a good one there." He glances at Penelope and gives me a fist bump before turning to talk to someone dressed as Cyndi Lauper.

Penelope takes my hand, and we walk through the house. Several girls wave at her, and she smiles as we head to the back. I feel like I'm in a dream. And here's the thing—I've had some kickass moments in my life, the time I won a state championship, the day I got my scholarship from Waylon, but nothing…nothing beats having her.

We step out into the yard, and I take in the wooden stage and the DJ bouncing around behind the stereo.

Penelope gets sidetracked by Charisma, and I head straight to him. After a few moments of explaining what I want, he shrugs and hands me the microphone. I tap it to get everyone's attention. "Hello, my name is Ryker Voss, and I have something to say." My voice echoes across the yard.

The music is turned down, and everyone slowly turns to face me. There's some whispering going on, and I see rustling in the crowd as some of the people from inside slip out to join us.

"We know who you are, QB1." I grin when I recognize Charisma's voice.

"Go Wildcats!" someone says.

"Great game!" another one calls out.

I rub my jaw, feeling sheepish, struggling with what to say. I had the confidence when the idea struck, but now as I look out at all the curious faces, I'm not so sure.

"Spit it out," someone yells, and I think it's Blaze.

My gaze searches the crowd until I see Penelope. She's standing on the right side of the yard and Margo is next to her. She arches her brows at me. *What the heck are you doing?* is written on her face.

I clear my throat. "We won a big game tonight…" The crowd cheers and I hold my hand up. "It's been a great season and it means a lot that you guys are supportive—especially after everything we went through last year."

I hear some murmurs of agreement and see heads nodding.

"First, I want to say thank you to the Chi Omegas for inviting us and providing these splendid outfits. I know they spent a lot of time deciding exactly how to best show us off, and the entire team appreciates it."

"Here, here!" Margo calls out.

"I want to see you dance in those pants!" someone else says.

I rake a hand through my hair, and my hand shakes. I clear my throat. Again. "But most importantly, I want to say that I love Penelope Graham."

The partygoers grow quiet. Some of them make *awww* sounds, and some search the crowd for the girl in question.

But I know where she is. I always will.

My gaze locks with hers, and she stares back at me, and maybe her lashes are wet—I can't be sure, we're too far apart —but fuck, I feel insanely giddy.

"Anything else?" someone yells.

"She completes me," I say simply before lifting the cup someone pressed into my hand. "Party on!"

The crowd erupts in cheers. She meets me at the bottom of the stage, her big gray eyes luminous.

I stare down at her. "God, Red. I wanted to be more eloquent. I got nervous—"

She kisses me and my arms go around her.

"It was perfect," she whispers into my ear. "*We're perfect.*"

EPILOGUE

TWO YEARS LATER

PENELOPE

I'm humming as I open the door to our penthouse. The smell of Ryker's spaghetti sauce is the first thing I notice, and I groan, inhaling the yummy spicy scent. It makes my stomach rumble.

"Shit! Pen! Give me a cigarette!" squawks Vampire Bill from his perch next to the window that overlooks Central Park in Manhattan.

"No sir," I tell him. "Smoking is bad for you."

I call out Ryker's name as I cross the room to check on my bird, but I don't get his usual *Hey Red* call. I assume he must be too engrossed in cooking, and I give Vampire Bill a little scratch on the head.

"The word of the day is *author*," I tell him, unperturbed by his glare. "I know. Easy, right. Well, today—and I'm telling you first because Ryker hasn't popped out to see me—I signed my first contract with a publisher! Isn't it great?"

Vampire Bill rolls his eyes.

"I know, I know, it's taken a long time, but with enough perseverance, dreams do come true. Isn't that cool?"

He shakes his head.

I grin. "Say *Pen is an author*. An awesome, deliriously happy author."

He picks up a piece of leftover food from the bottom of his cage with his foot and flings it at me.

I sniff, dodging it. "I know you're happy for me. You just have a hard time expressing love. Want a Ritz?"

"Shit! Yes!"

I give him one.

"Ryker," I call out as I leave Vampire Bill and walk into our ultramodern kitchen with its granite countertops, steel range, and white cabinets. Ryker and I bought it a year ago after he was selected by the New York Giants as the first pick of the draft.

After homecoming at Waylon two years ago, the Wildcats won the national championship, a first for our school. So, while he didn't come out with the Heisman, there's nothing sweeter than a championship ring that proves you're the best. Archer ended up being drafted in the third round, but his career stalled when he was arrested for getting into a fight outside a nightclub.

It looks like a tornado has come through the kitchen. There's a pot of delicious red sauce simmering on the stove and pans everywhere. I turn off the sauce and set it on the counter. Looking around, I see he's made a platter of caprese salad, complete with tomatoes, mozzarella cheese, and basil. There's also a bottle of champagne open with two flutes next to it. Several lit candles glow on the table. I grin, imagining him going to all this trouble for me.

Where is he?

Hmmm.

It's the offseason, thank goodness, and part of me wonders if he hasn't gotten sucked into watching old game tapes in his study.

I make my way down the hall, and when I hear a tortured groan coming from the bedroom, I detour and head that way. I open the door and freeze.

"What in the heck are you doing?"

Ryker's standing bare-chested in his jeans next to our nightstand, his face white as he looks down at his very sparkly and magenta pink chest and then back up at me. I blink.

His white shirt is on the floor as if he whipped it off in a hurry.

He runs a hand through his hair. "Oh, fuck, Red. I didn't think you'd be home for another half-hour."

I stride over to him and take the bottle he has in his hand, read the label, and look up at him. "Unicorn glitter lotion? Really? Where did you get this?"

"Some girly store. I thought you'd like it."

Part of me is pleased he's thinking of creative ways to make me laugh, but the other side is worried about his beautiful chest. "Is it supposed to turn your skin neon pink?"

He shrugs and then winces. "Oh, babe, it would have worked, but I think I'm allergic to it. I was trying to ride it out while I was cooking, but it started burning and itching, so I came in here to see what was going on…" He waves at his torso. "It doesn't look good." His lips quirk. "Do I remind you of Edward?"

I bite back a smile and give him a quick kiss. "He can't hold a candle to you. Now let's get this off ASAP." I tug him into the bathroom and turn on the shower. "Here, hop in and wash it off while I go find a Benadryl."

"I'm not getting in without you," he says with a little growl as he pulls me back towards him. "I've been waiting on pins and needles all day for you to get home and tell me the news. Did you get the contract you wanted?"

I throw my arms around him, not caring that the lotion may leave a stain on my white blouse. "I did. They loved my ideas! We have a lot to celebrate."

He kisses me hard. "Get in with me," he says against my neck.

"What about the Benadryl?"

"I'm tough. It can wait. My cock can't."

With a swiftness that proves he's a master at lovemaking, he removes my pencil skirt and blouse. My bra and lace panties are next. Whipping off his pants, he pulls me in the shower with him, his fingers already exploring the lines of my face, the hollows of my throat, the curves of my shoulders. He makes love like this a lot, memorizing me, touching me as if he'll never let me go.

I soap him up and scrub at his chest while he tries to kiss me. It's an ordeal and I'm giggling, but I finally get him rinsed off, glad to see his normal skin color underneath.

"God, I missed you," he says before biting my nipple, making me gasp.

"I was only gone for a few hours," I reply, gasping as his fingers slide down against my wetness. I toss my head back and press into his hand, and we go from zero to a million in a heartbeat.

My leg wraps around his. *I need him.*

"What's with the glitter lotion anyway?" I ask on an exhalation, my hand stroking his length, making him hiss as he bites his lip.

His eyes are low and heavy. "I wanted to surprise you."

"You did. You scared me." I laugh as my tongue toys with his chest, nipping at his skin.

"I love you." His hands tangle in my hair, and he pulls my head up to stare deep into my eyes. My back presses against the marble of the shower, and he kisses me hard with possession and love, but there's something different on his face as we pull back.

"What's wrong?"

He swallows and shakes his head, an uncertain look on his face. "I wanted to do this over a candlelit dinner. I wanted to pop off my white linen shirt and show you my sparkly chest… but now it's ruined."

I cup his face. "No, it isn't."

His aquamarine gaze is intense. "I don't mean it's ruined, I just mean it isn't what I planned."

"What did you plan?"

"This." With water coursing down his chest, he bends down on one knee and gazes up at me. "Penelope Jennifer Graham, will you marry me and make me the happiest man in the world? I promise to love you and cherish you no matter how many romance movies you make me watch. I promise to always wear shirts with buttons so you can tear them off. I promise to take care of you and Vampire Bill and any babies we have. I promise to be here for you and listen and cook you Italian when you're hungry. I promise to give you forever. You're my first love, my heart." He closes his eyes briefly. "Please say yes, because I can't imagine living without you."

Emotion builds and erupts as tears slide down my cheeks.

"I don't have the ring—it's hidden in the pocket of my white shirt, which is currently in the bedroom."

"Ryker."

He stands and our eyes cling.

"Yes," I say tremulously. "I accept, you silly man. Ring or no ring handy. I love you."

He kisses me and we stay like that for a long time.

My heart is full.

My love is complete.

And no matter what life throws at us, I know Ryker and I will weather it together. As one.

SECOND EPILOGUE

Draped in white gardenias and ivy, the cathedral is packed, and anyone who's anybody is watching as we stand before the minister. Even Viscount Connor is here with his new fiancée Lady Margo.

Dressed in his church finery, Lord Ryker's eyes are all over me, taking in my white lace dress, the way the neckline plunges just so.

He wants me. He always has.

"My lord, do you take Lady Penelope of Magnolia to be your lawfully wedded wife?" asks the minister.

"I do. She's mine," he says in his husky, deep voice. "Since the moment I saw her."

The minister turns to me. "My lady, do you take The Duke of Waylon to be your husband?"

I gaze up at him, and my heart knows it's home.

"I'll have no one else," I say softly.

THE END

Dear Reader,

Thank you for reading *I Bet You*. I hope you enjoyed Ryker and Penelope's story as much as I loved writing it. With that said, I must add that while historical romance remains one of my absolute favorite genres to read, I'm no expert when it comes to penning it. I hope you'll forgive any historical inconsistences you may find while also taking into consideration that Penelope's writing style is meant to be fun and slightly exaggerated. Xo

Thank you, again, for reading.

Go forth and live love, breathe love, and give love...
Ilsa Madden-Mills

PLAYLIST

"Iris" by Goo Goo Dolls

"Better Now" by Post Malone

"Wonderwall" by Oasis

"Truly Madly Deeply" by Savage Garden

"Perfect" by Ed Sheeran

"Not Afraid" by Eminem

"I Want It That Way" by Backstreet Boys

"Just Give Me A Reason" by Pink

"Jessie's Girl" by Rick Springfield

"Watch Me (Whip/Nae Nae)" by Silentó

"Something I Can Never Have" by Nine Inch Nails

"Treat You Better" by Shawn Mendez

"Leave Your Lover" by Sam Smith

"Hard to Handle" by The Black Crowes

"You Belong With Me" by Taylor Swift

"If I Was Your Girlfriend" Prince

"U Got It Bad" by Usher

Read I Dare You today, now a Top 2 Amazon Bestseller!

Badass Athlete: **I dare you to...**
Delaney Shaw: **Who is this?**

The late night text is random, but "Badass Athlete" sure seems to know who she is...

Delaney Shaw.
Good girl.
Lover of fluffy kitties and Star Wars.
Curious.

His dare? Spend one night in his bed—a night he promises will be unforgettable—and she can solve the mystery of who he is.

She knows she shouldn't, but what else is she going to do with her boring Valentine's Day? One sexy hook-up later, her mind is blown and the secret's out.

Maverick Monroe.
Bad boy.
The most talented football player in the country.
Just ask him.

Too bad for him Delaney's sworn off dating athletes forever after her last heartbreak.

But Maverick wants more than one night and refuses to give up on winning Delaney's heart. She isn't one to be fazed by a set of broad shoulders.

Will the bad boy land the nerd girl or will the secrets they keep from each other separate them forever?

ABOUT THE AUTHOR

Wall Street Journal, *New York Times*, and *USA Today* bestselling author Ilsa Madden-Mills writes about strong heroines and sexy alpha males that sometimes you just want to slap. A former high school English teacher and elementary librarian, she adores all things *Pride and Prejudice*; Mr. Darcy is her ultimate hero.

She loves unicorns, frothy coffee beverages, Vampire Dairies, and any book featuring sword-wielding females.

Join her Unicorn Girls FB group for special excerpts, prizes, and snarky fun!
https://www.facebook.com/groups/ilsasunicorngirls/

BOOKS AND STALKING

All my books are standalones with brand new couples and are currently enrolled in Kindle Unlimited.

Very Bad Things: http://amzn.to/2FfRNBW
Very Wicked Beginnings: (http://amzn.to/2sH6DPp
Very Wicked Things: http://amzn.to/2FifucO
Very Twisted Things: http://amzn.to/2C96hF4

Dirty English: http://amzn.to/2BCPlpv
Filthy English: http://amzn.to/2Cc8ijK
Spider: http://amzn.to/2GsXX1e

Fake Fiancée: http://amzn.to/2sHv3IG

The Last Guy (w/Tia Louise): http://amzn.to/2BFmMHR
The Right Stud (w/Tia Louise): https://amzn.to/2ClECjs

I Dare You: https://amzn.to/2Cp63Jp

Stalk Me:
→ Website: http://www.ilsamaddenmills.com
→ News Letter: (Free Book a Month): http://www.ilsamaddenmills.com/contact
→ Instagram: https://www.instagram.com/ilsamaddenmills/
→ Goodreads: http://bit.ly/2EESfM9
→ Bookbub: http://bit.ly/2GaR6cn
→ Amazon: http://amzn.to/2nY2pxT
→ Book+Main: https://bookandmainbites.com/ilsamaddenmills